THE TRUTH, VERY RARE

HANES SEGLER

THE TRUTH, VERY RARE

iUniverse books may be ordered through booksellers or by contacting:

iUniverse
1663 Liberty Drive
Bloomington, IN 47403
www.iuniverse.com
844-349-9409

ISBN: 978-1-6632-3524-4 (sc)
ISBN: 978-1-6632-3523-7 (e)

Print information available on the last page.

iUniverse rev. date: 02/10/2022

"I like my steak medium rare. I also like the truth, but it's *very* rare."

Source unknown.

Thanks to my friend Diane Weeks for helping me with some computer jargon and agreeing (albeit reluctantly) to provide a name and template for a character. Oh, and mostly for being my friend!

The killer had performed a number of jobs over a long career, and his knowledge, skill, and experience made him very good at his job. His chosen field flourished through good times and bad. No matter the economic climate at any given time, human conflict never seemed to wane. The killer was no philosopher, but he had analyzed the human condition enough to arrive at that conclusion, having operated in both ends of the economic spectrum and every shade in between.

In good times, when money and jobs were plentiful, everyone had more, spent more, did more…and got on each other's nerves more. The result? More personal conflict, not all of it resolved by a mere argument or in a court of law. Sometimes, it got down to a desire to rid one's world of the offending human, and since that entailed the death of said offending human, the killer was employed to handle the unpleasant business.

In bad times, there was less money, fewer jobs, less of everything to go around (except dissatisfaction and misery) less satisfaction with bosses, business partners, spouses, and brothers-in-law, so naturally, people got on each other's nerves more, resulting in…well, one could readily see the pattern.

The killer was in constant demand, and his stock was always on the rise as he carried out the mechanics of adjusting certain humans' time on earth, enough so that the innocuous term "mechanic" was often used in place of "killer," although the distinction wasn't important, certainly not to the subjects of his skills. And his own preference, had anyone bothered to ask his job title, would have been "killer," not mechanic, hitman, button man, muscle, enforcer, hired gun, or any other euphemism coined by popular culture.

To counter the killer's action, humans had developed laws, followed by those needed to enforce them. And that was the killer's usual nemesis, laws and their enforcement, both the institution of enforcement and the individuals selected, hired, and trained to implement its binding limitations on human behavior.

As a general rule, the parameters of law were clear, and those designated to enforce them followed those parameters. All the killer had to do was be mindful of the laws, their parameters, and the limitations and methods used to enforce them in order to avoid being apprehended, brought in, booked, indicted and convicted. Simple, really, and the killer was quite good at avoiding those involved in enforcing the laws by exercising extreme caution.

A successful performer in the business of killing for money also had to avoid running into the wrong job, or the wrong target. The very nature of murder-for-hire entailed dealing with a segment of society that didn't always play by the rules either, no matter which side of the law they claimed to inhabit.

In that vein, the killer had encountered a new enemy, an opponent far more intimidating than the prescribed rules set forth by legislators, judges, and courts. Those things the killer could understand, negotiate, avoid, hide behind, and thus, downright spurn. But this new enemy was in the form of a man who held his future in his hands—laws be damned and twisted—who was currently glowering over him as he set forth requirements that would enable the killer to keep practicing his trade and maybe even flourish—or so he said. The alternative was unthinkable, so he hadn't protested, even when given the news that the first three targets were to be taken out over a period of six days, a time span far too short for proper execution. He'd simply absorbed the information and begun his planning anyway.

"I don't care what logistical problems you have," the man was saying—again. "You just get the jobs done as I tell you about them. You'll have enough information to find the targets, figure out the tactics, and do the jobs—just like I told you."

"But I've always just taken out the target by the best means available," the killer argued. "And that means two, maybe three shots at the most. This business of kneecapping isn't my—"

"It is now!" the man cut in. "They have to be hit the same way, every damn one of them. If not, you know what's going to happen to you."

"Yeah, you told me—"

"That's right, I told you exactly what would happen. I explained it in great detail. And it will happen so fast, it will make your head swim. Is that what you want to happen?"

"No, of course not! But I can't guarantee that every one of the jobs will get done on time, or that every one will have their knees blown apart just the way you want it."

The man moved in closer, his face inches from the killer's. "Then we're wasting our time here, right? This discussion is over." He reached for his phone. "I'll just make the call—"

It was the killer's turn to interrupt. "No, no, you don't have to do that. I'll…just give me the information, and I'll get started. Right away."

The man smirked and slipped his phone back into his pocket, exchanging it for a single sheet of paper. "I'll give you an easy one for the first job. The rest of the information is all here. Get it done this week, no screw-ups, no excuses, no failures. Oh, and most important: no kneecaps—get it?" The man's smirk broadened at his inside joke.

The killer caught the irony and shook his head disconsolately, but seething below the façade of subservience. "Right. No kneecaps. I got it."

The man wasn't finished. "This had better be done right, or I make the call. I won't warn you beforehand, or let you know afterwards, I'll just do what I promised."

"Yeah, I told you, I get it!" the killer said again, his tone less agreeable than before. The killer, obviously no shrinking violet himself, had decided the man might need his expertise more than he thought; after all, who else could he get to take on the bizarre instructions and have half a chance at succeeding? That thought emboldened him more. "Just tell me this: just why does it have to be done this way? The kneecap thing?"

The man thought about it for a minute before responding. "Because it has to match up to another hit, one that took place recently. I want the guy who did it to look good for these jobs. So should you, by the way. It'll take heat off of you."

This time, the killer just nodded. It was a frame-up job; why hadn't the obnoxious man just said so in the beginning? Now it was making sense, although it seemed a long way around to accomplish something so iffy...which gave him insight into what he was dealing with, and he cursed the day he'd ever crossed paths with this one. Still, he couldn't resist one last question. "Do I get a look at this patsy I'm imitating?"

The man hesitated a moment. "We'll see. Get the first job done and I'll let you know."

CHAPTER 1

Had he thought about it, several adventures—and misadventures—had begun with a ringing phone. But *without* thinking that over, Carlton Westerfield poked "answer" on his cheap throwaway and waited for a voice to say something so he could get rid of the interruption and back to an old episode of *Miami Vice*. Although not recognizing the number or even the area code, he had to take it anyway. His rental car delivery gig entailed getting calls from all over, since one location or another always needed fleet inventory picked up someplace and driven somewhere else. Or, if not a job prospect, it would be a recorded pitch for an extended car warranty, help with student loan debt, or life insurance. Then he could go through the action of blocking the number against future calls, futile as that may be. Still, it gave him a sense of satisfaction to eliminate just one number from the thousands that phone marketing firms apparently buy in order to annoy the public.

He was surprised when the call turned out to be none of those.

"Carlton?"

"Oh, hi! Sorry, didn't recognize the number."

A laugh, the restrained, former girlfriend variety. *"Well, I took a few things you told me seriously. Like keeping a private phone and changing from time to time. And buying one on a trip to Milwaukee, so I'd get an out-of-state area code."*

"Glad to have been of some service, small as it was...no pun intended." The tone was more sarcastic than he intended.

Another laugh, this one better, more natural. *"Look, I was wondering if we could get together. I want to talk to you about something."*

The pause was a bit longer than she'd hoped for, but not unexpected. She knew Carlton to be a very cautious fellow.

"Uh, love to, but your new boyfriend isn't too fond of me, as I recall."

Her pause told him as much as the guarded response that followed. *"I don't know where you got that idea, you only met him once for about five seconds. Besides, I wasn't really planning on inviting him along. Or even telling him that I'd talked to you."*

For a cautious guy, Carlton didn't have to think long. It had been almost a month since the affair with Heather Colson had fizzled out, and he had to admit he was curious to know what had happened. And what *might* happen as a result of this proposed clandestine meeting. Still, he cursed himself as he delivered his answer too quickly.

"Okay, when and where?"

"How about the Italian place just off of West Avenue? This evening, about six?"

"Little Italy? That's fine, I haven't been there since we were there...uh, a while back. And six works for me."

"See you then."

Carlton snapped the phone closed and wondered about the conversation, which had started with promise—or had he read too much into it?—then ended with all the warmth of a business meeting confirmation. Then he realized he may have just witnessed what had gone wrong with their relationship—his inability to read her moods, her voice inflections, or her feelings and reasons for doing...well, *anything*. And not just the relationship with Heather Colson. Carlton didn't have the greatest track record with women in general; never had and likely never would. It seemed that something always interrupted relationships before progressing very far.

For the moment, though, it was time to record Heather's new burner number somewhere besides in his phone. It was a habit he'd formed long ago, deleting all calls and texts upon completion and never using the Contacts section for anything of an identifiable nature. Instead, phone numbers he might need to recall were recorded by means of pinpricks in a sheet of kitchen drawer liner paper. The digits were represented by a corresponding number of pinpricks arranged left to right, in columns, which could be seen by holding the drawer paper to the light. After pinpricking her number on the drawer sheet, he erased the call record, then removed the battery to reset the functions for good measure. As he closed the kitchen drawer "phonebook," he realized he hadn't needed the method with her other phone—he had memorized it, along with a lot of other details about Heather Colson.

Guess that means the bloom is off the rose—But, there's always this evening, about six!

The torrid affair with the pretty DEA agent had begun after the pair had been engaged in an unauthorized agency sting operation, which resulted in both of them being wounded, she seriously. Their joint recuperation at a resort in Mexico (also unauthorized) spawned a different side to their mild mutual attraction and continued upon their return to San Antonio, where her job dictated that she not be involved with the target of a recent Drug Enforcement Administration investigation. So, for weeks, they tiptoed around the DEA rules, with Heather able to dodge the heat as a perk for her role in the shootout. The resulting bust and death of a major drug dealer had boosted her to somewhat of a celebrity status at the local office, and the Special Agent in Charge gritted his teeth and looked the other way, despite his mistrust for Carlton, coupled with doubts about the details of the shootout.

Indeed, the relationship had continued even while Heather's employer tracked Carlton and *his* employers through a tumultuous gang war that spanned two months, two countries, over forty violent deaths, and resulted in Carlton's leaving the unlawful life for good, happy to be alive. And for a couple of months, things went swimmingly between them. Then...

As usual, he'd had no particular sign that troubled waters lay ahead, just a gradual lessening of interest that finally resulted in a parting of ways and Romance Silence, the worst kind. Two days later, he called again, but was unable to get beyond voice mail. Texts got no answer either. A message left at her workplace produced nothing.

A full week passed before he got a call late one night, whereupon she informed him that she had met someone *"more suitable"* for her, and *hadn't he known this would happen sooner or later? Oh, you know, because of their age difference, her career aspirations, a need for something else, (not yet determined)...but thank you for the lovely times, blah, blah, blah...*He almost expected an "I'll never forget you" proclamation, but it didn't happen, thankfully. The call ended with him feeling like Rick Blaine at the train station, watching while rain obliterated the ink on Ilsa's tender letter of explanation.

The very next day, of all the luck in the universe, they ran smack into each other at an old hangout of Carlton's, a burger joint called Good Time Charlie's, where Mulberry crosses Broadway. Carlton was alone, of course, there for a burger and beer; she, with Mr. More Suitable, apparently there for lunch, since it was one in the afternoon on the last Wednesday in April. Shaking hands with the guy, Carlton restated his own name and returned the guy's suspicious stare with his own best smile, the pleasant one that women said made him look almost boyish. He barely resisted the urge to tell him about his and Heather's good times in this same place.

Actually, his name was Darren Moore, not More Suitable, a nice-looking guy between forty and fifty, of medium build, with dark hair and brown eyes. Carlton surreptitiously appraised the decent rack suit, the conservative tie (even if it was tied a bit short) and shoes that had been shined recently enough. He could sense the guy sizing him up as well, and regretted that he was wearing casual khakis without much crease left and well-worn deck shoes, the look being salvaged by a cotton-silk blend shirt that cost over a hundred bucks at Penner's, thus leveling the fashion playing field. But the age difference scored a shut-out in favor of Heather's new flame, although it was tempered a bit by a few wistful glances in mature Carlton's direction, glances that did not go unnoticed by Mr. Suitable—uh, *Moore*.

In other words, it was the usual awkward introduction of Mr. Past and Mr. Present, with the two men eyeing each other, both trying to be cool, neither succeeding. After a brief exchange of civilized pleasantries, they parted ways to opposite sides of the noisy dining area, but not before Carlton caught Darren giving him a look that said "she's mine now, Bud, so watch your step." Again curbing his clever wit, Carlton neither rolled his eyes, nor winked lasciviously at Heather. Instead, he ate his burger too fast, chugged the beer, and retreated to his Cadillac. That afternoon, he suffered a stomach ache.

Of all the burger joints in all of San Antonio, she has to walk into this one...

Pulling into the popular Italian restaurant parking lot, Carlton regretted his quick acquiescence to this meeting. He should have declined, citing a recent realization that she had been right to dump him. Or maybe taking a harder stand, telling her he didn't want to be second choice, a replacement for the nights when her new guy was out of town. Or bolder yet, that he may be older, but was in better shape and arguably better-looking than anyone she knew within ten years of his age...

All of the unused responses sounded dumb as he played them over in his mind, so he wheeled the Caddy into a parking spot beside her blue Honda Accord. The car was empty, so he got out and headed for the entry, a double-door affair, approachable from two sides. As he approached it, a tall, heavy-set man emerged and turned to hold the door for Carlton. The man wore a rumpled suit with a white shirt buttoned to his throat, but no tie. It was a look that didn't get much play in San Antonio, Texas (or anywhere else, for that matter) more suited to a speakeasy gangster from the Twenties, or a well-dressed gunslinger in the Old West. However, his politeness at holding the door prompted Carlton to nod and thank the man as he entered the foyer.

"My pleasure, Carl," the man mumbled as he quickly turned and released the door, striding away as he spoke.

Surprised, Carlton turned to look at the retreating figure, wondering if he'd heard correctly. The man had addressed him by something that sounded like "Carl," not Carlton, but close enough to make him wonder where he might know the guy from. After a few seconds of gawking at the back of the man as he walked away, he shook his head and surmised the man might have been a past driver at Superior, one he'd met at some time but didn't recognize. Dismissing the encounter, he went inside to find his date.

It took a minute of wandering around before he found her in a booth in the back section. A glass of some kind of wine was already on the low side. When she looked up at him, the odd meeting at the door was immediately banished from his mind. He slid into the opposite side and glanced around before meeting her look, the blue eyes stunning as ever. Seeing her for the first time in a while, he wished for something clever, intelligent, or memorable to say to her, something to get this propitious encounter headed in the right direction.

Failing to come up with anything, he went with: "Hi! Sorry if I'm late. I was trying out some new scuba gear in my bathtub, and my flipper got hung on the soap dish."

The resulting smile gave Carlton a tiny flip-flop in his stomach, a feeling for which he immediately chastised himself. It had been that feeling he'd experienced in Mexico the first time they'd kissed, leading to a couple of good months, now ended and apparently forgotten—at least by her.

"You're a funny guy, Carlton," she said. "I like that, always did. A girl needs someone to make her laugh."

"Well, I'm your man, then. Carlton the Jokester, they call me."

"Okay, Jokester, but they'll call you something else if you don't watch where you hang your flipper."

A waiter appeared, toting a couple of monstrous menus. Carlton ordered a beer and gestured toward Heather's wine glass. She shook her head, and the waiter scurried away. Carlton flipped open the menu and began plodding through the selection of every form of pasta and sauce in existence, while Heather perused the salad section.

When she closed the menu, she looked up and went straight to the point. Her smile was gone. "Something happened that I need to ask you about."

The tone was unmistakable, her official DEA agent tone, the one that revealed her professional side and her true expertise. Carlton caught it, and tensed for what was coming. Not that he had expected *your place or mine?* or even anything close to that, but he hadn't thought about the possibility of this being a pure business meeting. He waited to hear her spiel, and the wait wasn't long.

"A local criminal was gunned down day before yesterday, a guy named Vince Peters. He was found dead in an alley on the West Side, not far from downtown."

Carlton shook his head, a somber look on his face. "Must be some mistake. Nothing like that ever happens on the West Side," he said, dead-panning the absurd comment. Both of them were acutely aware that the city's western area inside Loop 410 had some pretty rough sections, and bodies with bullet holes weren't that uncommon in the area's alleys.

Heather scowled at his weak joke, and moved to get her story taken in the proper context. "This is serious, Carlton, so listen carefully. Peters was shot in the head three times with a small-caliber weapon, likely a .22 or a .25, delivered at close range. They're still waiting on ballistics for specifics. But he had other wounds, made by big slugs, and that's the ones they're wanting to get analyzed first." She paused in her narrative and took a sip of wine.

Carlton, thinking she was waiting for him to theorize, didn't have to think long. "So two weapons, two shooters? That would make sense, sending at least two hitters for a big target like Peters, to make sure somebody got the job done while watching out for minders. If he was important in the local chain, he'd have had bodyguards."

Of course, she thought, Carlton Westerfield would know the tactics behind such a job. From his suspected former occupation, it was a no-brainer that two or more guys would be used to make sure the target's bodyguards didn't interfere with the job at hand. But that wasn't the point she was trying to make, and she shook her head impatiently to let him know it. Aloud, she tried to get back on subject. "The number of hitters isn't the topic of interest right now. Investigators think the placement of the bullets was intended to send a message."

Sensing trouble ahead, Carlton put on a confused look, something he'd had a great deal of practice with when conversing with women. "And you think I know what the message is?"

"I think you've sent that message before. So yes, I think it's possible you know."

Finally seeing where this was headed, Carlton rolled his eyes and groaned theatrically. "Heather, I've told you a dozen times to quit believing all the crap your boss *thinks* he knows about my past. He's grasping, trying to solve some old gangster hits here in the Alamo City.

"Or maybe he's succeeded in getting you to drink the Kool-Aid. It sounds like you've come around to his point of view about me, since there had to be some reason you dropped me like a bad habit."

"That has nothing to do with this!" she snapped. "So quit trying to make me the bad girl who dumped you because of office gossip. I'm talking about something entirely different here, and you might want to listen to me, just for once, okay?"

She stopped for a moment and took a deep breath while Carlton put up his hands in surrender. When she started again, her voice was calm and a few decibels lower. "Look Carlton, you shouldn't be surprised when suspicions arise about a guy who drives an expensive car, but doesn't have a loan for it, never did. A guy who dresses like a pro golfer from Dallas, vacays in Rio de Janeiro, and buys cheap phones by the case, but reported income last year to the IRS of less than thirty thousand dollars, earned by ferrying rental cars from one location to another. Sound like anybody you know?"

She paused in her lengthy diatribe, letting the just-acquired IRS information soak in while Carlton looked at her with no expression whatsoever. Clearly, he wasn't about to divulge anything to her that might clarify his past or present, not now, after their relationship had soured. Instead, he tried to recall anything he might have said during their time together, anything telling regarding his financial status. He didn't think so, and with good reason: some details of his past needed to remain a secret *forever*.

For Heather's part, she remained silent, waiting for the right moment to continue, while she thought about the mysterious man seated across the table, a quiet, trim, good-looking man in his early sixties who seemed a lot younger and was having a hard time leaving middle age for life's senior section.

Despite his claims to the contrary, recent DEA research had uncovered bits and pieces about Carlton Westerfield's past connection to a local gangster named Randall "Big Mo" Morris (now deceased). Murders of numerous unsavory locals spanning years remained officially unsolved, but Heather's boss, Stan Ikos, Special Agent in Charge of the local DEA office, had doggedly maintained that Carlton was a likely candidate to be good for the hits, performed while working for the old-school gangster known as "Big Mo."

Ikos' opinion had been bolstered after a closer review of Carlton's role in the parking garage shootout that had left him and Heather wounded and local drug kingpin Brujido Ramos dead. Some time after the shooting, a closer look at the mandatory autopsy report indicated that Ramos himself may have had a couple of extra bullet holes, with entry angles that Agent Colson could not have achieved from her position on the garage floor… badly wounded, lying on her back.

Another oddity preceding that gun battle: it seems that four of Mr. Ramos' gangbanger employees had met with foul play at an East Side car wash days before Ramos met his own bloody fate in a parking garage. Investigators found five spent shell casings with matching firing pin indentations, indicating five shots from the same .45 caliber weapon had resulted in four *armed* bodies strewn across the parking lot—a fine piece of marksmanship in anyone's book. Although a professional hitman didn't necessarily rely on fancy gunplay, Ikos was adamant in his position that Carlton Westerfield had been the shooter in that bloodbath.

The clincher came from an unlikely source, a *Nuevo Laredo*, Mexico investigator who provided Ikos with a preliminary report on the recent shooting of one Cletus Miller, aka Clive Millstone, a DEA contract operative who had been gunned down outside a restaurant in that city. The first report suggested a professional hit, with two or three gunmen involved. Therefore, thinking it well beyond the capabilities of a sole, sixty-something man, Ikos initially dismissed Westerfield from the killing of Miller/Millstone.

But a follow-up report revealed three new witnesses from a car in the restaurant parking lot who described an older Anglo man, well-dressed, who stepped from beside a trash dumpster and shot two men, then turned and confronted a third man who was holding a woman against him. When the woman escaped his grasp, the Anglo shot twice in rapid succession. The man fell to the ground, and the Anglo fled in a car with the woman, who was of indeterminate ethnicity, and a Hispanic man. Alas, the report went on to say there was no real progress in solving the case.

Three minutes had elapsed while Heather mentally replayed what she knew of the current state of a just-formed inter-agency investigation into the severe wounding of the DEA contract guy in February and its possible connection to the murder of Vince Peters just yesterday. Then, taking the last sip of her wine, she leaned forward and spoke quietly to Carlton, hoping he would stay calm and listen to what she knew—and maybe impart some information she didn't.

"Peters was shot with a large caliber weapon, either before or after the head shots that killed him. The ME may be able to determine which shots came first, but no matter. What matters is the placement of the large-caliber rounds, the ones intended to convey a message."

Carlton relaxed his stare enough to look inquisitive. "Okay, where'd he get hit with this message?"

Signaling to the waiter for another glass of wine, she pushed her menu aside and looked directly into Carlton's face. "Peters had both his kneecaps blown apart, just like Cletus Miller."

"*What?* Forget about Peters! Somebody popped caps on *Cletus Miller's* caps?" Carlton quipped sarcastically, raising his eyebrows in what he hoped she would take as genuine surprise.

It didn't work. It was Heather's turn for an eye-roll and a launch into a verbal scolding for his smart mouth, but both were saved from the battle by the waiter. Heather ordered a salad in great detail as to ingredients and dressing, while Carlton pointed out some kind of pasta/meat/sauce combo on the menu, one with a multi-syllable name straight from *The Godfather.*

Meal ordered, Heather started again. "Remember, I'm the one who told you about Miller working for us—"

"Yes, and I told you the sleazy, turncoat bastard shot my friend Tino in the face with a Colt .45," Carlton interrupted. "So forgive me if I don't have any sympathy for Miller getting his sticks shortened."

"I know, and I'm sorry for the loss of your friend. I get it, even if he *was* a drug dealer who needed to spend a few decades in the slammer.

"But cut the coy act, because right now, you're looking good for the stick-shortening job on Miller."

He stared at her in disbelief. "Oh, Heather, give me a break! As I recall, you wouldn't tell me anything about Millstone, Miller, whatever the hell his name is, not where he was, or even where he called home base, because you thought I was going after him for killing Tino. You said something like 'I don't know and wouldn't tell you if I did.' Remember?"

Heather was shaking her head as he finished. "That doesn't mean you couldn't find him on your own. Or with help from your buddy Reynaldo Gomez, who has more big-league contacts in Mexico than Major League Baseball has in Puerto Rico.

"Carlton, current thinking has you popping him in the parking lot of an Italian restaurant called *Restaurante Tomatillos* in Nuevo Laredo," she added, watching his face for any sign of hitting close to the truth.

Carlton stared at her in disbelief. "Oh, so that's why you wanted to meet here? In an *Italian* restaurant? Did you think that would jog my memory? If so, it didn't work, because I don't recall shooting Clive Millstone's kneecaps in a restaurant parking lot—but I wish I had. Tell your boss I said that if it will make him feel better about his hypothesis."

"He already feels pretty confident about it, after getting an anonymous package with a newspaper clipping of the crime scene, then a follow-up report from the *Nuevo Laredo* P.D. They found three wits who saw, quote, *'an older, well-dressed Anglo guy shoot two men dead, then shot another man twice before leaving in a car with a woman and a Hispanic man.'* I'd bet the shooter was you, the woman was Paula Hendricks, and the Hispanic man was Reynaldo Gomez."

Carlton shook his head emphatically as he smoothly lied to her. "Then you'd lose your bet. It wasn't *this* well-dressed Anglo guy."

After a few silent seconds, he decided to make one small attempt to learn something while she seemed in a talkative mood. "You mentioned Ikos getting an anonymous package, then an updated report from *Nuevo Laredo*, and now this Peters killing. And now, those three things are being tied together by an inter-agency investigation? Can you tell me the agencies involved?"

She swallowed some salad and thought for a moment. "I guess so, because right now, it's just an informal joint operation, the FBI and us. Their lead investigative agent keeps me, us, updated on progress."

She let the subject lie, and Carlton started thinking over what she'd said, putting aside her verbal slip for the moment. "Why the FBI? What's their interest in Miller?"

She shrugged and speared some more lettuce. "None, until Peters gets hit the same way. They were running a mole at Peters' operation, trying to get somebody inside. Their mole disappears last week, and Peters turns up dead and kneecapped. When they ran the MO at NCIC, they discovered the Miller job had the same touch."

"Huh? I thought you said Miller got popped in *Nuevo Laredo*. Isn't that still in Mexico? If so, how does a crime there end up in the NCIC database?"

"International cooperation, at least in Border regions, known in Mexico as *La Frontera*. After the successful bust on the *Golfo* cartel and the Benavides brothers, both the DEA and the PFM decided to cooperate in a number of ways. One of them is sharing data on crime statistics and MOs, among other things."

Carlton nodded, seeing where the connection had been made. A crime committed with a particular twist or special circumstance would be compared to a national database to see what other crimes had the same markings, thus providing information as to the possible perpetrator. Any law enforcement agency could access NCIC, the National Crime Information Center, for such comparisons, but top dogs like the FBI and the DEA get results a lot quicker than the Podunk, Texas Police Department, or maybe even the big San Antonio PD. Now the two countries were sharing the data, a disturbing piece of news for anyone who had seen Mexico as a safe haven. He started to ask more about Peters' illegal activities, but thought better of it, not wanting to reveal too much interest in the deceased gangster, certainly not to Heather, who was looking for any connection.

But now for the real connection, the one she didn't want me to know.

"So this FBI guy tells you where their investigation stands? He wouldn't happen to be your new beau, would he?"

An irritated look crossed her face. "Well, yes, Darren is the lead investigator, but don't make too much out of that. I'm his official POC with my agency, so there's nothing odd about him keeping me updated."

"Yeah, I'll bet. Oh, tell me again what POC stands for? Um, let me guess…"

Annoyed by her own slipup and Carlton's quick mouth, Heather laid her fork down and leaned toward him. "I think you got your revenge by shooting Cletus Miller in the knees. You didn't want to kill him, you wanted to punish him for a long time for murdering Tino. Then you sent the newspaper article to Stan Ikos, because you wanted to poke a finger in his eye. Now, for some reason, Vince Peters gets the same thing as Miller, and yes, it raises questions.

"Carlton, you think law enforcement is a bunch of dumbasses, don't you? Pretty cute, but you should have waited a while. You know the expression *'revenge is a dish best eaten cold,'* right?"

"Sure, I've heard that. But I've never been sure about its meaning. Or its veracity."

"Apparently not." She picked up her fork and pointed at his plate. "But I promise you, *that* dish is best eaten hot. So quit talking and eat your food."

He did as instructed, but not before smiling across the table at her. "I've always liked dining out with you."

Despite the fact that she'd managed to upset his usual quiet, mild-mannered persona, his proclamation was absolutely true.

CHAPTER 2

Leaving Little Italy, Carlton decided to drive around a while to think over the past ninety minutes, which had resulted in a lot of questions, mostly unanswered at this point. And he wasn't sure if they needed answers, but it would be nice to know what the inter-agency investigation was uncovering, if anything. Heather's dinner invitation (she'd even insisted on picking up the tab) might have just been a fishing expedition, he thought, a facet of the investigation assigned to her because of their past relationship. He smiled to himself as he thought about how short and inconclusive her report on their meeting would be.

But back to the questions: Who was Vince Peters, and why was he wounded in both knees, just like Miller/Millstone? Had someone who learned about Millstone's crippling wounds decided to use the nasty message on Peters for a similar reason—had Peters committed a vicious atrocity against someone, and a friend of that someone decided to make him think about it for the rest of his life? Or was it more twisted: was Millstone orchestrating this from his wheelchair, trying to set Carlton up by making him look good for the Peters hit? Carlton had to appreciate the irony behind that approach.

Other questions came to mind, a couple that were even more disturbing: Who were these new witnesses from the *Nuevo Laredo* parking lot, the ones who had seen quite a bit in the poor lighting behind the *Restaurante Tomotillos*? Another lie, perhaps, a piece of bait for Heather's fishing expedition? And why was Stan Ikos, Special Agent in Charge, so hot to hammer Carlton? Just plain dislike for a guy who'd been banging one of his female agents like a screen door? Jealousy, because *he* wanted to do the banging?

Jeez, take a look at Agent Colson; what man wouldn't want to check under the hood, take a test drive, maybe even sign a long-term lease, despite huge payments on that honey of a ride?

Or was Darren Moore, FBI agent and Heather's new flame, the source of all the brouhaha? If so, why? Carlton wasn't hanging around, stalking her like a love-sick teenager. He hadn't even called her for weeks, because as far as he was concerned, the deal was simply over, finished, time to move on. Poorly skilled as he was regarding long-term relationships with women, Carlton was smart enough to know when it was time to bow out. And he had—until his phone rang last night.

He pulled into a Valero and gassed up the car, then picked up a newspaper. He wanted to study what had been released to the press regarding Vince Peters without using the internet to do so. Indeed, until he discovered more about what was going on, he'd go to a library for any on-line stuff, wearing a long-billed ball cap for the security cameras every branch had installed over the entryway…Carlton Westerfield was nothing if not cautious. He only wished he could better control his smart mouth, like he'd done while working for Big Mo.

Once home, he scanned through the paper until he found the article. Not very informative, the piece simply described Vince Peters, a local man suspected of "ongoing illegal activities" as being the victim of a gang-style shooting. Carlton grinned as he ticked off the usual tidbits of information that comprised the rest of the story: *At this time, the assailant(s) are unknown, remain at large,* and are *considered armed and dangerous.* The article ended with another boiler-plate catch-phrase, *"a police department spokesperson said the investigation is continuing."*

Carlton had been hopeful to find out what kind of illegal activities Peters had been involved with in order to get a feel for who might have wanted to pop him and why, along with mangling his kneecaps in the process. Now it looked like that would entail a trip to the library to look at past newspaper articles after all, or a discrete inquiry among the city's underbelly, since he was only vaguely familiar with the name, much less with Peters' alleged criminal activity. He skimmed the rest of the paper, then tossed it into the recycle box under the kitchen sink before turning on the tube for an evening of television wasteland.

The next day started early, with a text from Ralph Lopez at Superior Auto Leasing. The San Antonio location had accumulated a surplus of small sedans and suffered a shortage of mid-size SUVs. Ralph wanted Carlton and a couple of other drivers to ferry the sedans to Houston and return with the needed SUVs, the sooner the better. Not enough to hire an eighteen-wheel car transport, they would simply drive down and back. It would take two trips to get the vehicles swapped out, so Carlton's take for the long day's work would be about a hundred and sixty bucks. Clearly, the gig with Superior was not a path to great wealth, he thought, a fact pointed out the previous night by Heather as she grilled him over dinner.

Recalling the evening, which had turned out fairly pleasant after a dubious start, her comment about his reported income nagged at him while he brushed his teeth. Why had she obtained the information? Easy enough for the Drug Enforcement Administration to get, but had she only asked, he would have saved her the trouble. I'd have made her a copy of my tax return, he thought, so she could share it with her boss and her new boyfriend, give them something to wonder about—or laugh about, more likely.

Evidently, his lifestyle had been bothering someone and had them wondering how he drove a late-model Cadillac, lived in a decent apartment, and wore nice clothes on pauper's wages. But hey, this is America, isn't it, where everyone is entitled to the Good Life? Besides, it's not as though he lived the exorbitant lifestyle of a gangster like Al Capone, whose blatant and heinous criminal activities went unpunished for years—until he was convicted for tax evasion. So *why* was Carlton Westerfield's paltry income such an item of interest? The inquiry must have something to do with their suspicions of him for popping Vince Peters, he surmised.

Perhaps someone at the two law enforcement agencies thought he was still making hits and earning big money doing it—and if so, they were wrong, at least for the several years just passed. Carlton smiled to himself as he dressed and mentally ticked off the four places where he'd hidden stashes of cash from his years as a mechanic, years now long done. Careful, infrequent visits to the caches enabled him to live fairly well, but not so well as to justify an inquiry to the IRS. So it had to be connected to the current inter-agency investigation.

He put the subject out of his mind as he headed out the door, telling himself that he need not worry about their investigation. The trail to the Miller/Millstone shooting was cold, notwithstanding the supposed new witnesses. If law enforcement had any proof, they would be on him like a duck on a grasshopper, jurisdiction problems be damned. And he *hadn't* killed Vince Peters and didn't know, or care, who did.

That mindset was about to change.

Ralph Lopez met him as he strolled onto the front lot after parking the Caddy out back with reserved rental units. "There you are! I'm glad you could make a couple of runs today. One of the others called in, can't make it. But Del Monighan will be here shortly," he added, opening the office door and motioning for Carlton to precede him inside.

The pair shook hands while Ralph looked his long-time driver up and down. "You look good, Carlton. Life taking care of you, I guess?"

"You bet, Ralph, everything's good on my end. How about you? Business is good, I see, since you need some cars shuffled around."

Ralph moved to the whiteboard behind his cluttered desk. "Yeah, we ended up with a bunch of butt-beater sedans out of New Mexico, and most of my SUVs have headed out to the Valley and Houston. Houston's the only place that will part with a few and accept the small gas-mileage cars in return." As he spoke, he pointed to the list of makes and models and their corresponding locations printed on the board.

Carlton looked at the indecipherable squiggles on the board, but couldn't discern what Ralph was referring to. "Ralph, that board is about as easy to understand as your desk. How do you find anything around here?"

Superior's manager grinned at the jab and opened the desk drawer. As he rummaged around for a pack of cigarettes, he explained his organizational skills, or lack thereof. "Actually, I keep it all in here," he said, tapping the side of his head. "The board is just for show.

"Which reminds me, a guy came in here yesterday, a guy with the FBI, of all things. He said pretty much the same thing about my board."

Shocked, Carlton turned quickly toward Ralph, then hoped he hadn't noticed the sudden movement or the surprise on his face. "Yeah? What'd he want? He looking for a missing weapon of mass destruction on your desk?"

Ralph grinned and shook his head. "No, but when he started asking questions about the car locations, I was looking at the board like I did with you, and I could tell he couldn't tell shit from looking at it."

"Neither could I. But what does a federal lawman have to do with rental cars? Just because they cross state lines?"

"Yep. Apparently, they are looking into a stolen car ring involving lots of lease cars. So they're checking smaller operations with agents wearing out shoe leather. The big boys, like Enterprise, Alamo, and Hertz get a whole team working at their headquarters operations and looking at computer printouts."

Carlton nodded again, though he still didn't understand. "I didn't know there was an ongoing theft of lease cars. Or does it go on all the time?"

"Don't know, but this has to do with that guy that got killed the other night off of Zarzamora. Some big crime guy, I think. Can't remember his name, but it was in the paper."

"Vince Peters?" Carlton blurted out, immediately sorry he'd revealed any knowledge of the guy or his demise. "I saw it in the paper," he added quickly.

"Yeah, that's it! Supposedly, he was the local go-to guy to get cars boosted around here. He owned a couple of body shops and they take the cars there for serial number alterations, false titles, or chop them up, sell the parts, whatever in hell they do with stolen cars these days.

"If the damn customers would care enough to take the key out of the rental, they wouldn't be so easy to steal. But hey, *it's a rental*, right?" he added, quoting the smart-assed quip from some movie or another.

Carlton nodded and turned to look out the window, glad to let the subject drop. And delighted with the information, meaning he wouldn't have to research Vince Peters.

But Ralph wasn't done with his story. "Yeah, this guy even wanted to know all about my drivers, even when and where they drove to and from. He got a list of names of everyone, even the part-time guys like you, along with trip schedules for the last two weeks and next week too."

"You gave him my name?" Carlton asked, surprised at this turn of events.

"Well, yes! I mean, he showed me his badge, he was an FBI agent, no doubt. What was I supposed to do? Tell him to eat shit and die? I guess I could have, but he'd have come back with a warrant or court order, right?"

Ralph's explanation and rhetorical questions all made perfect sense and Carlton calmed down, hoping he hadn't shown the surprise he'd felt inside. Trying to sound casual, he ventured to get additional information. "No, no, that's fine. I've got nothing to hide. I'm just wondering why they are going to such lengths as checking drivers' backgrounds when they've got the main culprit's body down at the city morgue.

"So what was this dude like, anyway, this FBI guy?"

Ralph thought for a moment before answering. "Um, maybe forty-five or so. Wearing a suit, just like you see on TV shows about FBI guys. Very polite and professional acting. Why?"

"Oh, nothing. I was just wondering if they really are like you see on TV shows. You know, wearing a suit and looking like…well, like an FBI agent."

Ralph shrugged. "Well, this one did, anyway. A neat haircut, shiny shoes, a fancy tie, all that stuff. And polite, but real pushy, you know?"

The additional description didn't fill in all the gaps, but it helped. Carlton wished Ralph would produce a business card left by the agent, but wasn't going to ask. Even so, he had a good idea who the inquisitive agent was. And he was pretty sure the guy didn't give a hoot about any of Superior's drivers except one.

The killer stood in the shadow of the seedy building's overhang. Just behind, a flickering neon sign in the window announced the place to be a bond bailsman's office, a popular place in this area. One door down, a tattoo shop was still open for the late-night crowd. Tonight's customers wouldn't be first to awake the next day wondering why they had let a buddy talk them into getting an obscene graphic inked into their skin...not only because it hurt like hell and looked ridiculous, but it had been expensive. The money could have been spent on more drinking...or some dope.

It was after eleven, but the bars in this, a crappy part of Houston's near northeast side, were just cranking up to full volume. Cars parked along the curb were still coming and going, with rowdy club-goers abandoning one venue and driving a few blocks to another. In another hour, the traffic flow would subside, with the hard-core drinkers and partiers anchored into their last waterhole for the night, the light-weights having departed for home and hearth in time to get some sleep, or maybe just to avoid having grief flung at them by the significant others left alone for the night.

The killer watched the bar across the intersection, cater-cornered from the building behind. The target had gone in over an hour earlier and, according to the information obtained earlier, seldom moved from bar to bar, choosing instead to pick one and stay until around midnight. And the target's car wasn't parked at the curb with all the other come-and-go folks. Instead, his late-model Jaguar was in a Park n' Pay lot behind the very building where the killer now stood, waiting for the target to emerge.

This part was miserable; the waiting was a monumental waste of time, time that could be spent elsewhere. And waiting for this guy to come out and head to his car was the worst possible expenditure of time. But it was necessary to do it this way, because the guy had to be hit just right, not just popped and left to bleed out on the pavement. If not, that fucking guy would ruin his life... unless I get a chance to use this big piece on him—*and* his *kneecaps, he thought grimly, despising the man and the day their paths had crossed.*

The thought made the killer aware of the extra weight of the two weapons in the pockets of the bulky black cargo pants. One in each side somewhat offset the weight difference, but one was a much larger gun than the other, necessitated by the particular nature of this hit. Just like the one a few nights ago in San Antonio, this guy needed to go down a certain way, a way that took considerable finesse and timing—

The killer's train of thought was interrupted by the opening of the bar's front door and a single black man emerging. Though still too early, it looked like it could be him, but he'd have to be followed and observed carefully, make sure he headed for the right car, the same car the killer had identified earlier and confirmed as the target's personal vehicle. So far tonight, the killer had only needed to follow two other drinkers, both of whom turned out to be false leads, since they'd both gotten into cars parked along the curb. Now, this guy was headed for the break between the bar and an adjoining business, which led to the rear parking lot. The killer pushed off the side of the bondsman office and hunched forward, crossing the street at a good distance behind the man, and hoping the parking lot wasn't busy with people coming and going.

The San Antonio job had been easier—the target was parked in his own private spot behind a body shop, one that he supposedly owned. Hitting this guy in a public lot was a lot riskier, but it was better to do it this way, to catch the guy outside the car with his entire body exposed. The target needed to be standing for the best results. It was the only way to ensure the target would be hit strategically, thus making it look right to the police so they would draw the right conclusions, file the right description in their report.

CHAPTER 3

The workday turned out to be a long one, since Superior's location in Houston was nearly halfway to Galveston on IH-45, beyond Hobby Airport. Carlton and two other guys made both trips, putting him back at his apartment after two in the morning, tired, but a few dollars better off.

The long drive had given him time by himself to ponder the FBI/DEA investigation, thinking about possible connections between Cletus Miller and Vince Peters and how Carlton Westerfield's name was so quickly moved onto the list of possibles. On that task, he'd struck out, and as he rolled through Seguin on the last trip, he decided to quit worrying about something that had to be a coincidence. As usual, the last thirty miles of the trip seemed interminable. All he wanted was to get home, take a long, hot shower and relax. It was not to be.

Seeing the missed call on his burner when he got out of the shower seemed like a stroke of good fortune at first. Recognizing the number, he hit "redial" and started talking as soon as the party on the other end answered.

"You called the Jokester, and he regrettably missed your call. But the Jokester is here now, at your service and dying to talk to you."

"Not if you knew why I was calling. Were you in Houston today?" Not even an opening pleasantry, her voice clipped and business-like.

Carlton took the phone from his ear and stared at it, as though a message on the screen might explain how she had known. Then, realizing he'd taken too long to answer, tried to cover it with more foolishness. *"Um, 'Ma'am the Jokester doesn't reveal his location to just <u>anyone</u> on his Missed Call list. May I ask who this is?"*

"Cut the crap, Jokester. Because another guy got popped tonight—make that <u>last</u> night—this one in Houston. And guess what? His right knee was blown away by a large-caliber bullet. Just one knee, the other one was hit, but not completely destroyed. Then he was popped with three small slugs in the back of the head. Lights out, of course."

"Well, gosh, fun as that sounds, I was way too busy to do anything like that. Two consecutive trips to that madhouse takes a while. No time to stop and have target practice. Only out of the cars I drove for two or three minutes, swapping keys with the lot manager. Oh, and the same thing on this end, just in case you find another kneecapped vic here in SA."

"Was someone with you during those drives? Because—"

"I'm sure your joint task force has uncovered what I do for a living and exactly how it works," he interrupted, trying to curb his tone, but not succeeding. *"But I'll give you a quick review: no pleasure rides in the country with passengers. I just drive lease cars to other locations, get out and hand the keys to the lot manager. Then I get in another one and drive back.*

"Remember, you saw my tax return. Look at it again, then call the IRS and ask them what that 'occupation' block means when it's filled in with 'Car Delivery Driver.' Then ask your boyfriend what he learned yesterday at Superior."

If Heather was surprised that Carlton knew of Darren Moore's visit to his employer's business, it didn't show up in her voice. She responded without missing a beat. *"He learned that you have a lot of mobility available to you, mobility in cars that are gone the next day, in another place, with lots of unaccountable miles and possible forensic evidence—useless evidence—from other drivers, that's what he learned."*

"Well, I'm sure he's a sharp lad, your boyfriend. He'll get over all those obstacles and find the perp. But it won't be me, because I didn't kill anyone, didn't kneecap anyone. He's wasting taxpayer money looking at me for it."

"I hope so, Carlton, I really do."

With that final remark, she broke the connection, leaving Carlton to look stupidly at the phone screen again, which was about as much help as his car's owner's manual—zero. He sighed and snapped it shut, shaking his head at this turn of events, none of which should involve him. Well, except Miller's fate, he admitted to himself, but that was water long gone under the international bridge at Laredo. Under ordinary circumstances, Cletus Miller's wounding wouldn't have raised an eyebrow with any legitimate law enforcement agency. The loud-mouthed Brit mercenary was a cold-blooded killer many times over who deserved to die a horrible death or continue living a horrible life. During his murky career, he had cheated the DEA and the American taxpayer out of hundreds of thousands of dollars. But so had every politician since Millard Fillmore, so no big deal there.

Carlton again wished Heather had told him more about the new kneecapped victim in Houston, although this time he hadn't even thought to ask. Now he would have to look it up, see if any news out of Houston would impart details of the shooting or the victim. The prospect of going to a library in the morning, or even a C-store to get a Houston newspaper didn't appeal to him. On impulse, he opened his phone and hit redial for Heather's burner. After four rings, it went to voice mail, and he shut his own phone, angry with himself for resorting to calling her for information. He considered going online anyway, despite the cookie trail his search for "Houston murders" would leave, but decided against it. He'd worry about it tomorrow; right now, the classic movie channel was running old detective mysteries, and he wasn't a bit sleepy. Maybe he could watch a couple and learn something about crime investigations—or better yet, extracting oneself from them.

CHAPTER 4

The next morning, Thursday, started out well, although sleep had eluded him until after five. He awoke just after eight and lay in bed wondering again about the Houston shooting and cursed the luck of it occurring on a day—make that night—when he was there; twice, in fact. He shook his head at the irony of being a suspect. He wouldn't have had time to pull off a crippling murder, even if he'd been so disposed. The absurdity of this whole thing convinced him to forget about it, at least for the moment. He got up, completed his exercise routine, and thought about where to get breakfast.

The good thing about being back in Castle Hills was the plethora of restaurants where one could get something besides a breakfast taco. While he'd lived in Tino's apartment on the far South Side, it was a ten-mile drive to find a conventional gringo breakfast like a good short stack, French toast, or ham that wasn't thin enough to read newsprint through, as was preferred by Hispanics. Though he loved Mexican food, he needed a break from time to time, so he headed for Denny's on Blanco Road, only five minutes away.

As he pulled into the parking lot, he noticed a car close behind him, a full-size sedan of indistinguishable make and unremarkable color with two occupants in front. In police jargon, the car was a "plain brown wrapper," intended to be inconspicuous. However, such vehicles stuck out these days *because* of their drab looks. Plain sedans were somewhat of a rarity at a time where everyone, even peon wage earners, seemed affluent enough to make the down payment on a slick new SUV, either red or silver in color, like what he'd been sent to Houston to get. Apparently, that's what everyone wanted to drive, even if they were just renting it to drive to the Riverwalk while visiting the Alamo City. Obviously, these guys on his bumper weren't tourists, or wage earners aspiring to look more successful than their station in life suggested.

Nope, they're cops, and not the ones who check insurance coverage and registration.

As he pulled toward the next suitable spot for the Caddy, the car stayed close behind, then pulled into the adjacent parking spot. When he got out, his peripheral vision picked up both front doors opening and the occupants, both males, getting out. Without even a glance in their direction, he figured he was having company for breakfast. The idea didn't appeal to him, but he quickly evaluated the situation and decided to make the best of it. Maybe they were just going to watch him, try to rattle him by their presence. Or, if they approached him perhaps he could get some information regarding the inter-agency investigation and the resulting scrutiny Heather Colson had warned him about. To do that, he reminded himself, he'd need some restraint on his smart remarks and be the quiet, unassuming guy he did best, the guy he'd been while he worked for Big Mo.

Without so much as a glance in their direction, he headed for the front door. Just inside, a waitress asked to seat him, and he motioned toward the diner counter. As he sat down, the front door opened, and the two men from the undercover car entered. Carlton didn't look their direction, but he could feel them looking at him, maybe fifteen feet away, while he pretended to study the menu. When the waitress saw the two guys, she moved to seat them in the main dining section; however, one guy said something, and she led them into the same section as the counter and put them in a booth almost directly behind him.

The waitress brought water and asked to take his order. "I want the French toast and two eggs, over medium."

As she turned to go, he heard a voice behind him. "Westerfield, at your age, you need to watch your cholesterol. You should have the oatmeal instead."

Hearing the voice, he knew who was behind him, at least one of them. He swiveled the counter stool around and feigned surprise at seeing FBI Agent Darren Moore. "Agent Moore! What brings you to this fine part of town?"

Moore shrugged. "Just grabbing a late breakfast. You live around here?" Carlton nearly laughed aloud at the dumb question.
You know exactly where I live, jackass!

Aloud he answered, "Yeah, about five minutes away. And this is a good place to load up on cholesterol, at my age or yours."

"Why don't you join us?" Moore asked, a smile on his face. "I'd like to talk to you."

"I'm not much of a listener before I eat in the morning."

"Oh, come on. You'll be interested in what we have to say. It'll improve your hearing." To emphasize his point he motioned for his partner to slide over and make room.

It was Carlton's turn to shrug, and he picked up his coffee and water and moved to the booth. When he placed his drinks down, he extended his hand to Moore's yet-silent companion and introduced himself. "I'm Carlton Westerfield."

"Dave Fowler." He shook hands and moved his own items over to make room for the new arrival.

As Carlton sat down, he took a quick appraisal of Fowler: older than Moore, maybe fifty, thinning gray hair, average build, a stern-looking face that had cop written all over it. The two agents couldn't have dressed more alike without looking downright comical; both had gray suits of similar cut, white shirts, and conservative ties of varying shades of blue and gray stripes. Carlton smiled to himself and wished Ralph Lopez were there to see the pair seated in the same booth, looking like central casting's idea of FBI agents.

Knowing they had followed him from his apartment, Carlton had several smart-mouthed observations he wanted to make, but reminded himself of the need to play it cool—at least for the moment. And taking Heather at her word, he wasn't going to let Darren Moore know they'd had dinner and a follow-up phone conversation. But that didn't include letting Moore think he was completely naïve.

"You must have really needed to talk to me, since you obviously followed me from my apartment," he began, keeping a pleasant smile on his face. "I doubt you guys just stumbled into Denny's at the precise moment I did. So what can I do for you?"

If revealing their tailing ploy upset him, Moore didn't show it. "We're in involved in an investigation that's begun to take on characteristics much like a serial killing spree." He waited, an expectant look on his face, as though Carlton might throw up his hands and blurt out an admission to being a reincarnation of Ted Bundy.

Instead, Carlton took a sip of coffee and said nothing. A long moment passed before he met the agent's look and arched his eyebrows in surprise, as though he'd only just realized Moore was waiting for a response. "*Really?* A serial killer operating here in this city?" he said with genuine concern, looking back and forth between both agents. "That's pretty scary. How many does it take to qualify as serial murders, by the way?"

"The Bureau has an official internal designation of three murders of the same pattern or very similar characteristics. However, other factors can change that number."

Already knowledgeable of what Moore had just said, Carlton nodded. "Not sure how I can help you with that. Unless you're looking for someone to pose as a possible target and lure this guy out. Do I fit the profile of the victims?"

It was Fowler who answered. "No Mr. Westerfield, in fact, you fit the profile of the *killer*."

Carlton did a fair job of turning quickly to his right to face Fowler, a look of amazement matching his open mouth, which was uttering nothing, so he shut it. A quick recovery and a switch to a look of real concern was amplified by setting down his coffee cup a bit harder than necessary. Of course, the two agents had seen indignation played out before, and Carlton's act, superb though it was, didn't appear to faze them. Both continued to stare at Carlton as though waiting for him to come clean.

But Carlton played out the scene as he'd seen it evolve, keeping calm and pursing his lips reflectively, as though thinking through the reasoning behind the implied accusation. "Well, I guess most serial killers *are* single men. I don't recall reading about any of them with a nice little house and picket fence, a wife, two-point-three kids, and a dog...but then I don't study that stuff as I'm sure you two guys do." He let the observation lie, as though waiting for an explanation of their theory. They didn't keep him waiting long.

"It's not that part that fits, not how you live," Moore said, taking the lead back from Fowler. "But you're right, serial killers aren't usually the guy next door, unless you happen to live next door to Jeffrey Dahmer."

Carlton allowed a smile to show he was able to take the little joke in stride and wait for the lawman to divulge exactly what aligned him with other serial killers in history.

Instead, Fowler leaned forward in the booth, and took the ball for a run. "It's how you *shoot*, Westerfield, how you shoot people you really don't like, or maybe someone you think needs to send a message to others. *Making a statement*, the psychologists call it, or a *signature* that differentiates it from other crimes and criminals."

Carlton timed his response to start five full seconds later, as though he were having to think about Fowler's explanation. "I'm not following you," he said carefully. "I haven't shot anyone, I don't even own a gun. And if I recall my time in the military, I didn't shoot very well then, and I haven't tried to improve in the last forty-some-odd years.

"As to sending a message, I don't get that part at all. Whoever's getting shot probably gets the message, right?"

It was Moore's turn, but instead of addressing Carlton he looked across at his partner and spoke. "The SAC over at DEA told me he was good at being evasive by being acting dense as to the subject at hand. I'll have to say, he's pretty convincing." Then, turning to Carlton, he qualified his remark. "But not convincing enough, not for me."

Carlton knew the meeting was going nowhere, not for him or the agents. They weren't going to get anything from him, and he wouldn't learn anything useful, not in this environment. They weren't going to mention Vince Peters or the guy who'd been popped yesterday in Houston. They weren't going to ask his whereabouts at the time of the murders, like they did in all the cop shows on television. They weren't even going to reach back to Cletus Miller and his pre-wheelchair days, ask about their relationship during the big drug war in Mexico. No, they were just tossing softballs and waiting for Carlton to get nervous and spill something useful to *them*.

Hiding his exasperation, he met Agent Moore's inquiring countenance with an unwavering look of his own. "I'm not trying to *convince* you of anything, because if you're not going to arrest me or take me in for questioning on an official basis, I don't need to. In fact, all I need to do is eat my breakfast," he added, leaning back to let the waitress set his plate in front of him before she turned to the agents and took their orders.

Carlton dug into his meal, and the two agents took a break from their tag team tactics to sip coffee. While he ate, he made every effort to appear relaxed by avoiding looking at them and concentrating on his meal as though sitting alone. If the lack of conversation bothered anyone, it didn't show. Within a few minutes, the pair of lawmen had their food, everyone was eating, and the awkward silence abated for the moment.

Carlton had finished the eggs and was halfway through the French toast before speaking. "I'm not sure why y'all are so interested in me, but you're wasting your time. Whatever source is giving you information pointing to me is simply mistaken, or trying to set me up for something I didn't do. Either way, I'm not interested in your problems. But I am concerned when you try to make *your* problem *my* problem. You might try too hard."

With that, he reached for his water glass and dipped his napkin into it. Then he carefully wiped the coffee cup and his eating utensils with the dampened cloth, while the agents stared at him with curiosity. Then he rose from the booth and addressed them both. "I'm sure you can find something else with a hard surface from which to transfer my fingerprints onto something that will incriminate me, but it won't be this morning's breakfast dishes—the breakfast you guys rudely interrupted and didn't learn anything from.

"Oh, by the way, my cholesterol numbers are perfect, much better than either of yours, I'd bet. So to celebrate my good health, breakfast is on me." He leaned across the booth, collected the three separate checks and placed two twenties on top of them before turning away and sauntering out the door.

CHAPTER 5

Walking to his car, Carlton tried to calm down and evaluate the near-comedic encounter, but he noticed a slight tremor in his hand as pushed the unlock function on the key fob. Contrary to his promise to himself to play it cool and try to learn something, he'd become irritated within minutes of the encounter, sparked by the certainty that the agents had been watching his apartment and followed him to Denny's, and not the chance run-in Moore initially claimed. Then, the pointed hints regarding shooting and "sending a message" did nothing to further a friendly discussion. Clearly, the federal agents had wanted to direct the interview, manipulate the discussion, and not give away anything. The tag-team ploy and cocksure manner of good law enforcement was designed to intimidate the subject of questioning, and those two guys were pros at it. Plus, anyone dealing with a large federal agency would be foolish to overlook the vast legal power and technological advantages at their disposal. They could afford to be sure of themselves.

However, despite his past work history and the more recent activities involving a shootout in Mexico, Carlton was fairly immune to intimidation tactics, reasonably certain that law enforcement didn't have anything concrete, not yet anyway. If so, he would be sitting in their office fielding questions, not eating breakfast with them. And while it might not have been the best move to embarrass them with his parting act, the look on the pair's faces had been worth it.

After removing the battery from his phone while in Denny's parking lot, he drove to the Walmart at Loop 410 and 281 to purchase another burner. Back in his car, he rehearsed his opening line for brevity, then powered up the new phone and placed a call to Reynaldo Gomez, punching in the number from memory and hoping his friend still kept his private line on his person and turned on.

Faustino "Tino" Perez' boyhood friend and the architect behind the disastrous venture in Mexico, Reynaldo was the only person who might have the necessary connections to check on Cletus Miller's status, and only if the British gunrunner were still in Mexico. Knowing Reynaldo wouldn't recognize the new number of the incoming call, Carlton wasn't surprised at the silence on the other end. He opened the conversation himself without a greeting.

"Can you still get information on our former friend down south, the one with the ambulatory problem?"

A pause while Reynaldo fielded the cryptic question and collected his thoughts for a cautious response, one that couldn't be used to pinpoint or identify either participant in the conversation. *"I think so. I'll need to contact my sources there and get back to you. Call you at this number?"*

"Yes. And can I buy your dinner in return for your services?"

A laugh at the other end. *"Absolutely! And it better be a good one, someplace expensive."*

"Perfect. I'll await your call, and we can fix a time to meet at our usual spot for important conversations."

"It's your lucky day. I'm not far from your city, checking on my…uh, agricultural interests. I'll make some inquiries and get back to you."

"As always, I appreciate it."

The call ended abruptly, both parties snapping their burner phones shut after less than forty seconds. Anyone listening in wouldn't likely figure out that the subject of the call was Cletus Miller, who'd had his knees destroyed and was supposedly recuperating in an expensive Mexican medical facility, probably on the tab of the American taxpayer. Reynaldo had indicated he was at his ranch near Sabinal, checking on his livestock, and his choice for dinner would be Ernesto's, where the pair had previously met for quiet, private dining and conversation.

The precautions were probably way overboard, but Carlton's recent visit with the smug FBI agents reminded him that his adversary had the upper hand when it came to technology and the ability to track anyone, anywhere. It was a lesson he and Reynaldo had learned soon after the debacle in *Nuevo Laredo*, when the DEA had tracked them through South Texas and picked them up at a truck stop in Encinal.

Both had escaped charges being filed, mainly because of the bloodbath across the Border, which had resulted in a huge success for the DEA and its Mexican counterpart agency, the PFM. For reasons known only to the federal agencies, Carlton Westerfield and Reynaldo Gomez were allowed to skate, perhaps because the DEA's biggest fish, Faustino Perez, had died in the melee and the *Golfo* drug cartel was severely damaged, which had been the goal of the PFM. Now it appeared the federal law enforcement agencies—or someone—had reunited in a campaign to hang Carlton with this serial killer rap, despite his departure from illegal activities. But *why*?

Soon after Tino's funeral, Carlton and Reynaldo had decided to leave criminal activities to those who liked it and reveled in the daily exposure to danger and intrigue, the inability to trust anyone, plus the need to look over one's shoulder twenty-four/seven. Both men had adequate resources to give up illegal income; Reynaldo from a successful construction business in Wichita Falls and Carlton from his paltry car-driving gig and a substantial stash from previous years' of contract hit jobs.

Carlton's departure from illegal activity made the current situation all the more perplexing. All those years with Big Mo, with lots of contracts being performed, often as many as twice a month, he had never had a run-in with law enforcement, never was connected to a victim, and thus, never suspected, picked up, or questioned. The reasons for this success were several: Carlton's penchant for caution, planning each job thoroughly, researching the subject, using cold weapons, and most importantly, working alone and only through one intermediary: Randall "Big Mo" Morris. The trouble began with Big Mo's death and the beginning of dealings with Paula Hendricks and her half-brother, Tino Perez, who had been a mid-level drug distributor in San Antonio.

The violent end of that tumultuous three-year relationship signaled a new beginning for Carlton. Life should have been much quieter and less stressful, as befitting a man nearing Social Security's full benefits bracket. But here he was, making secretive calls for information on his last job and planning a clandestine meeting with a former partner in crime—and he'd done nothing illegal in months!

No good deed goes unpunished, he thought grimly, chastising Big Mo for getting killed and ending a good thing for both of them.

He drove home watching his mirror, but saw nothing to indicate the morning's encounter had been anything beyond Heather's new boyfriend pricking with him. The closer he got to his apartment, the more that thought irked him. Wishing he had a garage, he parked in his covered spot and headed to his apartment, pondering the turn of events, knowing he'd best get back in his old ultracareful mode, the one that had served him so well during his working days, but had become rusty during the past three years. Luckily, the old suspicious nature kicked in at his front door.

When he turned the key on the deadbolt, he noticed it failed to travel as far as usual. He'd become accustomed to turning his key past a tiny burr in the lock mechanism in order to extend the bolt fully into the door frame. It was an unimportant problem, one he hadn't bothered to report to maintenance. Instead, he'd grown used to twisting the key another quarter inch to extend the bolt and securely lock the door, just as he had done this morning on his way to Denny's. Now, the bolt slid back too easily, telling him it hadn't been completely engaged. Clearly, he'd had a visitor. He pulled his key, quickly stepped to one side and carefully pushed the door open with his foot.

The open apartment entrance yawned back at him, leaving him feeling a bit foolish, but only for a second. This was exactly what he had been thinking about while driving home only minutes earlier—it was time to be vigilant and stay that way. He entered and shut the door behind him, then stood still, listening for any sound of movement. After a full three minutes of dead silence, he relaxed and thought about the possibilities, all of which included his presence at Denny's being verified and somewhat controlled. Since no one awaited inside and he had nothing incriminating in his possession, it was very likely that something had been left, something he needed to find—and now. He took a deep breath and stood back to look and think. The exercise was worthwhile; within seconds he thought he knew *what* to look for, if not the exact spot.

He started in the living room, the first room past the entryway foyer. Searching his place wouldn't be difficult, since his lifestyle precluded collecting much in the way of "stuff." Indeed, basic furniture and appliances made up the bulk of items in the apartment, so within fifteen minutes or so, every obvious nook and cranny had been exposed and the back covers unscrewed from the refrigerator, washer, and dryer. Next came the toilet tank, between the mattress and base, all the drawers and cabinets. Still nothing, so he started on clothes, checking each jacket pocket and shoe box, in and behind the cedar chest holding blankets. No luck.

Knowing what it was narrowed down the search a bit, but time was getting short. He needed to find it quickly and figure out how to deal with it. Despite seeing no one following him, his car was now parked in the lot, so he could be nabbed here in his apartment and connected to whatever had been secreted here. No amount of explaining would work, of that he was certain. Tamping down panic, he started again, looking closely at every possible place for a removable panel or board and becoming more anxious by the minute. He'd never noticed anything of that nature in the four or five months since he'd moved in, and he was sure he wouldn't spot one now.

But he did.

In the hall closet ceiling, barely visible at the rear, was a sheetrock panel set into thin wood trim. About eighteen inches square, it was apparently used to access the crawl space above his, a top-floor apartment. The push-up sheetrock panel and adjacent trim had been painted over so many times it had become camouflaged—almost. Now, a few flakes of paint lay on the carpet, dislodged by recent movement.

He ran to the kitchen and grabbed a footstool and stood on it to push the panel aside. He reached up and felt around, reaching farther with each circuit, but when his hand brushed the object, it slid farther away. Cursing, he got down and ran to get several books to increase the height of the stool. Climbing on the now-precarious perch, he reached in and grasped the gun, wishing he'd used gloves, but knowing it was more important to get rid of it in the next few minutes. Thinking frantically, he discarded a couple of plans and dashed to get his laundry basket. He wiped the gun thoroughly on a tee shirt and tucked it under the other clothes before heading to the door, grabbing a box of detergent on the way out.

The minute or so trip to his car was the most nerve-wracking walk of his life, at least in the past few months. He felt as though the laundry basket had a big sign on the side announcing "murder weapon hidden here." By the time he started the car and pulled out, he was sweating and certain that his pulse rate was off the chart for a man his age. Taking several deep breaths, he recalled tighter spots he'd been in and concentrated on remembering where he'd seen a laundromat. It took over ten minutes of driving around to spot one, and his anxiety was building again as he got out and toted the basket and detergent inside, scanning the rows of machines for the nearest vacant one. He put all the clothes into the first available washer, even the tee shirt bundle, and started digging in his pockets for change. Not surprisingly, he didn't have eight quarters.

Dreading the trip to the change machine (which would surely be out of order) he was reminded of why he willingly paid a higher price for his apartment, one equipped with a washer/dryer. Incredibly, the change machine worked, and he returned to the washer and deposited enough money to start the wash cycle. Leaning close to the machine, he retrieved the wrapped gun and tucked it into his pants before closing the door and starting the machine. Resisting the urge to look around, he strolled to the restroom at the far end of the building.

Inside, he locked the door and removed the top of the toilet tank, then pulled the bundle from his pants. He unwrapped the gun and took a few seconds to look it over. It was a large caliber auto-pistol of a make and model he didn't recognize, so he assumed it to be of foreign manufacture. Whatever the case, it wasn't important; instead, it was imperative to get the thing stashed and out of his life. He wiped it again thoroughly with the tee shirt and held the barrel between cloth-covered fingers as he lowered it into the rust-stained water, making sure it didn't interfere with the float mechanism. He flushed and watched the tank refill before replacing the cover.

Back at the washer, he took a seat and waited for the laundry to finish, relieved that the gun was out of his hands, but antsy to get farther away from it. He tried to relax by taking deep breaths and telling himself he'd dodged disaster—for now. While the interview with Moore and Fowler was uncomfortable enough, imagining his apartment being broken into at the same time elevated the danger to a whole new plateau. Not knowing *who* was behind the set-up was perplexing, but the question of *why* was becoming maddening.

He forced his mind to go over the event, to analyze what had happened in the past few hours. Of one thing, he was certain: despite TV shows to the contrary, picking a lock, especially a commercial deadbolt used by apartment builders, wasn't easy. It took more than a hairpin in the hands of a MacGyver wannabe to do it. The break-in technique pointed to a professional, whether law enforcement or someone outside the law with extraordinary skills.

Thinking about the timing, it now seemed possible that the FBI was involved in planting evidence, and he had an involuntary shiver thinking about the glib remark he'd made to the agents about transferring fingerprints to something incriminating. Maybe that exact thing had occurred, but the thorough wipe-down and immersion in water had nullified their efforts, and his anxiety morphed into a smirk. With luck, the piece wouldn't be found until the laundromat called a plumber to fix the toilet—months or years from now.

Or, Miller's helper—or someone—had simply watched him leave for breakfast and used the opportunity to break in and plant the gun. In that scenario the FBI was not involved, except they or the local police would soon get an anonymous call about the hidden murder weapon. If so, they'd surely need a search warrant, since he'd done nothing to give them probable cause to search his place without one—or so he hoped. In any event, catching it from two fronts would make it difficult to avoid being set up for an indictment by the independent actions of one or the other.

Another alternative was the possibility that the FBI and Miller were actively working together—not likely, but possible. Millstone/Miller had bilked the American government for huge amounts of money in the past. Maybe the feds—DEA and FBI—had hired him to do the dirty deed that would be Carlton's undoing. If that were the case, the odds against him were enormous.

Carlton had spent years being extremely cautious in his actions, relying on a minimum of contact with anyone who might compromise his solitary lifestyle. He had steadfastly avoided relationships that might get too involved, or turn into a conduit for deep, introspective conversation. For the second time in an hour, he was reminded that everything had changed when he met Paula, and his solitary, ordered life hadn't been the same since.

Frowning at the thought, he threw the bundle of damp clothes into the basket and headed for his apartment to dry them.

CHAPTER 6

It was just after noon on Friday when Reynaldo called. He kept the conversation short, simply telling Carlton he had some news and they should meet at the "usual spot tonight at eight." Carlton was pleased with his friend's prompt response. He prepared by having a light lunch and saving his appetite for Ernesto's, knowing that would be the place to enjoy an evening meal and a couple of beers—along with learning something useful, or so he hoped. Then he turned off the TV and sat down to think through—for the third or fourth time—the various scenarios which could have led to his being a suspect in the ritual killing of two people. Studying the problem a piece at a time meant applying the possible reasons or rewards to each individual and group involved in his recent history. It seemed the only way he could come up with a plausible explanation and a way to escape the net law enforcement was tossing his way.

What had begun as a curious conversation with Heather Colson had become serious with her follow-up call regarding the Houston victim. Then, the discovery of the large-caliber weapon in his apartment had elevated the situation to a full-blown crisis. He had to figure out who, if anyone, had anything to gain by shooting people in the same fashion he'd shot the turncoat mercenary gun runner for killing Tino.

As he had first considered, that made Cletus Miller the first and most obvious choice. As revenge for being confined to a wheelchair, he was orchestrating the copy-cat shootings in order to have Carlton moved to the top of the suspect list, indicted, and convicted. Knowing the legal system as he surely did, he'd accurately predicted the method of the shootings would lead law enforcement to suspect the perpetrator in the *Nuevo Laredo* shooting. But why go to the trouble and risk to kill additional people instead of simply informing his former employer—the DEA—that he'd been shot by Carlton Westerfield? The SAC, Stan Ikos, would be more than happy to have his suspicions about Carlton confirmed and take him down for it.

Or better yet, why not orchestrate the same punishment on Carlton—without the final bullets to the head—and let him feel the same pain and helplessness of being crippled for life? Wouldn't that be the ultimate payback, plus a lot easier than arranging some shaky plan that involved lining up other unpredictable victims? It didn't make sense. But maybe that's what being stuck in a wheelchair for the remainder of one's life did to the thought process, Carlton reasoned. Maybe Miller liked spending time and effort calling in old markers to set Carlton up for conviction. No doubt, the Brit had the necessary contacts in the underworld to carry out his vendetta in such a manner, including breaking into his apartment and planting a weapon, almost certainly the gun used in one or both of the recent shootings. The last part of the scenario had Carlton wishing he'd just squeezed off three at Miller's center mass before hopping into Reynaldo's car…much cleaner, leaving no one to make nefarious plans now, months later.

A second scenario had Stan Ikos, Special Agent in Charge of the San Antonio DEA office, blaming the shootings on Carlton out of pure dislike. Cops don't like to be fooled, and Carlton had done so with his unpleasant and uninvited involvement in the Ramos shooting, followed by his delightful and delicious involvement with Agent Heather Colson. Add to that Carlton's little package in the mail, anonymous though it seemed, may have been an obvious red flag to the savvy law enforcement agent. One didn't get to be SAIC in the DEA by being dumb, and Carlton knew that, but he hadn't been willing to let Ikos' top mercenary-for-hire continue receiving accolades for being such a stellar employee, when it was clear that Cletus Miller was a turncoat dirtbag who had clipped everyone in sight for money and lives.

But the DEA connection didn't quite hold up. Even though the two recent victims hadn't been community leaders, the car booster wasn't in the drug business, unless the stolen cars were loaded with illegal drugs and moved across state lines. That type of operation would be complex and have a lot of players, but it would get the DEA involved, as well as the FBI, who, according to Heather, was the lead on the case. As to the graphic method of shootings, maybe Heather had enhanced her dinner date spiel by inserting the part about the kneecap destruction…

A third possibility put Darren Moore as the architect, but why? His girlfriend Heather might have a tight grip on Darren's nose ring, a practice known to cause extreme bouts of jealousy, but he had no reason to send Carlton Westerfield to prison or the gas chamber to keep him away from her; he was already out of the picture and knew it. And again, it would be far easier to take me out, Carlton thought, by orchestrating a no-knock entry warrant and, *regrettably, the subject was shot when he resisted arrest.* Moore would have Heather to himself and she wouldn't cry for him, not any more than…hell, *Argentina* would! That thought brought the only smile to the analysis session and prompted him to give up and take a nap.

He woke up at five, feeling refreshed and rested for the first time since the all-nighter to Houston and back. He took a long walk through Hardberger Park, then got home in time for a long shower and shave before heading to Ernesto's, a long-time favorite place for quiet, upscale dining. He looked forward to seeing Reynaldo again, eating a good meal, and getting some useful information.

What he got was surprised.

Arriving just before eight, he asked for a secluded table and ordered a *Dos Equis.* A few sips later, two people came in the front door, but Carlton barely glanced in their direction since the man entering the dimly lit dining area was accompanied by a woman. Only as the pair approached his table did Carlton look up to see his handsome friend's trademark smile, one suitable for a *telenovela* star.

And why wouldn't he be smiling? Carlton thought as he stood up to greet his dinner guests, going with "greet ladies first" etiquette and smiling at the woman by his friend's side, ignoring Reynaldo for the moment. She was of indeterminate age, but looked to be somewhere north of fifty and south of sixty. Carlton immediately saw that she was either genetically gifted, well-preserved, or both. Nice hair of some reddish-brown tone he couldn't name framed a pretty face with good cheekbones and wide-set brown eyes. Her hair almost reached her collar and had a texture that outright invited stroking. However, even those positive factors were overshadowed by the pleasant, level gaze locked onto his face as she extended her hand.

"Hello! My name's Diane Martin."

Her voice matched the look; pleasingly soft in tone, but unwavering… *and a bit disarming*, Carlton thought as he reached for her hand. "Carlton Westerfield."

He was surprised by the firm grip, while her eyes never shifted away from his face. Her eyes were locked onto his like a Stinger missile guidance beam. Carlton didn't recall ever being such a willing target and had to resist the urge to tell her so, while reminding himself to release her hand.

"I'm pleased to meet you, Mister Westerfield. I've heard a great deal about you."

"The pleasure of this meeting is all mine, I assure you. And please call me Carlton.

"But you can't believe everything you hear, especially if it's from the man by your side." He turned in Reynaldo's direction, then shifted his smile to him as they shook hands. "Hello, my friend," he said. "It's good to see you."

"It's good to see you, too, Carlton."

The conversation stalled when the proprietor came over to seat Diane while the two men remained standing. Carlton handled their drink order before sitting down and turning again to his friend, who was taking his seat next to Diane on the other side of the table.

"You're looking good, Reynaldo. How're things?"

"All good for me. And I hope it is for you, although your request made me wonder." His smile dimmed slightly as he studied Carlton's face with concern.

Carlton tilted his head to one side in a shrug. "Just wanted to check on something, see if there's a connection," he said. Then he amended his statement quickly as though just realizing they weren't alone. "But we can do it another time if—"

Picking up on the reluctance in his voice, Reynaldo interrupted. "Oh, it's okay! I already briefed Diane on your—*our* situation."

Carlton glanced at Diane, then back to Reynaldo, a questioning look on his face. Seeing the look, Reynaldo continued. "I'm sorry, Carlton, I should have explained about her role in getting the information you need. She's my assistant, she takes care of background checks for my construction company, both on new hires and prospective customers. She has the necessary skills to do that type of work without being detected, so she's the one I turned to in order to check on our friend."

Carlton, still looking dumbfounded, could only nod. Since when do construction companies need to check out new customers with the aid of a computer sleuth? he wondered. And didn't employment agencies check out workers for drug use and criminal history?

"No secrets here, not from Diane," Reynaldo added, as if to dismiss any trepidation regarding a private discussion in her presence. Indeed, his tone implied an invitation for an open discussion about anything and everything.

If she was embarrassed by the broad statement, she didn't show it. Instead, she turned from Reynaldo to Carlton and again fixed the guidance beam look on him. "As Reynaldo said, I'm his assistant, and the assistance I'm best at is finding out about people and organizations he deals with in the construction business.

"But that can extend to other areas, of course. Given the right information going in, I can find out about a lot of things and people, not just those involved in construction contract dealings. That ability makes me *useful*, just as you have been described, but in another way."

Carlton waited a beat, trying to frame his response carefully. "Then you know about me and Reynaldo, our recent past...difficulties?" he asked, hoping his choice of wording didn't convey too much, which seemed unlikely, given Reynaldo's earlier endorsement.

"Yes. After you contacted him for intel on Miller, Reynaldo took the liberty of telling me about you and him and Tino, and the conflict with Cletus Miller aka Clive Millstone. I needed the back story to understand the assignment fully," she added in explanation.

Carlton nodded again, still unsure of what he should say, if anything. The fact that this stranger—trusted by Reynaldo or not—knew about his past activities made him nervous. It contradicted everything he'd believed in while working for Big Mo, and his attitude on the matter was supported by the turn of events he now faced. Only in the past twenty-four hours he had promised himself to revert to his pre-Tino and Paula days, go back to his earlier penchant for secrecy and caution. And now Reynaldo had apparently opened the file on him and turned it around for inspection by... Ms. Laser Beam, for crying out loud!

His musings were interrupted by their server who placed drinks before Reynaldo and Diane and inquired if Carlton needed another beer. "Not just yet," he replied, wondering if he should push the beer aside in favor of a Margarita—a strong one.

Diane leaned forward slightly to speak again. Carlton had noticed she had not averted her eyes during the drink interruption. The level gaze continued, reminding him of a cheetah in hot pursuit, its entire body and tail gyrating all over to maintain balance at full speed, while the head never bobbled, never lost sight of the prey.

Lowering her voice a bit, she picked up the thread. "Just so you understand, I'm not a stranger to either side of the laws of our land. And I'm not opposed to exploring business on both sides. Reynaldo has described you and your...um, *utility* in great detail, hence my remark about hearing a lot about you. And I want to assure you that nothing he said about himself, you, or Faustino Perez evoked any judgment from me.

"In other words, I'm on board here, Carlton," she stated emphatically.

"That's good to know," he replied uncertainly, then amended it to soften any negativity she might attach to his tone. "Please understand that I've always tried to be very private about my life, my dealings, my finances—everything, in fact. I have no family, no one depending on me, and I depend on no one, so it makes sense to keep things to myself. I was just taken by surprise, that's all."

She nodded almost imperceptibly, then expanded on her position. "I understand that completely, and I couldn't agree more for someone in your line of work. And being a loner, you have to depend on self-sufficiency. But when Reynaldo gave me the assignment, I wanted background to determine which direction to take my inquiry. For example, did you want to know the medical side of Miller's recovery? That would entail an entirely different set of facts coming to light: which specialists are attending, what medications he's taking, what rehabilitation program he's doing, what's the prognosis at this stage, versus immediately after the incident—that sort of stuff. It might be useful if you're investigating him for insurance fraud or some other insurance scam in order to have him arrested.

"But when Reynaldo explained your connection to this guy, I assumed his medical *arrangements* weren't the issue. I figured you wanted to know if he's recovered enough to come after you, and the short answer is 'no.' Then it made sense that you wanted to know if he could send someone after you;

if so, who is he seeing, communicating with, talking to by phone, etcetera. The answer to that is 'probably.'"

It was Carlton's turn to nod, this time in agreement. What she said made sense to him, even though he thought Reynaldo could have steered her investigation in the right direction without disclosing the whole sorry episode…but he had to admit, he was impressed by her quick perception of the vague assignment given her by Reynaldo.

Their meeting was again interrupted by the server, who gave a verbal spiel of menu standards and specials, then assured them that Ernesto's kitchen could mix and match anything and he would see to their satisfaction, a fact already known to Carlton. He knew the proprietor's accommodating pitch was for the benefit of Diane, whom he had not seen in his restaurant before tonight. The method had been passed to him by his father, the restaurant's founder, and was a big part of the restaurant's appeal for regular patrons, including Carlton. At his suggestion, it didn't take long for the three diners to decide on a basic entrée and leave the details in the proprietor and chef's hands.

As he walked away, the discussion picked up where it left off, with Reynaldo telling of the initial efforts regarding Miller. "I contacted the people I used in *Nuevo Laredo*, the couple who supplied the…uh, *tools* for that night. They were able to find out he's in a private rehab facility on the southern outskirts of the city. But when they tried to find out details of his arrangements or visitors there, they met a brick wall, which told me someone powerful is footing the bill. From his background, I figured the DEA, since he burned his bridges with the *Golfo* Cartel and the Benavides family. And the Rendón brothers aren't likely to be fond of him either, after the big bust."

"Neither are we," Carlton agreed. "That's what working both sides of the street will get you."

"And I'm surprised the PFM hasn't waltzed into the rehab place and handcuffed him," Reynaldo continued, referring to the Mexican counterpart to the Drug Enforcement Administration, who had been involved in the nasty cross-border incident. "I saw it was going to be a bit more complicated than bribing the head nurse for a visitors list, so that's when I confided in Diane."

"Yeah, the DEA is the most likely the only supporter Miller's got left in the world," Carlton agreed. "And according to Agent Colson, her boss thinks Miller is the greatest thing going, so that doesn't surprise me. What I don't get is *why*. I would have thought government agencies had their pick of military vets with the necessary skills to do that kind of work. And they choose *that* guy, who has all the loyalty of a rabid heyena."

"I think I can help with that," Diane offered. "I was able to glean pretty extensive information about Cletus Miller aka Clive Millstone's past military service. Seems he was a Special Air Services soldier from 2001 through 2016, achieving the rank of Squadron Sergeant Major, which is pretty high up. His military record before SAS is sketchy, but he was decorated three times in Northern Ireland, when he served as an enlisted man in the regular British Army. I didn't search for further details, but I would say the moral shortcomings he exhibited with you two were not related to a shortage of balls."

Carlton and Reynaldo both smiled at the crude analogy coming from a pretty face and delivered with a soft, cultured voice. For some reason, discovering Reynaldo's computer geekette assistant could talk like one of the boys made Carlton lose some of his earlier apprehension. As to the accuracy of her assessment, he had to admit that Miller/Millstone didn't shy away from dangerous situations, notwithstanding the problems with his moral compass. Thinking about this facet her research had revealed, Carlton wondered what made an honorable soldier, a seasoned member of an elite, close-knit military group, become a mercenary, then a turncoat without scruples or loyalty, beholden to no particular individual or group, not even the one who hired him.

Diane seemed to be reading his mind. "After his departure from service in 2016, Miller was attending meetings for a period of several months with a group of veterans, all of whom suffered from PTSD. Apparently, there are various support groups who function much like Alcoholics Anonymous or grief support groups. Many are self-funded, paid for by dues from attendees, but Miller's group was funded by a British relief agency. The agency collects data on groups it funds, and that's where I found out about Miller belonging to it. I got the names of everyone who ever attended one of their meetings," she added, looking between the two men to gauge their reaction.

With effort, Carlton shifted his look from her to Reynaldo. "We can look through the list of names, see if anything jumps out. But if he has a guy pulling these shootings, and it's a bud of his from the meetings, we wouldn't recognize it."

"Shootings? What shootings?" Reynaldo looked confused, and with good reason.

Carlton suddenly realized this meeting had taken such a quick trip from introductions to drinks to details of Miller, the pair seated across from him didn't have any idea what was going on to prompt his renewed interest in the Brit mercenary. "Sorry, we've gotten ahead of ourselves. My fault, I need to explain what brought about my interest in Cletus Miller."

He proceeded to relate the story, beginning with the phone call from Heather, their dinner date, and its troubling information. By the time he had told of the second maiming/murder, his weird breakfast encounter with her new boyfriend, and the frantic search and discovery of the weapon, both Reynaldo and Diane's eyes were open wide. They turned to look at each other, then turned back to Carlton, speechless.

Carlton was amused by the confusion his omission had caused, but he set forth to clarify things. "I'm sorry, guess I should have explained it a bit in my phone call, but by then I was paranoid about who might be listening in, so I kept it short and vague. A bit *too* vague, I guess."

Reynaldo waved off the apology. "No, not a problem. I mean, I knew you weren't getting information on him to know where to send flowers, but I had no idea it was this serious. I can understand you need to know who's been in contact with him that would pull off these hits and saddle you with the blame."

"So maybe the list of his cohorts from the support group, former military buddies, *is* the place to start looking?" Diane persisted. It was apparent that she had developed skills at following threads of digital information through a logical progression, a path that often led to the right answer.

Carlton still had his doubts. "Miller's plenty crafty and I think he would use someone as shady as he is, somebody who changes names like we change socks. I just can't see him or her showing up on a list from his past military experiences."

"No, not likely," Reynaldo agreed. "The other trainer went by the name of Mendoza, but I'd bet that was another *nom de guerre,* just like Millstone/Miller."

Carlton noticed a tiny change in Diane's facial expression, maybe a hint of disappointment at the rejection of her theory. Not wanting to dim the laser-beam eye contact he was beginning to like, he resisted the urge to ask if she ever blinked and instead asked, "How many names on the list?"

"I think between one hundred and one-thirty, something like that. And not all attended every meeting or were attendees during the same time period as Miller. I couldn't pin it down in that much detail."

The intel session was again delayed by the arrival of their food. By this time, Carlton was glad to get off the subject of Cletus Miller and onto the subject of Ernesto's fine food. For the next hour, the trio put aside the grim matter and enjoyed the meal and each other's company. At Carlton's inquiry, Diane gave a brief background of herself: born in Massachusetts, moved around a great deal after college, finally settling on work in the media/communications field. That led to a job with a computer security firm in Virginia, where she had worked for over a decade before relocating to the Midwest to work for a lobbyist, then Miami for another security company, then to New Orleans before moving to Wichita Falls a few months ago. She made no mention of husband, past or present, children, or any human connection whatsoever. Carlton thought that odd; most women seemed compelled to offer some insight in that area.

Neither did her abridged auto-biography clarify how she had gone to work for Reynaldo in Wichita Falls, but Carlton wasn't about to ask how the attractive woman seated across the table ended up in San Antonio tonight, giving two felony-dodging men information on a crippled British mercenary gun runner who was currently holed up in a rehab facility in Mexico.

Might be best to leave some stones unturned.

He knew Reynaldo had recently divorced his wife—Esmerelda?—in *Cuernavaca* and hooked up with Paula Hendricks, the mother of his twelve-year-old daughter, who was now residing in *Mexico City, Distrito Federal,* with her foster parents...

Whew, there but for the grace of God... No wonder I like being a loner!

When the meal was finished, Reynaldo insisted on dessert and after-dinner drinks. Carlton didn't want anything else, but opted for a kalua and coffee, as did Diane. The remainder of the meeting was spent with all three tossing around theories as to how, why, and who might be pulling off the murders, which resulted in several possibilities, but nothing Carlton hadn't already mulled over *ad nauseam*. Diane presented a few ways she could expand her searches with the new information she'd gotten tonight, including, at Carlton's urging, searches on Vince Peters and the Houston guy, name as yet unknown.

"That's a good idea," she said. "Maybe those two guys have a common thread that will point to the doer. At the same time, we can see about a connection to you or Miller. I can work on that tomorrow."

Carlton saw that she didn't take any notes, and seemed undaunted by the task ahead, making him feel better about her involvement, if not yet totally comfortable.

Besides, why not have competent help that's plenty easy on the eyes to boot?

As promised, Carlton caught the tab for dinner, then suggested the trio meet again on Sunday afternoon at Brackenridge Park, an old meeting place he had used back in his days with Big Mo. It was full of people on Sundays, with the crowd providing anonymity and privacy. Plus, it was a pleasant way to spend an afternoon and go over any new findings, courtesy of Reynaldo's attractive digital bloodhound.

Carlton hoped for some inspiration in the setting. Perhaps a return to simpler times in his career—when he had to trust no one but himself and the fat, greedy gangster who'd always arrived with thousands of dollars in one-hundred-dollar bills—would enlighten him. And maybe Diane would do more to earn the trust of both himself and Reynaldo. Back then, the trust he'd had in Big Mo was fueled by the fat man's own greed for the money involved; Carlton had always known the gangster would do nothing to endanger his meal ticket, the quiet, unassuming man who did the dirty work. And Big Mo had no reason *not* to trust that meal ticket. It was the perfect symbiotic relationship.

The memory reminded Carlton that he and Reynaldo were trusting Diane Martin to do her job efficiently and quietly. Her earlier remark about being "on board here" resonated in his mind as he recalled Clive Millstone giving Reynaldo and Tino the same impression—scant hours before killing Tino and barely failing to do the same to him and Reynaldo.

It was an uneasy ending to the otherwise pleasant evening.

The killer had been informed that this one was different. Not the method and manner, those would be the same, or close, depending on logistical details. But the target, the next appointed victim, would be different from the others in a major way. This time, a woman was the target who would be struck in the same manner as the other two, shot and killed, but with both knees left mangled, too, in order to intensify the focus on the poor schmuck being framed.

While not one to be squeamish, killing a woman was, nevertheless, not a desirable box to check off. However, this woman was special: she lived and breathed the life of crime, and thus was a fair target and necessary to entice law enforcement to expand their investigation, pick up the pace.

Like the first two, the woman was a criminal; no question about that. Raquel Pembrooke operated a string of underground brothels, believed to number five in all. She catered to a shady clientele, mostly underground figures themselves, but also the occasional politician or law enforcement officer looking for some of life's seamier entertainment. Raquel's locations—all known as "Rocky's"—could accommodate both major sex categories, plus any of the modern offshoot groups, no matter which letter of the alphabet described them. Regardless of sexual persuasion, Rocky's staff could provide, for a price, whatever form of debauchery a customer favored. Additionally, Raquel indulged in the occasional practice of laundering money. A portion of her shady clientele had a need for cleaning their own ill-gotten gains, and the cash-intensive brothels produced the right product to create several symbiotic relationships within the city's network of least-desirable citizens.

The killer had to research this one carefully, and it turned out to be a tedious task. Rocky's didn't have a business website, a public information office, and no news releases touted the owner's activities and personal appearances via Twitter or Facebook. The target's daily location was not highly publicized, and she could be present at any of her establishments on a given day—or night— collecting money, handling problems, interviewing new hires, or firing those who didn't perform up to standards, such as missing work or failing to please an important client.

Therefore, the killer had to partake of Rocky's services in order to gain the needed personal information, an unpleasant but necessary facet of the assignment. Luckily, by the third visit, he had enough information to choose the next encounter with some precision and nail down the details of Raquel's itinerary. The fourth visit was to the Rocky's location in a business park on North Broadway, a place disguised as a sports bar, which cleverly advertised "Covering Sports of All Kinds."

Generous tips and discrete questions during the killer's second and third visits had finally resulted in the killer being informed that Rocky herself preferred to spend Tuesdays and Thursdays at the Broadway location, which served as somewhat of a clearinghouse for Rocky's various services of the kinkier sort. Patrons in the know could inquire of any waiter or waitress about the particular "sport" available, along with a one hundred-dollar bill "inquiry fee," and get a recitation of the evening's entertainment specials. If the inquirer's particular diversion wasn't on that evening's menu board, he, she, or it was informed of an address where the special service could be found—for an additional fee, of course.

By hanging out in the main bar area for three nights running in mid-May, the killer finally had an opportunity to lay eyes on the target as she strolled across the floor, heading to a back office marked "Private Sports." A friendly waiter—too friendly, in fact—pointed out the establishment's proprietress to the killer as he casually laid a hand on the killer's shoulder before sliding it down to a zone of dubious comfort. The move prompted the killer to leave quickly, but not without handing over another big tip for a description of Rocky's parking spot, plus a wink that hinted at future accommodations.

A weekend of research and physical tailing resulted in the killer learning Raquel's address, a garden home in an up-scale area off of Vance Jackson, north of Wurzbach Road, west of where it became Wurzbach Parkway, according to Google Maps. The knowledge was a disappointment, because it revealed the difficulty of hitting this target. Another three days (and some night hours) were spent determining how to overcome the logistical obstacles.

The biggest problem had been getting around the security employed by the target, as well as that of the Home Owners' Association, which had all the appropriate measures in place: signs, controlled access, cameras, and worst of all, nosy neighbors who valued their privacy and seclusion. Luckily for the killer, Ms. Pembrooke was more open with her private life connection to social media platforms than her neighbors. With some study, a solution presented itself in the form of LinkedIn and Facebook profiles that labeled the female gangster as an avid bicyclist and gym member. Though no details of her affiliation or schedule were given, it only took the killer a week to decipher a rough pattern, one which could be utilized to do the job safely.

A regular at McAllister Park on the northwest side of the city, the brothel madam/money launderer bicycled its trails a couple of times each week, affording the killer ample opportunity to saddle up and scope out the target without danger of being spotted among the dozens of riders who flock to the park daily. Although the surveillance meant staking out her neighborhood gate from a convenience store parking lot, the killer's patience payed off on the third evening, and it was easy to follow the target to the park and casually unstrap and mount up on a bicycle for the tailing surveillance.

The Pembrooke job had been a long, arduous task, with the research and surveillance period overlapping the first two jobs. Maiming and killing those two criminal types was easier because of their shady personas and bad-side-of-town lifestyles, but upon adding the third, higher-profile individual, the surveillance and planning periods became exhausting, almost overwhelming, even with capable assistance. The killer was relieved when the first two were done, leaving only the third, which finally started coming together nicely. Still, the killer vowed not to jam up future jobs and create the conflict this one had, no matter what orders he got from the bastard pulling his chain.

At the end of three weeks, the killer knew enough to set the date for the event. Rocky's thriving enterprise would soon need a new person at the helm, because Raquel "Rocky" Pembrooke would not live to see another workweek.

CHAPTER 7

Saturday turned into the usual bachelor cleanup day for Carlton: time to do laundry, clean the apartment, wash the car. All the things he could easily put off through the week wouldn't make it through Saturday without being completed, on that he was firm. It was a ritual he had long practiced for no other reason than falling into the habit at some long-ago point in his life, and now it gave him a sense of accomplishment. Beginning right after breakfast, he worked through the day with only a brief break for lunch, and by five everything he owned was spotless.

While doing the housework, he had wondered about the meeting with Reynaldo's new assistant and how the attractive woman really fit into his friend's life. He wasn't quite ready to accept that Reynaldo's construction business had to have a cyber-sleuth around to check on things. So where was Paula? What was she doing these days, and what did she think of Reynaldo traveling across the state with Diane in tow? From personal experience, he knew Paula Hendricks was not a woman who shared much of anything, certainly not a man she had an interest in, as she surely did in Reynaldo Gomez. On impulse, he texted Reynaldo on his new burner asking for a return call at his convenience. His phone rang immediately.

"I'll bet you've just finished cleaning your house and doing laundry." Reynaldo said without preamble, opening with a ribbing to his friend about his Saturday compulsion.

Carlton laughed, knowing he had to take it in stride. *"Yep, you remembered. When I moved in here on a Saturday, you and Paula helped me and made fun of my schedule for that day."*

"Of course I remember. Paula thought it was hilarious that you were more concerned with doing laundry than getting your new place arranged."

"Like I told her, I'm a creature of habit," Carlton answered, pleased that the turn in the conversation made the next part easy. *"By the way, I was wondering about her, but wasn't about to ask last night,"* he said, using a tone that implied bringing up Paula in front of Diane wouldn't have been wise. The ensuing pause told him a lengthy explanation might be coming, and he was right, judging by the sigh from the other end.

"Well, you know Paula. She's prone to launch off on some project or another and get completely caught up in it. Right now, she's got a lot going on. She likes Wichita Falls okay, but she travels back down here at least twice a month. In fact, right now she's at Marta's place visiting people she knew from here. You remember Raul and Catalina?" he asked, referring to an older couple with whom Carlton had worked while carrying out a dangerous project for Tino. The couple had posed as decoys in a sting operation, and Carlton had come to know them and greatly respect their bravery. Soon thereafter, Paula had become fast friends with Raul's wife, Catalina.

"Sure, I remember them. How are they doing?"

"Fine, I guess. And I'm sure I'll get a full report from Paula, if she ever finds time to get back and talk to me. She sure stays busy.

"Believe it or not, she's on a kick to learn archery. She goes to a range in Wichita Falls at least two or three times a week. She's even started taking lessons from a pro there."

"Archery? You mean...like a bow and arrow? And there's a guy who teaches it at a range?"

"Well, that's the only kind of archery I know of, so I suppose so. And her instructor is a woman, not a guy. But I haven't asked her to show me her Robin Hood credentials."

"Who? Paula or her instructor?"

Reynaldo laughed. *"Neither one, and I'm not going to. I'm smarter than that."*

Carlton gave a snort of agreement. *"I know you are, Reynaldo, you're a survivor, not inclined to do dumb things like ask a woman any questions, no matter how curious you are about what she's doing.*

"Oh, and tell me this, my survivor friend: What does Paula think of your new assistant?" he asked, abandoning finesse and opening the door a crack to get to what he had wanted to know in the first place. This time, no hesitation, no sigh.

"Oh, she's met her a few times when she comes by the office. They seem to get on just fine. And she knows Diane is just an employee," he added in a tone that almost sounded convinced.

Carlton smiled at the response, which he thought was a bit naïve on his friend's part. He knew Paula Hendricks to be a superb actress, and whatever she was thinking wasn't likely to be advertised on her face or in her speech, but it wasn't his place to remind Reynaldo of that.

Aloud he said, *"Well, that's a plus. A man doesn't want the woman in his life getting her panties twisted over an employee. Anyway, I just wondered what was up with her. Tell her I said 'hey.' That is, if you see her again."*

Reynaldo chuckled on the other end. *"Will do. And we'll see you tomorrow at the park."*

"You bet. See y'all then."

The phone call ended, and Carlton sat back to ponder what he'd heard. Paula was here, in South Texas? Had the trio ridden down here together? Or flown down in Reynaldo's plane...*together*? That thought brought to mind an old expression about old pilots and bold pilots, but a combination of the two does not exist.

And neither will Reynaldo if Paula gets a whiff of any hanky-panky with that shiny computer whiz, he thought, then shrugged off the problem as someone else's and concentrated on finding a good place to eat dinner.

Sunday turned out to be a gorgeous day, and the park was crowded. Reynaldo and Diane were at the agreed area near the Brackenridge Eagle Train Depot well before two, sitting at one of the picnic tables. Carlton strode up promptly at two, and found he was too late to get in on the hot dogs Reynaldo had stood in line for. Declining Diane's offer of half of hers, he told the pair he'd learned his lesson: be early, or lose out on getting a hot dog—or anything else, judging by the crowd now surging toward the snack bar and the ticket line for the Eagle.

"I'll eat after while," he said. "Maybe we can go down to Good Time Charlies later, it's only a few blocks. But right now, I wanted to give you and Diane some information on other possibilities of what's going on."

"Oh, and what did you find out about Vince Peters and the other guy, the one in Houston?"

"It didn't take long to get the scoop on the Houston vic," Diane began. "His name was Jamal Isaac Crenshaw, a small-time hood with a string of prostitutes who doubled as dope slingers. He'd been busted a dozen times, but nothing would ever stick. He always had a slimy defense lawyer who managed to find a PC issue to throw out the evidence.

"Jamal was a real peach of a man; his claim to fame was a courthouse-steps proclamation that he didn't have any girls working for him, but if he did, *'they could spread dope as easily as they spread their legs'*. His quote didn't quite make the newspaper, but it entertained everyone in hearing distance."

Carlton had to laugh. "A regular orator, that guy. I'd say he ought to run for mayor of Houston, but he might win. Any connection to Vince Peters, the San Antonio car thief?"

"None that I could find, but I have two more databases I want to check for commonality in prison stints or even jail time at county lockups when they might have met. Then I can look for someone they both knew who wanted them crippled and dead."

Carlton shook his head at the news, disappointed that she had not yet found any obvious connection between the two thugs that might give a clue about their fate being the same as Cletus Miller's. He then proceeded to lay out his theories regarding local SAIC Ikos and FBI Agent Moore, this time including every detail of the breakfast with Moore and his partner, even his own puerile stunt at the end. Reynaldo grinned broadly at the breakfast check trick, citing it as "perfect."

Diane rolled her eyes and shook her head, but showed she had been listening intently when she intervened with a couple of questions. Again, there was no sign of a notebook or pen for recording what she heard. "Do you know of any previous connection between Darren Moore and Stan Ikos?"

Carlton didn't, but her question raised an interesting point, one he didn't get to explore before she asked another.

"How about his partner, Dave Fowler? He and Ikos know each other before this?"

Another head shake. "Not that I know of, but how would I? They sure didn't tell me about their background, except for their expertise in nailing serial killers like me."

"Hmm. Just wondered."

As to Reynaldo, he knew the basics about Ikos of the DEA, but this was the first he'd heard of Agents Moore and Fowler of the FBI. Nevertheless, he was quick to tie the two names to Agent Heather Colson, Carlton's past love interest, and he wasted no time in filling Diane in on all the details. Two minutes into it, Carlton groaned and threw up his hands in a "halt" gesture.

Facing Diane, he explained. "My friend Reynaldo has big shoes to fill since Tino's gone. Between those two old gossips, a man couldn't have any privacy in his life whatsoever. And what they didn't have gossip for, they made up. Reynaldo's just trying to make up for Tino's absence, so don't take anything he says at face value."

Diane smiled at his dilemma, while Reynaldo tried to effect a hurt look at Carlton's accusation, prompting Carlton to add, "I just wanted you to know the other players and see if you had any thoughts about their possible involvement."

Still smiling, Diane focused her intense look on him and ticked off a few points, all of which Carlton had mentally covered. It didn't make sense for either of the law enforcement agents to frame Carlton for the recent pair of maiming/shootings, no matter their personal viewpoints about his recent connection to Agent Colson. They could find easier ways to jam him up on something, surely easier than planting the weapon.

"The big agencies have plenty of time, money, and talent at their disposal," she added. "But from what you've described about your relationship with this Colson woman, I can't imagine it rising to the level of a full-out plan to put you away for murder. That involves way too many moving parts."

"That's what I think. But I wanted you to know more about the only people I can think of who have any reason to put me away—besides Cletus Miller."

"And I can't see the DEA boss going to bat for him, no matter how much he likes his work," she persisted. "All those contract guys know what they're hired to do and the risks involved. They get paid plenty to take those risks. And unless there's more to the relationship than we know about, the DEA has plenty more of those people knocking at their door."

"It seems more likely that some nut has picked up on the Miller job and just decided to copy the method," Reynaldo offered.

"Except for planting the gun in my apartment," Carlton reminded him. "Which brings us back to a stand-in for Miller."

"Unless that copy-cat nut knows you and knows about the Miller thing you did. He's just trying to put it on you to protect himself. Maybe it's not a retaliation thing at all," Diane countered. "It's just a survival tool."

"Since we seem to be at a dead end on this at the moment, I think you should get out of town for a while," Reynaldo suggested. "Somewhere that's a documented destination with lots of receipts, like a cruise or two-week stay somewhere far enough away to give you an alibi for the next one—if there is a next one, of course."

Carlton was mulling the idea over for a minute when his phone, the older of two he now carried, rang and he pulled it out to check the number. He recognized it and raised a finger to signal its importance and to request a moment to take the call. He didn't put it on speaker, but held it away from his ear and waved the pair closer so they could hear the caller as well as his end of the conversation.

"Well, hello there!" he opened, trying to keep his voice cheerful, not displaying the wariness he felt. *"You've reached the Jokester."*

"Afraid I have upsetting news for the Jokester," came Heather Colson's official voice.

"Are you joking? You dare to joke with the Jokester?"

An exasperated sigh at his silliness, just as he expected. *"Not for a minute, and neither should you. Where've you been since Friday afternoon?"*

Sensing danger in the question, Carlton paused, then said cautiously. *"Um, here in the city. Dinner at Ernesto's Friday night, stayed home all day Saturday—"*

"Cleaning your apartment, I suppose?" Heather's comment bordered on sarcastic. Across the table, Reynaldo rolled his eyes in appreciation of his friend's widely known habit before turning to Diane and giving her an "I told you so" thumbs-up. Out of respect for Diane, Carlton resisted the urge to flip him off.

"As a matter of fact, yes. And Saturday evening I had supper at Chalula's on Broadway, near MacArthur High School." He paused again, glancing around furtively, wondering if the DEA agent was fifty feet away, watching him for a telling reaction to her interrogation. It was worse than that.

"*That's not far from McAllister Park, where the bicycle paths begin, isn't it?*"

"*Not sure, I'm not a bicycle guy. Why? Did someone get their bike boosted and your federal joint task force is bringing in the usual suspects?*" Carlton's apprehension rose another notch, wondering where this was headed. When he found out, he didn't like it.

"*A woman was shot last night in the parking lot by an unknown assailant. This time it was a long-range shot, probably a medium-caliber deer rifle. We'll know by tonight.*"

"*Shot? As in killed?*" he asked dumbly. Dreading the answer, he clutched his phone so tightly he thought it might break. "*Uh…who was the vic? I mean, was she…anybody I've heard of?*"

"*Yes to the first two questions. Again, not sure which came first, the two knee shots or the one to the head. But no matter to the vic, not now.*

"*As to the identity, her name's being withheld right now, but she was a local bad girl who ran a string of prostitutes out of four or five locations around the city. They're disguised as dive bars, titty bars, and sports bars, depending on location.*

"*And just so you know, you're going to be brought in for questioning.*"

His phone went blank and Carlton didn't even bother to look at it. He snapped it shut and looked at his companions' shocked faces.

"Wish you'd suggested a trip out of town before last night, Reynaldo," he said. "That would have been a good move, but too late now."

CHAPTER 8

After Heather's call, no one was in the mood for a pleasant afternoon in the park, but Carlton insisted they stay a while and look relaxed, in case his paranoia about being observed was accurate.

"I don't want to look like a scared rabbit doing a runner, even if that describes me pretty well right now," he explained. "Not sure who will pick me up for questioning, but I don't want to appear on the run to a watcher or whoever comes for me. It'll give them something else to grill me about."

"Did you keep your receipt for your dinner last night?" Diane asked, glancing around nervously as though someone in the crowd might approach their table with proffered handcuffs.

Carlton shook his head. "No, and the place was busy while I was there. Don't know if the girls working the tables would remember me or recall what time period I was there eating. And being at Chalula's isn't much of an alibi, anyway. It's less than two miles from McAllister Park, so that puts me in the wrong place at the wrong time, rather than providing an alibi."

The trio thought that over for a minute before Diane spoke up, changing gears on the event. "Why did this Agent Colson call and give you the heads-up? You've described her as a straight-arrow DEA agent."

Carlton shrugged. "She is that, for sure, and very ambitious about her career. I think that's the reason she dropped me from her personal agenda. It was fun for a while, but she figured out that hanging with me wasn't good for her future. In any respect," he added, smiling.

"But she's taking a chance by calling you with investigation information." Diane's statement made it clear she wasn't going to let it go.

"Despite everything going on with things pointing toward me, she knows me well enough to figure out I'm not the doer. I didn't exactly disclose my entire career and philosophy on life during our time together, but you sort of get a feel for the type of person you're with, you know? Besides, she's a good law enforcement agent. They can spot a criminal a mile away and tell when someone is blowing smoke.

"And when that mess in Mexico was done, I told her I was out of it for good, and I meant it."

"So maybe she's trying to help you with inside information, hoping you can use it to expose the real culprit. You certainly have an incentive to do that. But she's putting herself at risk. Better hope she keeps that burner phone hidden from her co-workers, even if there's nothing in the Contacts directory. Plus, she needs to delete the call history each time, just in case."

"She does that, I'm sure," Carlton responded, impressed with Diane's quick uptake on safely using a burner to its full potential, citing all the things he'd impressed upon Heather, Tino, Paula, and Reynaldo. "Heather's already well-versed in this stuff and a quick study when she wants to pick up on something."

He didn't tell Diane that his cautions hadn't always been heeded. Of the four, only Paula had been remiss in following his instructions regarding burner phone secrecy. Ironically, her stubbornness had turned out to be a life-saver. Months before, she had kept contacts in her phone that enabled Carlton to find her daughter after she'd been kidnapped. Recalling the incident now, it seemed like another lifetime. Even the pressure of dealing with crazy Brujido Ramos and Paula's kidnapped daughter paled in comparison to the current dilemma—mainly because it was *his* neck in the noose this time, he thought ruefully.

"Maybe we should go to your place and check it for anything you didn't put there," Reynaldo suggested, fidgeting around on the hard picnic bench as he spoke. He'd obviously had enough of the family park for one day.

"That's a good idea," Diane and Carlton said, almost in unison.

At Carlton's apartment, it didn't take long to search every possible spot, since he'd gone through the same motions a few days earlier. Within fifteen minutes, they gave up and decided to get dinner somewhere quiet enough to talk and loud enough for privacy. After a brief discussion, it was decided that Italian would work for everyone, and Little Italy was the place. When they walked out, Carlton turned to lock the door, paying attention to the positioning of the sticky deadbolt. In the parking lot, dinner plans fell apart.

Carlton spotted the plain sedan that had followed him into the Denny's lot the previous Thursday, sitting in a tenant-assigned spot three slots from his car.

"Don't look now, but I don't think I'm going to join y'all for dinner," he told his companions. "Before they roll up here, just peel off and go to your car like we're splitting up," he mouthed quietly to Reynaldo. "Go to Little Italy, and we'll see how this plays out."

Reynaldo and Diane followed the instructions, leaving Carlton to walk another fifty or sixty feet toward his car alone, still ignoring the FBI car's presence. In his car, he thought he had been mistaken. The plain-wrap sedan hadn't moved, and it was impossible to determine who, if anyone, was seated behind the dark-tinted door glass. He started his car and pulled out of his spot, intentionally turning in the direction of the sedan, heading for the rear exit of the apartment building. As he rolled by the front of the car, he caught sight of two people behind the windshield in his peripheral vision, but didn't want to look closely enough to determine if it was Moore and Fowler.

He pulled onto West Avenue from the side street, turning right, in the direction of the restaurant. He watched his mirror for the next few minutes as the unmarked sedan kept pace, hanging back fifty yards or so, but moving up to catch the green light at Blanco Road. When he wheeled into the restaurant parking lot, he expected the sedan to follow, but it cruised by in his mirror without slowing. Apparently, the federal agents wanted to monitor his movements, not haul him in for questioning—just yet.

Inside, he found his friends had already been seated in a booth in the same area where he'd met with Heather at the beginning of the copy-cat shooting debacle a mere five days before. After ordering, he proceeded to relate that recent event to them in greater detail, hoping one of them might interpret something from the DEA agent's actions that would help. Neither could, but it was clear that Diane didn't understand Agent Colson's intentions regarding keeping Carlton informed, but she was on it like a dog on a bone.

Dinner went well, and the conversation strayed from the business at hand to a casual catch-up session between Carlton and Reynaldo. Diane seemed quite entertained by learning additional tidbits of information regarding the pair's past activities, including a few references to Tino and his main operation, the legal one. The discussion led to both men promising to take her to the flea market for a true South Texas experience, one which would "further her education." The unwavering gaze swept back and forth between the two grinning men as though trying to determine if she were being led astray by their description of the dozens of tiny, cramped stalls comprising the massive market. Sensing her apprehension, Reynaldo assured her the experience would change her mind about shopping, and the exploratory venture was set for the next day.

"Wish I could go along," Carlton said, "but I think I have an appointment elsewhere pretty soon. I don't know what they were up to this afternoon with that stunt. If it was Moore and Fowler, they *have* to know that I'd recognize the undercover car from their visit at Denny's."

Reynaldo voiced the obvious answer. "It's got to be intimidation. What else could that move accomplish? Did they think you'd walk over to their car, open the back door, and climb in to chat with them?"

Diane had another idea. "They're out to spook you, that's for sure. But I think it's because they're hoping to rattle you and make you slip up by acting guilty. They may want to see if you'll break and run. I'd bet they will put a tracking device on your car and probably on Reynaldo's too, if they haven't already. If they see either of those vehicles headed to the airport, they may or may not race to intercept you, but it will give them something to hammer you with when they pick you up."

Carlton agreed with both assessments, but wondered if there might still be a way to disprove whatever theory the federal agents had making him good for the shootings. "It would have been great to be out of town during this latest shooting," he said. "Instead, I was having a meal within a rock's throw of the new murder. I need some better luck."

"There have been three shootings in the last five days or so. If that pattern holds, another one will occur in the couple of days. If I left now and another one occurred during my absence, that would work to throw the heat off of me."

"I think it might put more focus on you if you left now, though, and another shooting *didn't* occur pretty soon," Diane said. "And it might make you lose your information source, the only ally you have from their camp. She may start to have doubts if you do a disappearing act now."

He couldn't argue with that, knowing Heather Colson as he did. And as to her motive for feeding him the latest information on the shootings, she might be doing the same as the two FBI agents, trying to frighten him into running and thus cementing his guilt, he thought—but he wasn't inclined to suggest that to Ms. Laser Beam, whom he could sense had taken a dislike to the DEA agent without having laid eyes on her. Being a woman, he was concerned that Diane might use her computer skills to do something really devious—like put a digital hijack on Heather's Victoria's Secret credit card.

Talk about getting your panties in a wad, now that would do it!

He sighed and reached for the check, but Reynaldo beat him to it.

"The least I can do is spring for a good meal now," he declared. "You missed out on the hotdogs, and your next food might be a bologna sandwich in a holding cell."

"Gosh, thanks! Wish I could have clipped you for a hotdog, too."

"I'll buy you one to celebrate when you get out."

Carlton reached for Diane's hand and assisted her from the booth. "That's why he's my friend," he told her solemnly. "Always looking out for me."

The trio split up, with Reynaldo and Diane headed back to Sabinal to his ranch, while Carlton drove back to his apartment to mull over—one more time—the trap from which there appeared to be no easy escape. As he pulled into the apartment lot and drove toward his parking space, he noticed the sedan. It was now parked in a visitor's slot not far from the office. As he rolled by, he tried again to determine the occupants, but the dark windows did their intended job. As he pulled into his space and parked, he saw the sedan roll up behind him, effectively blocking his car in.

He felt his pulse quicken and took deep breaths to calm down, reminding himself to do a better job than he'd done at Denny's a few days ago. He realized these guys had to be good at their job, or they wouldn't have lasted long with the Federal Bureau of Investigation. The agency's well-trained manpower and superior technology put them in position to counter any slick trick he could come up with; they had seen it all and heard it all.

So answer their questions, don't expound on anything. Maybe a successful session with these guys will actually do me some good.

"Mr. Westerfield, I'm Agent Darren Moore of the Federal Bureau of Investigation. This is Agent David Fowler. We'd like you to come with us to our office and answer a few questions. Are you willing to do that?"

The formality was a far cry from their previous meeting, and Carlton figured the agents must be under the scrutiny of body cams, dash cams, and/or recorders this time. He had just opened his car door when Moore appeared beside him. He could sense Fowler standing toward the rear of the Caddy, at the rear quarter, but didn't bother to turn his head and look. Their speed and smoothness told him they had done this before. By moving quickly from their plain wrap into positions too far apart to keep both in a clear line of sight gave them a safety margin, plus a psychological advantage. It was another example of what they did best—intimidation, their stock in the trade. But having discussed that very subject only minutes earlier with Diane and Reynaldo gave Carlton an edge; he easily suppressed any sign of alarm or apprehension at the tactic.

He exited his car and closed the door, then clicked the fob to lock it before turning to face Moore. "Alright," he said evenly, keeping his voice even and devoid of inflection.

His one-word response seemed to take Moore off guard judging by the slight hesitation and double eye-blink before he proceeded. "If you'll just step over to our car and take a seat in the rear, please," he said, stepping back two full steps and gesturing toward the sedan. As they covered the fifteen or so feet, he moved ahead of Carlton and spoke again while he opened the left rear door.

"You have stated you are willing to go with us and answer questions, so you are not being handcuffed for this trip. This is an informal meeting you have agreed to, correct?"

"Yes, that's correct."

The process was painfully formal, but Carlton resisted the urge to say, *"come on, Darren, cut the crap, let's get this over with. Come on up to my apartment and we'll talk."* He knew the drive to the FBI office, the ushering into the building, and the seating in a stark interrogation environment were all intended to be advantageous to the law enforcement agents. This

THE TRUTH, VERY RARE

time, he was determined to stay cool, play by their rules, and hope it worked better than exercising his clever wit like before, satisfying as it had been to rattle their cage over breakfast. Walking between the pair, he steeled himself to have his own cage rattled. It began immediately after receiving the Miranda warning.

Fowler started. "Please state your full name for the record."

"Carlton Delano Westerfield."

"What is your occupation?"

"I drive rental automobiles to various locations."

"Is that a lucrative occupation, Mr. Westerfield?"

"Lucrative enough."

"Not as lucrative as working for Faustino Perez, though, is it?"

"No."

"How much were you paid to kill Vince Peters?"

"Nothing. I didn't kill Vance Peters."

"Cute," Darren Moore interjected, a smirk on his face. "It's *Vince*, Mr. Westerfield, not Vance. But you knew that, didn't you? You're full of cute tricks, just as you've exhibited recently."

Carlton didn't respond. He waited for the softball session to end, for these guys to get on with the interrogation.

"Did you engage in murder-for-hire for Faustino Perez?" Moore continued, apparently taking the handoff for the next stage.

"No."

"What did you do for him?"

"I worked at his flea market, the big one on 16 South."

"That's State Highway 16? That goes to Poteet?"

"Yes."

"What did you do there?"

"Stocked merchandise in the stores, cleaned up the parking lot, emptied trash cans, mowed the grass."

"Did you kill anyone while working for Perez' flea market?"

"No."

"Where were you on May 22?" Now Fowler was on the mound, trying a curve ball regarding yesterday, not months ago.

65

Nervous, Carlton had to think a moment to change the time frame recollections. "I was at home almost all day, cleaning my house, doing laundry. In the evening, I went to a car wash on West Avenue and cleaned my car. Later that evening, I ate at Chalula's, over on Broadway."

"What time was that?"

"I don't recall exactly, but between six and seven or seven-thirty."

"Where'd you go then?"

"Home."

Moore tried another smooth one, a mere knuckleball this time. "What car wash?"

"I don't know the name. The one where Rhapsody tees into West Avenue."

The questions ceased then. At a glance from Moore, he and Fowler got up and left the room without a word of explanation. Carlton leaned back in the chair and wondered what this part of the charade was designed to accomplish. Undoubtedly the tone of the questions would change when the pair started again. In less than a minute, he found out.

"Did you work for Big Mo?'"

"No."

"We have information to the contrary. You were a button man for Big Mo, weren't you?"

"No."

"Your name was found in Big Mo's records, the ones he kept at his main pawnshop on San Pedro. Records that indicated he paid you to kill people."

Carlton didn't respond, knowing that this tack was pursuant to Stan Ikos' mission a few months before. The DEA chief had old crime scene records perused by his staff, trying to find information tying Carlton to the deceased gangster. Heather Colson had mentioned the quest to Carlton, but he'd heard nothing of its results. Now he was banking on the fact that this was a red herring, and that Ikos' crew hadn't found anything, because Big Mo, being a successful thug for decades, surely didn't keep records of his illegal activities.

After almost a minute of silence, Moore spoke again. "You said you'd cooperate. I asked you a question."

"No, you didn't," Carlton answered, his ire growing. "You made a statement. There was no question mark at the end of your statement, incorrect though it was."

"Incorrect? How so?"

"My name was not found in Big Mo's records unless I pawned something at one of his pawnshops. If I did, I don't remember."

"Did you kill Jamal "Spreadum" Crenshaw?"

The question came from Fowler, taking Carlton by surprise; so much so, he almost asked *"who?"* Diane had told him the name of the Houston victim, but he wasn't prepared to have the name thrown at him in the context of his infamous courthouse speech. Hoping his slight hesitation wasn't too long, he answered "no," and vowed to give future responses quickly.

"Did you kill Raquel Pembrooke?"

"No." He'd counted on that one coming next, and that the name, which he'd never heard, had to be that of the slain woman who ran a string of whores.

"You answered that one a lot faster than the previous one, Mr. Westerfield. What are we to take from that?"

Carlton had at least four smart-aleck responses, but opted to go with a shrug and "I don't know."

Now Moore tag-teamed back into the fray. "Why did you answer Agent Fowler so quickly on that one? Is it because you didn't have to stop and think about it, like you did with Crenshaw? Because you killed Spreadum, didn't you?"

"The answer was a quick 'no' because I didn't kill *anyone*, so I didn't have to stop and think at all."

"Where were you on May 18th?"

Carlton looked directly at Moore and feigned thinking about the date. "What day of the week was that?" Since Tuesday, May 18, was the day he'd gotten the first phone call from Heather, he thought it might be possible that Moore knew of the dinner meeting and was trying to catch Carlton in a lie—or at dinner with his girlfriend, neither prospect very appealing. Wondering how he was going to keep Heather's name out of it—or hurt her new boyfriend's feelings instead—he held his breath while Moore looked at his notes.

"Tuesday."

"On Tuesday, I read most of the day, watched TV, dinner in the evening. Nothing in particular that I can recall."

"You did absolutely *nothing* all day?" Moore pressed, his voice dripping disbelief.

"I told you, I read and watched TV, but nothing *in particular*. I may have taken a nap before dinner. I'm retired, you know."

"Do you know a man named Bert Morris?"

"No."

"Have you ever heard of Bert Morris?"

"No."

"Did you ever kill anyone for Bert Morris?"

"No."

Again, the questions stalled, and again, Carlton wondered what was next while the agents retreated to somewhere else. He thought about the last three questions regarding Bert Morris. He'd never heard the name and decided it must have been due to an error in the research abilities of Ikos' team, the staff he'd assigned to look into any connection between him and Big Mo. The fat gangster's name was *Randall* Morris, not *Bert*, but by asking him with the wrong name, Carlton had told the truth: he'd never heard of Bert Morris.

Guess ol' Stan is too much of a bigshot to check over his minions' work product.

When the agents re-entered the room, it was Moore who spoke. "Ok, that's it for now, Mr. Westerfield. We're done here. Let's go, we'll take you back to your apartment." The last part came with a smirk, as though the whole exercise had been a joke.

Stunned, Carlton was caught off guard, but recovered quickly. "Thanks, but I'll catch a cab."

Now a smirk was plastered on both agents' faces, but it was Fowler who spoke for them. "What's wrong, Westerfield? You don't like riding with us?"

The negative implied in the question left Carlton no choice but to slip in one tiny example of his smart-mouth, despite his earlier promise not to.

"Yes, I don't," he said tonelessly, pulling his burner as he stood and walked out of the room, recalling that Yellow Cab's number was a bunch of twos—easy to remember. Behind him, he could feel their stares as they thought about his answer.

CHAPTER 9

Back in his apartment, Carlton was relieved and mystified at the same time. The short, inconsequential meeting couldn't have been designed to further the investigation, he thought—that is, unless the agents were counting on a quick confession out of fright and guilt. Or maybe they were just looking at his response times and hoping to get a glimpse into Carlton's long-past life for some leverage with which to open the door to the current crime wave. He'd been plenty nervous, as would anyone but the most experienced criminal, so maybe they'd been planning on tripping him up with the tag-team effort and out-of-sequence questions, plus a few that made no sense whatsoever. And oddest of all, there had been no mention of the details of the recent murders. The signature kneecapping that each victim had suffered, the main thing that had Carlton Westerfield tied to the recent spate of shootings, hadn't even been mentioned. If their intent had been to confuse, then the interview was a success, he decided. In any event, he hadn't given them much to go on, of that he felt confident.

He wondered if Heather would get an update on today's activities. He hoped so, and he hoped she would call and enlighten him on what their goal had been and what they had learned. With luck, his responses had been just right, and the spotlight was easing off of him for some reason or another. That would be great news.

Maybe another suspect has surfaced, one who actually had a motive, he thought hopefully. Not being able to establish a connection between himself and any of the victims was the only thing keeping him from arrest. Of that he was sure, because opportunity had been present in all three murders due to his location at the time of the crimes, especially the Houston one.

Why couldn't that have happened in El Paso? Or better yet, Butte, Montana?

And the similar MOs had to be an ongoing, nagging factor to the investigators, reminding them to stay focused (at Stan Ikos' directive, no doubt) on the suspected sender of the gory newspaper story depicting a man with both knees destroyed. Carlton shook his head at the thought of the time and effort he'd spent to get the newspaper story, cut it out, print the smart-assed reminder of Miller's vulnerability on it, and mail it to the DEA boss. All that, just to get myself looking good for three murders I had nothing to do with, he thought, cursing himself for the juvenile stunt.

Maybe it would be worth it if I'd seen the look on Ikos' face!

It was after ten when his burner phone rang. The number wasn't familiar, and he answered cautiously with the last four digits of his number.

"This is four, six, six, one."

"It's me." Heather's business voice was unmistakable. *"I heard your day took a bad turn."*

Carlton managed a weak laugh. *"You might say that. But it didn't go badly at all, actually. They asked some questions, I answered them, and then I went home—"*

"In a cab, yes, I heard," she interrupted. *"You realize, don't you, that a twenty-six-dollar cab ride doesn't do much to support your claim that you only deliver cars for a living?"*

Carlton thought quickly. The cab fare had indeed been exactly twenty-six bucks, so the feds had gone to the trouble to contact the cab company and get the information. Aloud, he added to Heather's pointed comment. *"Yeah, plus tip. And I'd have paid twice as much to keep from riding with those two."*

She laughed. *"I heard them talking about your answer to their offer of a ride home. They were discussing the nuances of the English language when using double negatives, or whatever you were doing to them."*

"Just having fun. Like they were doing with me during the interrogation."

"They mentioned that you weren't overly talkative during the meeting."

"Just as I intended. They asked, and I answered. Without embellishment. By the way, did they say why they asked all those questions that have nothing to do with anything?"

"No, but that's standard practice. It's not always like on TV when everything is clear and the questions and answers fit right into the plot line. That's for TV audiences who surf over to watch wrestling during commercials. In real life, sometimes you have to make stuff up, fish around a while just to find the motive."

It was the opening he'd been waiting for. *"Well, I hope their fishing expedition was successful and they learned that I didn't do any of the shootings, because I had no motive."*

"The transcript will be passed around and discussed on Tuesday. That's the time for the weekly meeting of all investigators. It's gotten larger now, with the woman's death. SAPD is back in, because the SAPD Vice squad had an investigation going already. And there's talk that the Texas Rangers are interested. It turns out that, believe it or not, she had friends in influential places. Someone contacted the governor's office, and he may send in a Ranger investigator if something doesn't break soon."

"Oh, you mean bigshots have been trading money and favors for sex in low places? Imagine that!"

"I know you're surprised to hear that influential people have base desires. And now one of them is calling in a marker, even if this sleazeball didn't run the best little whorehouse in Texas. Or maybe she did," she added. *"I wouldn't know."*

The part about the Texas Rangers wasn't something he'd expected to hear, and he didn't know whether that was good news or bad. He didn't need any more heat, but maybe the famous state law enforcement group wouldn't be looking at him because of personal grudges, girlfriend/boyfriend jealousy, or some crusade to solve ten-year-old murders of San Antonio's least-favorite miscreants. He opted to tiptoe around the issue for the moment and see what Heather's agenda was—if she would tell him.

"When you see the transcript, I wish you'd call me and give me your take on it. I mean, you've been sticking your neck out to tell me about these murders. I appreciate it, but I don't know what to think about that."

Heather was silent for so long he thought they had lost their connection. When she finally spoke, it wasn't all he'd hoped for, but not an outright dismissal, either. *"Well, I don't know what to think about you either, or your possible involvement in this mess.*

"Carlton, unlike my boss, I think you come across as a decent guy on many levels. But the statistics of three shootings just like Miller's are really weighing against your being innocent."

Carlton thought about that for a moment. *"Why is it automatically assumed that I was involved in the Miller shooting? We've been through this, Heather. That guy had more enemies than Israel's government and Donald Trump put together. He was probably being hunted by four or five people he screwed over—"*

"You were the one with the biggest motive to do it, Carlton. You were exhausted that day we picked you up in Encinal, so you may not remember. But the look on your face when you told me about Tino being shot told me everything I needed to know about your intentions for Miller. There may be a lot of others who could, and would have done it, but the timing, the motive, the opportunity…all those factors point to you. And don't forget your little newspaper clipping stunt.

"Oh, and the new wits from Nuevo Laredo. It seems they've been questioned again by the locals, and they were insistent that the gringo pistolero was, quote, 'incredibly good, like watching an action movie.'"

Carlton groaned. *"So the Mexican police have convinced the fabled FBI and DEA that some drunk partiers who watch too much TV are now marksmanship experts? They ever think about going down there and grilling these witnesses themselves? Or would that interfere with donut hour?"*

She ignored his sarcastic observation and continued. *"Plus, as to the three current murders, nothing points in another direction, so a SODDI defense is looking weak."*

Carlton knew the SODDI defense stood for "Some Other Dude Did It." He heard and read it dozens of times in books and on TV, usually used by a scofflaw with a shady past, no alibi, and no other defense in sight. Now, he was being painted with that brush, and he struggled to control his anger.

"Well, before I forget, let me inform you of a SODDI event that I witnessed with my own eyes. While I was having a delightful breakfast with your boyfriend and his boyfriend, someone broke into my apartment and stashed a gun in the attic access. I only caught it because my door lock is sticking, and I noticed it wasn't locked all the way."

"Are you serious? What did you do with it?"

"It went away."

"Maybe you should have told Moore and Fowler about that incident."

"And tip them off that I'm smarter than they are? So they can plant something more carefully next time? No, I'm waiting for them to bust in with some trumped-up PC and a search warrant, so I can laugh at them when they don't find their plant."

Heather was quiet for almost a minute. When she spoke, her tone was different. *"That's incredible, Carlton. I don't know what to think. I can't believe the FBI would do something like that, no matter how bad they want a collar. But I do know there's currently not another suspect."*

"<u>What?</u> You're telling me that not another suspect or even another person of interest is out there? That's unbelievable! No one can find a connection between me and any of the three victims, so your boyfriend had to plant one. Besides, where's the motive for me?

"As to opportunity, there are one-point-four million people in this city who had as much opportunity to kill them as I did, and four-point-five million in Houston who could have popped Jamal what's-his-name. What happened to all the standards of crime investigation? Are they not politically correct any more, or is someone so hell-bent on hanging this on me—"

"Another good point, Carlton," she interrupted. *"Maybe that's why I keep you informed. And maybe that's what is keeping the DA from filing charges he knows won't fly and a grand jury won't even nibble on, providing you don't screw up."*

Heather's interruption of his rant was followed by a break in their connection; their terse conversation was over. For a brief moment, Carlton seethed. He wondered if he should have disclosed the planted weapon to her, then decided it made no difference. All the points he had made to her were accurate, but it seemed that this task force was bent on hanging the three shootings on him, regardless of a lack of motive or any real proof he'd done the crimes. Instead, it was simply a lack of anyone else to look good for the crimes.

Then he calmed down and thought through the entire exchange, especially her closing lines, the ones she didn't stay on to debate. It sounded like Heather Colson and the state's chief prosecutor weren't convinced he was the doer, but it remained to be seen if either had enough stroke to alter the direction of the other tunnel-vision investigators. Also on the plus side, it sounded like she was keeping him informed for those very reasons while subtly reminding him to stay cognizant of that—in other words, "you're in the clear legally, but you'd better work to stay that way."

Another thought regarding the victims occurred to him during the phone conversation. With the death of the female brothel operator, an interesting pattern was beginning to appear: all the victims were miscreants, individuals on the wrong side of the law. The first two didn't have any obvious connection to each other, and now the third, in a different line of criminal enterprise, didn't have an obvious connection to car theft or ordinary street hookers and drugs. The underground brothel gig was a different twist.

On the surface, that made the murders look like the work of some kind of vigilante, someone who had a grudge against lawbreakers of every stripe, these three, anyway. And that pointed to someone connected to law enforcement, or perhaps just someone who had experienced frustration at the justice system, but had official connections to crime-related intel. Who else would have ready access to the scofflaws' identities, their activities, and know their movements? He wondered if the pattern would be apparent to the task force and if it would change the direction of the investigation.

I'm certainly not part of law enforcement, and my only connection to those fine folks just hung up on me...the pretty one, who dropped me like a hot rock!

He gave up on the puzzle for the time being and added her new cell number to the kitchen drawer directory. Then, before placing the sheet back under the tableware tray, he memorized both numbers and found himself hoping to see one or the other pop up on his screen—soon, and with good news. It was the only help he could hope to get from law enforcement.

The next day was Monday, the day that had been set to show Diane the flea market operation. Since Carlton had finished up his business with the FBI, he texted Reynaldo that morning, saying he was finished with his "interview" and able to go along. A return text said to be ready at ten.

In fact, Carlton relished the idea of doing something different, visiting with a few of the merchants he'd come to know while working in Tino's giant Southside operation. Plus, spending a few hours with his friend and his new assistant sounded good, even with the mystery of what Paula must think of the arrangement, with all its opportunity for coziness. And it certainly beat what he'd been doing—worrying over something that had no clear-cut solution. Almost any nine-to-five job could provide that kind of frustration.

When they arrived, Carlton was a bit surprised, but pleased, to see Paula sitting next to Reynaldo, while Diane had taken up residence in the back seat.

So much for the mystery of what Paula thinks!

He opened the other door and got in next to Diane. "Good morning, Diane! And good morning to you, Paula. How've you been?"

"Just fine! How about you? Still driving cars to different locations?"

"Yep, that's my claim to fame and fortune now. And I like it; a lot quieter than some of my past activities," he said, giving his former girlfriend a smile. "Reynaldo said you like Wichita Falls, but come back down here pretty often."

"Yes! Can't give up my old friends. I've been visiting with Raul and Caterina, stayed at their place this trip. They asked about you, of course."

"Maybe we'll see them today. How're you, Reynaldo?"

"I'm good. I thought you'd forgotten me, or just chose to ignore me," he said, grinning in the rear-view mirror.

"When you drive these two around, you should expect to be ignored."

"I can't disagree. You eat breakfast already?"

"Yeah, about four hours ago."

"Well, we didn't, and these ladies are hungry."

Breakfast turned out to be at the La Madeleine in North Park Center, very near the scene of the Ramos shooting nearly a year ago. As they pulled in, Carlton looked toward the parking garage some one hundred yards away and thought about all the repercussions that stemmed from the shootout between Brujido Ramos' drug dealers and himself, assisted by three off-duty DEA agents. Before the event was over, several people had died; among them, Ramos and three of his henchmen. All of the DEA agents, including Heather Colson, were injured, along with Carlton. Rehabilitation and full recovery had consumed months of their lives.

Additionally, SAPD had joined the fray that day—after frantic 9-1-1 calls reported gunfire in the Target parking garage—and scooped up eight more of Ramos' group and four of Tino's men. The best result—and the least publicized—had been the recovery of Paula's daughter from a kidnapping situation engineered by Ramos himself. Other events that had evolved directly and indirectly from the shootout comprised a mixed bag: the affair with Heather Colson, Paula hooking up with Reynaldo, the plan to take over a portion of the *Golfo* Cartel action, the huge firefight in a Mexico warehouse, Tino's death, the fizzle-out of the relationship with Heather...it was a long chain of occurrences that had kept Carlton Westerfield in danger or on edge almost non-stop during the past eight or nine months.

Paula was getting out from the front seat and caught Carlton looking in the direction of the shootout in which he had been wounded taking down Brujido Ramos and rescuing her daughter. The kidnapping of her daughter had been one of the most harrowing experiences of her life, and she knew its successful resolution had been due to Carlton's involvement, as well as that of the DEA agent, Heather Colson, who was also severely wounded.

She looked at Carlton and smiled. "Celia is doing fine. Brenda contacted me—*us* this morning," she said, referring to herself and Reynaldo, the girl's father, and Brenda Ramos, the girl's legal guardian.

Carlton returned the smile, glad to be shaken from his grim reverie upon seeing the scene of the shootout and reliving, for a few seconds, the pulse-pounding gun battle and its painful aftermath. "That's good news, Paula," he said, taking a deep breath to cover a rare wave of emotion. "They still living in *Distrito Federal*?"

"Yes, and Celia likes her new school and new friends. Brenda says she doesn't seem to miss being here at all."

"I guess youth has advantages, like being able to adapt to new surroundings, new people, different food. A whole new life, I suppose."

"Yes. And it's turned out that way for me and Reynaldo, too, and we have you to thank for that."

Hearing the remark, Diane, who had been quiet during the short drive, turned to look at them. Reynaldo stood by the driver's door, saying nothing, but having some of the same thoughts as Carlton. He turned to face Diane. "It's a long story. Get Carlton to tell you the whole thing. He was the hero of the hour. Still is, for that matter."

Embarrassed, Carlton rolled his eyes and shut his door, wishing he could shut the door on this conversation. "Let's just get these women something to eat Reynaldo. That's more important than some old story I've already forgotten." Walking around the car to Diane, he whispered, "Get the story from Paula. I was a bit under the weather at the time, so I'm sure she remembers it better than I."

Breakfast turned out to be a pleasant affair. The women chatted away, seemingly comfortable in each other's company, but the kidnapping-and-rescue story didn't surface again. Carlton was pleased that the discussion hadn't continued in the restaurant; he wasn't sure this was the time to add another chapter to Diane's growing file of information regarding Carlton Westerfield. But he knew that the smart computer geekette wouldn't let go of it now that she had learned of a source from which to hear all about it. He wished it hadn't come up.

There was a lot more important ground to cover: he hadn't had a chance to tell Reynaldo and Diane the entire story of the interrogation session and didn't want to bring it up around Paula, though she was quite familiar with Carlton's past. For someone who didn't like even two people rehashing his troubles, an audience of three would have caused him more unease than he could stand. The update would have to wait.

Visiting the flea market soon became a reunion with people Carlton hadn't seen since soon after the Nuevo Laredo massacre, during Tino's memorial service. Of course, all of the merchants remembered him and greeted him warmly, along with the taciturn woman who ran the snack bar, Beatriz, and Jese, another laborer who had worked with Carlton at daily tasks around the market. Raul and Caterina Vega showed up, alerted by Paula that Carlton would be there. Both of them hugged Carlton like their long-lost son, and he was happy to return the gesture to the Cuban refugees with whom he'd shared a dangerous adventure.

Looking around as they wandered through the market, he was relieved to see that everyone greeted Reynaldo cordially. When they'd arrived, it occurred to Carlton that many people in the close-knit community had lost family members in the gun battle in *Nuevo Laredo* a few months earlier. While everyone had attended Tino's funeral and exhibited a strong community bond during the immediate aftermath, Carlton had wondered if the camaraderie of the time would last, or if the passage of a few months might give people time to think about the sacrifice and loss caused by the debacle, which was the result of Reynaldo and Tino's ambitious overtures toward the *Golfo* Cartel. But if anyone harbored ill feelings, it wasn't present today.

During a stop at the snack bar for drinks, Reynaldo announced an idea to go to Corpus for a few days. "It's Monday, so we can go down until Thursday and come back before the weekend crowd starts showing up."

Paula looked at Diane, Diane looked at Carlton, and Carlton looked embarrassed. "Uh, sure. I need to get out of town and hope something happens while I'm gone. Something I can prove I wasn't a part of," he added.

"Good!" Reynaldo said. "We've got our stuff already, so we'll just take you by your place to get your gear."

Carlton shook his head and looked sheepishly from face to face, realizing this had been planned without any input on his part. Diane smiled at his discomfort and admitted the whole thing. "We talked it over last night at the ranch and decided it would be a good thing for you. Plus, I've never been to Corpus Christi, so it's a necessary trip for me, too."

Within the hour, the group was pulling into Carlton's apartment complex. Reynaldo swung into the back lot and pulled into an empty slot. Carlton opened his door to get out. "It'll only take me about five minutes, but y'all are welcome to come up," he offered.

The rest decided to stay put, and Carlton, warming to the idea of a short trip out of town, hurried to get an overnight bag. Coming back down the stairs, he glanced in the direction of his parking spot near the end of a covered section. His blue Cadillac was in its spot, sparkling clean from his Saturday ritual. The sight brought a grin to his face as he recalled the ribbing his ingrained habit brought him from friends.

At the bottom of the stairs, his field of view changed, and a movement near his car caught his attention. A man was walking beside it, looking around in each direction, then back at his car, and clearly up to no good. Something about the man's stature and movements seemed vaguely familiar, and Carlton trotted over to Reynaldo's car.

"Hang on a second here," he said, dropping his bag beside the rear passenger door. "There's a guy at my car, looking around as though he wants something. Maybe he backed into it or something. I'd better go check."

Circling in front of Reynaldo's car, he was hidden from the man's field of vision long enough to approach without being seen until he was under the carport cover and very near the intruder. When he was about twenty feet away, the man turned and looked at him without a sign of surprise or apprehension. At that moment, Carlton recognized him as the same man who had opened the door for him at Little Italy, the night he'd gone in to meet Heather Colson. Then, he'd appeared oddly dressed, reminding Carlton of someone out of place or time, trying to effect a look that was reminiscent of a long-ago dandy gunfighter, one who had a chrome-plated derringer up his sleeve, in addition to a six-gun on his hip. This time, the odd ensemble of clothes didn't seem so out of place. In fact, the shirt buttoned to the throat covered by a rumpled sports jacket looked a bit rakish, Carlton thought, if not stylish in a traditional sense.

"Hello, Carl," the man said. His voice even sounded familiar, though it grated on Carlton's nerves to be addressed by the diminutive of his given name, one he'd never used or even tolerated.

"Can I help you?" Carlton asked. His tone didn't match the words— more appropriate would have been "what the hell are you doing pacing around my car?"

"I hope so," the man said. "I need a job done. A couple of jobs, in fact. They pay—"

"I don't want a job," Carlton interrupted. "I'm retired. What I would like is for you to tell me why you approached me the other night and why you've followed me to my home. I didn't sign up on any job-seeking sites."

The man held up both hands in a surrendering gesture. "I know, and I apologize for upsetting you," he explained in a voice that suggested Upper Midwest, maybe Chicago or Milwaukee. "But I wanted to meet you in person and offer you the work, because you come highly recommended. In fact—"

"The only work I've done in years is sweeping up at a flea market and driving rental cars to various locations," Carlton interrupted, not bothering to sound civil. "It doesn't take a reference to locate someone to do that, so tell me who you are and what you want, or I'll call the police right now."

"My name isn't important until…" His voice trailed off as Carlton pulled his burner phone from his pocket and punched two digits and held his finger poised over the second "1" of 9-1-1.

"Okay, okay. I'll tell you my name, then you can decide. But there's no need to call the police. You don't want them coming here any more than—"

"Bert? Bert Morris?" The incredulous tone of the question being uttered right behind him made Carlton whirl around to see Paula Hendricks looking over his shoulder at the intruder, a look of amazement on her face. She had approached them quietly from Reynaldo's car using the same indirect path Carlton had moments before. And though posed as a question, her words answered Carlton's inquiry and cleared up a number of things in the process while opening up a bunch of additional mysteries.

Thinking quickly, Carlton decided to use the revelation to convey his wishes in no uncertain terms. "Mr. Morris, I don't know you, and I don't want to. I don't know anyone whom you know, certainly not anyone who'd recommend me for a job—"

It was Bert Morris' turn to interrupt. "Big Mo was my brother, and I believe he was qualified to recommend your skills as far back as nineteen seventy-nine." He pointed toward Paula, "Ask her—"

Carlton was ready for it, already shaking his head. "That name—and yours—keep coming up, thrown at me by people I don't care to associate with; not now, not then, not ever."

"If you would just hear me out—"

The insistent request was disrupted again by Carlton. "One more digit to press." He held up his phone to show he was a half-second from summoning the police, no matter the consequences. He didn't think the situation could get much worse for him, and Big Mo's long-lost brother was not likely a stellar citizen who could withstand much scrutiny from law enforcement.

"Okay, I'm leaving." His resigned tone of voice sounded convinced of Carlton's next move. He turned to go, walking in the opposite direction from where Reynaldo was parked.

When he was about three steps away, Carlton decided to make a point, not something he was usually inclined to do. "And Mr. Morris? After we're done here, it would be in your best interest if you forgot this address and forgot me. Because I won't forget you, and you won't like my waiting for your return. And to make certain you understand, I want you to get in my car."

The look on Morris' face said he hadn't expected this turn of events. "Uh, where are we going? I mean, I understand what you told me. I won't come—"

"I said get in!" Carlton shouted, pulling his key fob and pointing to the passenger door of the Caddy.

Morris shrugged and walked nonchalantly toward the car. When he reached the door, Carlton hit the fob twice. The resulting click made the man smile before reaching for the handle and sitting down gingerly in the passenger seat and pulling the door shut.

At that moment, Carlton noticed Reynaldo and Diane had approached at some point, adding to the strange scene unfolding here in the parking lot. Without explanation, he strode around to the driver's side and got in. Holding the key fob, he slowly reached for the Start button, watching Bert Morris' face in his peripheral vision for over five seconds, waiting for the man to break. Instead, Morris simply looked straight ahead, so Carlton started the car, put it in gear to pull forward a few feet, then stabbed the brake and put it in reverse. He backed into the same place and killed the engine before turning to face his passenger.

"Okay, Mr. Morris, get out, walk away, and don't come back. Just remember what I said about my waiting for your return."

Morris pulled the door handle, then got out of the car and started walking away. After a few steps, he slowed and turned around to face Carlton, as the others looked on, mystified by the scene. "If I had put a bomb in your car, I wouldn't have gotten in with you," he said, a smarmy smile on his face. "Because neither of us would have gotten out. You would have activated it with your key fob and blown us both to hell when you started the car."

Carlton stared at him without expression, but he was impressed with the man's apparent knowledge of using the key fob transmitter to begin the flow of power to a bomb's timing device. That method precluded a possible problem with a dead—

His thoughts were interrupted by Morris' next statement, which expounded on his tutorial. "It's the best way if you don't want to wire into the car's power source and have to worry about the battery going bad.

"I can see your problem, Westerfield, just as my brother saw it," he continued. "He said you were smart, but maybe you're too smart for your own good, because you don't realize there are some *other* smart people out there. And right now, you've got a real problem with a few of them. I hope I've gotten your attention."

With that, he turned and walked away.

CHAPTER 10

Reynaldo insisted on dropping off Carlton's car at the flea market and storing it in one of the garages, a precaution Carlton couldn't argue with. After informing Beatriz of the car, the four piled into Reynaldo's Lexus and headed for Corpus, running a bit later than planned, but feeling better about leaving Carlton's car in a safe place.

The first fifteen minutes of the drive were quiet, the only sound being that of tires on the pavement if IH-37. Carlton sat leaned against the door, his body language not inviting any intrusion into his thoughts. Right now, he was fully absorbed in the encounter, analyzing what it told him, and wondering what he might be missing from Bert Morris' troubling visit.

Most concerning was Morris' mention of Carlton's connection to his brother and alluding that Big Mo had imparted information regarding his job skills. Also, Paula had recognized him from some previous time in her life when she had dealt with Bert's brother, and Bert had pointed to Paula while saying something about asking her…It was a topic that begged some serious discussion, he thought, recalling that Paula had plenty of mystery surrounding her own past. He couldn't fathom how to start that discussion, though, without sounding like an interrogator.

Not until they had passed South Loop 1604 did anyone utter a word. At that point, Carlton had calmed down and couldn't bear the uncomfortable silence any more. After all, it was *his* connection to Bert Morris, tenuous as it was, that had caused the ugly confrontation and set the current mood. It wasn't the fault of his companions in the car, not even Paula, with her sketchy history.

This can't go on for the entire trip, we're supposed to be having fun. Time to get things back to normal…if such a thing exists.

"Well!" he began, startling everyone amidst the silence. "I'm glad Bert didn't use his stronger method to get my attention, or I'd be car-shopping instead of headed for the beach."

The comment ended the silence, and everyone laughed, if nervously. But at least the tension was broken, and the next fifty miles were spent discussing the old San Antonio gangster's wayward brother, who, according to Paula, was from Bloomington, Minnesota, giving Carlton the satisfaction of having placed the man's accent with fair accuracy.

"I met him once, years ago, when I worked at Big Mo's Pawnshop, the one on Nacogdoches Road," she began. "He came in, dressed like a medicine show peddler in an old movie, and announced who he was, where he was from, and said he was looking for "Randy." It took me a second to connect that to Randall, because he never went by anything but Big Mo. He didn't even sign payroll checks with 'Randall' or 'Randy;' it was always just 'Big Mo.'

"So I buzzed the office and Mo came right out. The pair went back and closed the door without saying a thing to each other. They were in there all afternoon, I guess. I left at the end of my shift, and when I came in the next day, not a word was mentioned about it. And I certainly didn't bring it up, because it was plain to see that Mo wasn't comfortable having Bert come around. I think they had different opinions of how to conduct their business ventures."

"That makes two of us," Carlton said. "When you said his name, I realized why the FBI had questioned me about someone named Bert Morris. I thought they had made a mistake about the name, or that Bert was Randall's middle name. Instead, they just made a mistake about the timing and the nature of our new relationship—one I'm now wishing didn't exist."

He proceeded to go over the entire interrogation session, not really caring at this point about Paula's presence. The strange run-in with Bert had put aside—for the moment—any qualms he'd held about discussing his circumstances with all three of them, and he went on to describe his brief encounter with Bert on the night he'd met with Heather, and thinking all along that the oddly-dressed man looked familiar. "Now I can see the family resemblance, but at the time, it was just a feeling, like déjà vu, or remembering something from a dream."

"But what is he doing here, trying to get you to do a job for him?" Reynaldo asked. "And how could his timing be any worse?" he added, voicing what everyone in the car had been wondering since witnessing the confrontation.

"I suppose he was just following me around the other night, getting close enough to identify me and speak to me. But why would he approach me right out in the open today? Since the FBI is throwing his name around, they obviously knows he's in San Antonio, so you'd think he'd lie low, or go back home, wherever that is now."

"I never heard exactly what he did, but he didn't seem much like his brother," Paula said. "Big Mo, for all his faults, knew the shady side of every business in the city. He knew every illegal game being played, and all the players, but he didn't showboat or comment on it."

"Whatever it was that you did for him, Big Mo must have given a good recommendation for Bert to remember you after all these years," Diane said, her tone inviting a clarification, while her unsettling visual concentration never wavered from Carlton's face.

Carlton didn't respond at first, wondering if the astute woman beside him had simply overheard Bert's words and connected himself and the deceased pawnshop owner, or if Paula had filled her in, including details of *exactly* what he did for Big Mo. The more he thought about the expanding circle of people who knew, or were learning, certain things about his past life, the more...*concerned* he became, despite his earlier concessions to social contact. Not that he mistrusted anyone in the car; it simply went against his nature, honed over the past thirty years, to have his history aired. It was time to shift the conversation to another facet of his life—the current spotlight that was shining on him.

He asked Diane if she thought there might be a connection between Bert Morris and any of the recently slain miscreants. "It's quite a coincidence that he shows up here while people are getting popped and capped, asking me if I would work for him."

"I wondered when you might mention that," she said. "And I brought my laptop, I'll work on it tonight.

"But one question for you first: Why did you get in your car and start it if you thought there might be a bomb? What if he had really placed one in your car?"

Carlton shook his head, smiling. "I don't think he would have done that in broad daylight. He wanted me to know that he knew how, though, down to the details of activating it without worrying about the power source running down. Anyway, I felt pretty sure he'd come clean when I made him sit with me in the car while I started it, no matter how it was wired, or how good he is at keeping a poker face. Then when I put it in gear, in case an explosive was wired to go off at forward or reverse movement, he *still* didn't show much expression. I began to wonder if I'd bluffed myself into serious trouble."

The look on Diane's face said what she thought about such bluffing. She looked at him closely with the laser-beam mode powered all the way up for a few seconds. Then she composed herself and went on to explain the threads she would follow to ascertain any link between Bert Morris, Randall Morris, and any of the three recent murder victims. She also reminded him to check his car for a tracking device.

Carlton sighed. "Between that guy, the FBI, and the DEA, my car may wired be like a NASA spacecraft. I'll look, but if I find anything, I'll just get another car and let them all think they've got me tracked. Or I may take the device off of my car and stick it on a long-haul truck headed to Pittsburgh. That will keep them busy for a while," he added with a smirk.

Diane opened the laser beam aperture a bit at that remark. "That's pretty clever. I'm beginning to see why Big Mo highly recommended you."

They pulled into Corpus Christi as the sun fell in the west, behind the forest of refinery towers looming beside the interstate. Reynaldo had reserved adjoining rooms at the Radisson Hotel on North Beach, and Carlton felt somewhat apprehensive in the elevator, wondering what, exactly, were the sleeping arrangements his friend had procured? He glanced at his elevator companions, but no hint was forthcoming from the trio discussing dinner plans and tomorrow's beachwear.

He needn't have worried. Both rooms were large, spacious suites, with separated bathrooms and sleeping areas. Either one could have accommodated all of them without any privacy problems. Diane must have seen, or sensed, his relief as they walked into the first one and looked around. "Did we have you worried for a while?" she asked, mischief replacing the disarming laser beam look for a moment.

"Huh? Oh, no! Uh, this is really nice. I just wasn't sure what—"

She burst out laughing, the first time he'd experienced that emotion coming from the woman he had internally labeled Ms. Laser Beam and Ms. Computer Geekette. While both nicknames were intended as compliments, he hadn't been prepared for anything as...*human* as an outright guffaw. He turned to her, feeling his face redden. It was one of those times when nothing anyone said would come out right, and they both knew it. He felt compelled to try anyway.

"I didn't know what the sleeping arrangements were, and I didn't want anyone to feel uncomfortable, that's all. Especially *me*," he added with a grin.

"Okay, I'll confess. Reynaldo thought it would be great fun to set this up and keep you worried. He said you were a tad reserved when it comes to things like this, that you would have gotten four separate rooms if left up to you. Paula and I were more than happy to go along with his joke."

"Yeah, well, I can hear him coming up with something like that. I guess he knows me too well. And he's just like our departed friend Tino; never miss a chance to make their shy Anglo friend uncomfortable."

Diane thought about what he'd said for a long moment. "You three were close, weren't you?"

The question was a leading one. Carlton knew he was being played for some new file information, but he didn't mind. He'd agreed to take this mini-vacay in order to get his mind off the ominous murder accusations, so he plopped down in a chair facing the bay and motioned for her to take the other one. Outside the window, gulls were hanging motionless in mid-air as the stiff onshore breeze passed over gently flapping, curved wings, equalizing lift, thrust, drag, and weight. Meanwhile, the delicate balancing act didn't stop them from shrieking their heads off.

"We certainly became that way after sharing what we did and going through a few nightmarish experiences together. Of course, he and Tino go back to childhood and prep school. I'm a newcomer, about three years. But yes, we became good friends, despite having differing opinions on some matters."

"So I gathered. Reynaldo told me all about the mess in *Nuevo Laredo*. He said you were against the idea from the start, that you really opposed going up against the *Golfos*."

Wow! Doesn't take this gal long to cut to the chase!

He shrugged that one off. "Like I said, just a difference of opinion. It could have gone the other way, and they would have been in position to make a lot of money."

She thought about that for a long minute. "Could have gone the other way, except for Clive Millstone."

"Aka Cletus Miller, the turncoat bastard," Carlton responded, more venom in his voice than he'd intended—but not as much as he felt.

"And now he's causing more trouble, even if he's not directly involved in setting up these shootings. You should have just killed him, Carlton."

"Don't I know it! The problem was, he was holding Paula in front of his body as a shield. Finally, I could get a shot at the right knee, so I took it. When he let Paula loose and spun to his right, he exposed his left knee. So I took that shot, too. If I had walked over and put one between his headlights, it would have prevented him from causing any more problems."

"But a copycat shooter—if that's who's doing them—might still have thought it a workable idea to make you look good for what's going on now."

"I know, Diane. We've been all through this a dozen times, and we can come up with scenarios that work, but no way to prove or disprove any of them."

"I'm going to work on connecting dots tonight, see if I can put any of the players in the same place at the same time. Maybe that will give us some new ideas, anyway.

"But first, I want to get something awkward out of the way, before they call us with dinner plans," she said, rising from her chair and leaning down toward Carlton.

He looked up to see the steady gaze zeroing in on his eyes for about two seconds before she came too close to focus on. By then, her eyes were closed, and he made the wise choice of following her lead.

So this is what "connecting dots" means…I need to get out more!

This one would be a lot more difficult, an operation with too many variables. The killer hated it, but there was no alternative. Just like the others, there was no way to turn down this job. The price for failure was too high.

First, the killer had to work alone, no assistance other than information, and it had been sparse so far, hard to get, and harder still to understand.

Second, the victim had to be hit here in San Antonio, then taken somewhere else to be dumped. Just where the dumping would take place was the sparse part on the information. Hauling a shot-up corpse wasn't a pleasant task, and though the killer had performed many unpleasant jobs, transporting a dead body to God-knows-where wasn't a chore that would ever become easy. The transport vehicle would have to be fully protected, then sanitized, not just cleaned. Modern forensics could find anything, and the magical technology it employed removed many of the liberties taken for granted back in the day. In short, a simple scrub job with soap and water wasn't enough.

The only alternative was to use a disposable car, and that meant stealing one. Itself, not a difficult task, but just one more piece added to this assignment, which was becoming more complicated with each phase. To further compound the problem, the car had to be acquired the same day as the target, not beforehand, because there wasn't a good way to hide the car and wait for the time to pick up the target. According to the only information that was not sparse, the target, a loser named Gabriel Mason, would be leaving his shithole apartment around ten o'clock on Monday night, the 24th.

At six in the evening of that day, the killer waited for a disposable car at an HEB store about three miles from Mason's dump. Having taken a cab to the grocery store location on the west side, the killer had only to hang around until dusk, scoping out possible cars. By eight that night, it would be time to get more aggressive, but not until time grew short.

It was just after eight and the killer was growing anxious, dreading the thought of having to carjack the next reasonable-looking candidate, when the perfect car showed up and pulled haphazardly into a parking spot near the street. The driver, a young woman carrying a baby and leading a toddler, slammed the door and rushed toward the store to get something. Seeing her haste, the killer quickly wandered over the car, a junky old Toyota Corolla. The key was in the ignition, likely because the woman didn't give a crap if it was stolen or not—it was her boyfriend's piece of shit car anyway, and was nearly out of gas, just as the boyfriend was nearly out of money.

The killer jumped in, started the car (Toyotas were best, even the old ones always started and ran) and drove away, hoping to make a gas station before the thing sputtered to a halt. Thirty-seven bucks worth of gas later, the killer backed the Corolla into a spot at a different store, this one near the target's apartment. Backing into the parking slot hid the rear license plate from cruising cops, at least a little, so the hot car would retain its usefulness. The front plate had long ago disappeared, but cops didn't bother with minor stuff like that anymore.

Now it was time to wait, so the killer hunkered down in the seat and killed an hour before heading to the target's address. The entire hour was painful, with the killer wondering when a police car would pull up…exactly the kind of foolish, amateur action the killer hated, but couldn't avoid in this rushed-order job. Seeing that the damn clock didn't work in this junker, the killer had to keep checking time on the cell phone, another amateur move, almost guaranteed to be noticed by the security patrol making the rounds of the parking lot.

Finally, it was time to get busy. The killer cranked up the Corolla and headed toward the guy's place, hoping he would be leaving around ten to meet his connection, as he always did.

By ten o'clock, it was completely dark, so when the target emerged from his dump of an apartment at twelve minutes after ten, following him was fairly straightforward. No one paid much attention to derelicts or ratty cars following them in this part of the city. By moving ahead and front-tailing the guy, the killer was able to pick a spot and wait for the target to turn the corner and come into view a half-block away. By the time the target approached the killer's crappy car, the hood was up and the killer was poking around under the hood. Clearly flummoxed by the trouble, the killer, seeing the man approaching, offered a twenty-dollar bill if the man could help him by removing the air cleaner. The target, always in need of money, was happy to oblige, just as he was happy to accept the offer of a ride when the junky car started without a problem. Driver and passenger got in and drove away…for about three blocks, when the driver inexplicably pulled into a dark parking lot. As passenger Mason looked inquiringly at the driver, the gun's muzzle came up and a small-caliber round entered his forehead from about twenty-eight inches away. As he slumped over toward the windshield, two more found their way into his left temple. Four more rounds were administered to Mason's legs, these from a much larger handgun, but the angle was wrong for direct hits to the knees, which would have been excruciatingly painful had Gabriel Mason not already been dead for twenty-one seconds. The killer calmly pulled out of the parking lot and took Southwest Military Drive to Interstate 37. At the last red light before the interstate, the killer finally relaxed and started thinking about where to lose the two weapons.

The next stop would be Corpus Christi, the Sparkling City by the Sea, according to that city's Chamber of Commerce brochures. For the target, now victim Gabriel Mason, it would be his final stop.

CHAPTER 11

Dinner was at a place called Harrison's Landing off the People's Street T-head pier. If San Antonio represented the mecca for Tex-Mex food, Corpus Christs had a good shot at the title for seafood, and the group enjoyed the outing. By some unspoken mutual consent, nothing was said about the weird meeting with the out-of-state gangster or Carlton's ongoing drama with three—or was it four, now?—law enforcement agencies trying to indict him for three grisly murders.

After eating, they returned to North Beach where enough daylight remained to walk down the beach sidewalk and take in the view. One direction led to the big World War II era aircraft carrier, the Lexington, anchored in the bay and serving as a first-class WWII museum and memorial. Beyond that, the Texas State Aquarium held Diane's attention. Her roots on the East Coast made her an ocean-loving person, but she thought the chillier Atlantic waters were probably a far cry from the bathtub-warm Gulf of Mexico and its selection of sea critters. Though it was closed for the day, the aquarium made the cut for the next day's activities.

After lingering near the huge aircraft carrier for a while, the mosquitoes found them, and the group headed back to the shelter of the hotel. All agreed on a final after-dinner drink, then retired to their respective suites. As the door clicked shut behind them, Carlton was glad Diane had put the "awkward" moment to rest earlier in the evening. He wondered if a glass of wine and the couch, combined with the TV on a soft jazz channel, would be a good starting point. Or let things find their own way, which would probably result in "Good night, see you in the morning."

Come on, Carlton, you gotta' be positive—and proactive!

He began scanning the room for the remote, but the computer sleuth had other things on her mind right now. "The group we're looking at has expanded, so I need some input from you about the Big Mo era," she started out. "I'm going to try every way I know to find out about both the Morris brothers' prison records; where they served time, and when. Then I can cross-reference each of their stints with Millstone/Miller and the three murder victims to see if their paths ever crossed in time and in the same facility. That will tell us—"

Carlton interrupted her. "I don't know about Bert Morris, but it won't tell us anything about Randall, because he didn't spend any time in prison, not even a night in county lockup, during the many years I knew him."

Dianne seemed mystified. "How could he avoid at least some time away if he was around for thirty years doing hinky jobs? As I understood it, he ran a pawnshop chain, not a church daycare center. Pawnshops in general are notorious for things like stolen property, fencing all types of merchandise, and laundering money.

"That's not to say all pawnshop owners are crooks; it's just the nature of a multi-faceted, cash-based business that deals with cash-strapped people. Combine that with Big Mo's sideline action, for which he needed your skillset, and odds are he's bound to have run afoul sometime over the years.

"Just because you were never even questioned doesn't mean all his action went that well—unless you were his only employee, of course, and performed all his jobs."

Carlton smiled inwardly at her accurate take on the widely accepted pawnshop industry's reputation and her textbook assessment of reasons for its shady reputation. But she had missed the mark with Randall Morris. The obese gangster had many shortcomings, but brains and street-smarts weren't on the list. And he avoided any interaction with law enforcement like the plague. Aloud he said, "He had other employees, I'm sure. But Mo was very careful, as I am. I guess we made a good team.

"He certainly wasn't headed for sainthood, since he ran afoul of someone about three years ago. He was found murdered in his main store. He'd been tortured and knifed, a grisly ending for Mo. It was ruled as some connection to his way of life that went bad, nothing that law enforcement was a part of. Anyway, the investigation led nowhere, another unsolved murder."

He didn't tell her the entire story, or what he knew to be the entire story, as told to him by none other than Paula Hendricks, Mo's one-time employee, Reynaldo's current squeeze, and Diane's newfound friend—the woman in the adjoining suite at this very moment.

As Paula had later related to him, Big Mo had visitors pounding on his private entrance door on the evening of his death, and he insisted that she take his briefcase and hide in his walk-in vault while he met with them. While quietly waiting and scared out of her mind, she overheard the commotion and remained in the vault during the horrific torture session, not emerging until the assailants were gone and Big Mo was headed to the Big Pawnshop in the Sky. However, that story changed when Big Mo's briefcase full of money went missing and turned up later in Paula's possession…Carlton groaned to himself as he recalled the questionable attributes of the woman he'd slept with for over two years. He kept his face as neutral as he could and hoped Ms. Laser Beam wasn't reading his mind, as she sometimes appeared to be.

Diane shifted tactics and started in another direction. "Ok, no law enforcement, so let's start with your part. What did you do that made you such a highly-sought employee by his brother years later?"

By now, Carton was shaking his head. "Okay, okay. It seems you're dying to hear everything there is to know about my career with Big Mo. For about thirty years, I carried out contract work for him. I never knew how he located the jobs, and I didn't want to know. He and I kept things compartmentalized. What I didn't know, I couldn't tell, under any amount of pressure. That way, he never had to worry if I were taken in for questioning.

"But back to your question, I think he had sources who contacted him when a contract was let, or maybe individuals wanting something done contacted him directly. I did the jobs and got sixty percent of the contract, he kept forty."

"Exactly what kind of work did the contracts entail? Mostly fencing stolen goods for pro thieves?"

Carlton gritted his teeth, uncomfortable with this line of questioning. He plunged ahead—warily. "I'm afraid it was a bit more serious than that. But suffice it to say, since neither of us was even questioned, it's not likely that you'll find anything on file about Randall Morris." He paused a few seconds, then raised an index finger upward to signify an important fact. "Remember, Diane, he was a successful businessman first, and a slimeball gangster second. He was good at keeping the two lives separated."

"So you're not going to tell me?" A sly grin replaced the laser beam for a moment, giving him the uneasy feeling that any man in a personal relationship with this gal had better walk a straight line.

"Diane, I don't think I need to spell it out for you. I'm sure Reynaldo told you enough, and if he hasn't, then Paula has—or will."

The hypnotic look powered up again, maybe to lie-detector mode. "They didn't give me any details, but they told me you eliminated people. I wasn't sure if that meant you intimidated them into leaving someone alone, or leaving town. Or if you murdered them."

If she was watching him for some kind of reaction, she had to be disappointed. Carlton met her stare with one of his own as he answered. "I don't know of a way to sugarcoat it. That last sentence is a pretty accurate job description for Carlton Westerfield during the 'Big Mo era' as you call it."

She didn't even blink. "And I told you when we met that I don't mind exploring work on both sides of the law, so sugarcoating isn't necessary. Carlton, I'm the last one on earth to judge people's actions by how they make a living."

He wondered what that last part meant, but wasn't about to ask. In any event, it made him feel more comfortable with her—just not comfortable enough to lay out details of the murder-for-hire career he'd led for over three decades, not yet.

She relented and turned on her laptop, smiling as she did so. "I guess I'll have to stick with the other shady characters, then. Seriously, we've got to find some common thread between all the players, including Bert Morris, to make any progress on why they were killed in the manner they were—by someone who wants to maim the victims, either before or after their death."

"I hope you can, because right now, *this* shady guy sitting here with you is the only connection to the *one* shooting I did, and I don't like being this popular."

When her computer booted up, she began the mysterious process of sifting through several databases, plugging in the names of the three late murder victims, Millstone/Miller, and both Morris brothers, writing down any hits she found, then entering the others under a different filter, like a time frame or matching location, trying to find a connection. At least, that's the way she described the basic process to Carlton, who found it incredibly tedious and boring.

Two hours later, she had found only a couple of common denominators between the three victims, and those were court appearances before the same judge. No surprise there; all three vics were repeat offenders, and the revolving door of justice, even in a city of San Antonio's size, had to hit such miscreants in the butt from time to time. The only oddity at all was Jamal Crenshaw, who was arrested and arraigned in a Bexar County court in July, 2018, on a charge of possession with intent to sell. It seems Jamal had come to the Alamo City to pick up his goods and decided to sell a bit while here, before driving back to Houston. The other two, Peters and Pembrooke, appeared in court before the same judge, but years apart, so no time together in lockup.

All the data regarding Bertrand Gayle Morris put him in Minnesota for his entire adulthood, no connections to any of the vics or Millstone/Miller. He had applied for and received a license to operate a pawnshop in 1970. Thereafter, he had only a few minor incidents relating to improper pawn procedures. And his brother, Randall Carver Morris, had no criminal record, and only a few minor brushes with the law regarding stolen property, fraudulent credit card use, and similar pawnshop procedure misdemeanors. All of the bigger incidents involved inquiries only, no indictments.

She sighed and closed the laptop. "That's about all I can do with what we've got right now. I'm just not finding a connection. It's as though everyone in this mess is a random individual, the only commonality being illegal, or at least shady, activities to make a living.

"And even stranger is the complete lack of information on one of them."

By now Carlton was sleepy and had to think about the last comment before asking, "Which one?"

"Carlton Westerfield. Except for a driver's license, a bank account, and a military stint over four decades ago, he doesn't exist. You could be dead, except I couldn't find a death certificate."

That woke him up. "Well, that's comforting. The part about no death certificate. I feel better already."

"I'd like a glass of wine," Diane said, rising from her chair and changing gears instantly from the ugly business of murder research to seeking relaxation in the form of a grape product.

Carlton rummaged through the minibar and came up with some that would do, along with a cold *Dos Equis* for himself. Feeling more on sound footing with this line of activity, he tuned the TV to a Latin Jazz channel that was featuring a *Sergio Mendez & Brasil 66* album and headed for the couch. Diane followed him and shed her shoes on the way.

Two hours later, Carlton was sold on the value of "connecting the dots." He was quickly developing a different viewpoint of Reynaldo's computer geekette with the intense, unsettling eye contact, which had suddenly become quite appealing.

The four met for breakfast in the hotel restaurant just after eight, where Reynaldo and Paula already had a table. As Carlton and Diane approached, it was clear that something had occurred. Carlton eyed Reynaldo and noticed the brilliant smile was considerably dimmed this morning, replaced by a somber look. He was afraid to inquire, suspecting a tiff between him and Paula, but he was curious to know, in case it involved the turmoil in his own life.

"What's going on with y'all this morning?" he asked cautiously as he pulled a chair for Diane and remained standing, waiting for the answer.

"This."

Reynaldo reached to a nearby chair and handed him the day's copy of the *Corpus Christi Caller-Times*, folded open to the Metro Section. An above-the-fold article described the discovery of a man's body in a seedy section of downtown, not far from Crosstown Expressway. The man, as yet unidentified, had been shot multiple times in the "legs and head." Carlton didn't have to speculate long on what that meant.

"Damn!"

His rare use of an expletive caused Reynaldo and Paula to look at him, a bit surprised. Diane didn't know him well in that regard, but surmised from the others the impact the news had made on her new…computer research client. She turned her face upward to see him still standing there; frowning, scanning through the article a second time. Spotting nothing further of value, he sighed and tossed the paper back on the unoccupied chair and pulled his own out to sit down.

"This is just dandy," he said, trying to keep the harshness from his voice while frustration increased by the minute.

"It's plain to see that someone is able to keep up with your movements and use that to their advantage," Reynaldo ventured, not wishing to say aloud what was on everyone's mind.

Carlton thought for a moment. "When you brought this up yesterday, we were at the flea market snack bar. Was anyone close enough to overhear our plans?"

All four looked at each other and began shaking their heads. "I don't think so," Reynaldo said. "Not that it was a big secret, but the three of us discussed it earlier, at the ranch, and when I brought it up at the flea market, no one was anywhere close to our table."

Diane's knowledge of electronic surveillance short-stopped the uncomfortable moment. "Besides a tracking device on your cars, any of us could have a bug in our luggage. Or even on our person. We need to go to an electronics store and try to find a detector."

"Actually, it wouldn't take an all-out surveillance effort to know where we were headed once we got on I-37," Carlton said. "I mean, we could have cut off on 281 and gone to the Valley, but two couples traveling together would likely be going to Corpus."

"So anyone could have just followed us from your apartment parking lot to the interstate and figured out we were probably going to Corpus Christi," Reynaldo agreed. "No electronic stuff or multiple vehicles required, certainly not after we passed the Three Rivers turnoff to 281. The only logical destination is Corpus."

"Hotel reservations can be hacked pretty easily," Diane stated, getting an eye-roll from Carlton, who could barely *make* a reservation, much less hack one. "So that would narrow things down considerably, once they knew which general direction we were headed. Anybody with reasonable computer skills could do it."

"Yes, but that degree of sophistication is pointing more toward a law enforcement action," Carlton insisted. "No matter how motivated, I just can't see a copycat shooter going to all this trouble to calculate our movements, just to pin the next victim on me. It could have waited until I returned."

Diane understood the point he was making. "Tracking us—you— would be doable, but it would take a lot of resources and skill to get down here, find the victim, maim and kill him—all in the past eighteen or so hours. That's not a trick your average bad guy could pull off, is it?"

"Nope. But maybe this victim was hit in San Antonio, then bagged up and brought down here. That would make it easier for the shooter. And easier to pin on me, by the way, since that's where I hang my hat. A case could be made that I knew the victim."

"Maybe tomorrow's paper will have the victim identified," Diane said, already thinking ahead to more computer sleuthing.

Paula, who had remained quiet, spoke up. "Well, at least you have three people to say you were with them the entire time, not out shooting somebody."

Carlton managed a grin at that. "I was so angry at seeing the article, I hadn't even thought of that."

Reynaldo brightened at the reminder. "I guess I was also thinking only of location, not actual opportunity, or an alibi from three people. We'd just as well make the most of our little vacation and quit worrying over something we can't do anything about."

After breakfast, the four set out to do exactly that. Plenty of new sightseeing for Diane: the aquarium, and making the loop to Padre Island, then north to Mustang Island, Port Aransas, Aransas Pass, and back to North Beach took up the day. The only reminder of the current problems came when Diane called for a stop at an electronics store where she bought an instrument she thought could detect any tracking devices they might have acquired. Sitting in the back seat with her, Carlton watched as she perused the data sheet packaged with the gadget, skimming over it and quietly commenting on its various functions, along with advantages and shortcomings.

After a few minutes of technical talk, she summarized the equipment in layman's language. "This will work pretty well to expose most common locater and tracking devices that use radio frequency waves. There are some really sophisticated ones out there that use microwave technology, and this won't detect those. We'll just have to go with this and see what we find."

Carlton shook his head at her quick lesson, impressed with her knowhow. At the same time, he was disappointed, almost embarrassed, by his own lack of knowledge. He wasn't totally ignorant of common electrical circuitry or basics of most general scientific theory, but she was talking about modern tracking equipment that used the latest digital technology, which no doubt was far advanced from anything he'd ever studied. It made him feel helpless, realizing that his fate was being manipulated, at least in part, by something he could not see, nor even understand.

Listening to her, he wished he could confront the perpetrator of this mess with a piece of equipment that he, Carlton, *was* comfortable with—a Colt .45 auto-pistol. It would even the playing field in a micro-second, with only ounces of pressure applied to the trigger. He held the thought for only a few seconds, though, then dismissed it. It showed a lack of control, and that was a weakness he loathed.

In reality, Carlton didn't even care for guns, except for their utility. He didn't own one, didn't want one, and had only procured them in pursuit of completing a job, then disposed of them. It was a necessary piece of equipment that had made him a good living, not something he needed as a crutch to bolster some macho image of American male culture.

He had discovered his natural ability with a handgun while in the military, but hadn't thought much about it at the time. In fact, his military trainers had chided him for his poor shooting form, even though the results were almost phenomenal. As a young soldier of minor rank, he was soon delegated to other tasks, and gave handguns no more thought—until his career took a turn from the military to being Big Mo's top button man. Even then, he seldom had to rely on marksmanship skill to complete an assignment, since they were usually attended at point-blank range.

Indeed, only after Big Mo's death, during Carlton's association with Tino Perez did he have need for his extraordinary natural skill: first, at a car wash while being confronted by four gangbangers sent to collect the ransom for Paula's daughter; and second, in a retaliatory gesture against the Brit mercenary, Clive Millstone. Those more recent episodes were now serving only to make Carlton wish for a confrontation with his electronics-savvy adversary, one in which he would clearly have the upper hand. Nevertheless, it was not a train of thought he wanted to dwell on, like some hotshot gunslinger in the Old West. It wasn't what Carlton Westerfield wanted to be.

Besides, my "natural talent" with a big handgun is what landed me in this problem to begin with.

At a Port Aransas parking lot, Diane got out with the tracker finding device and went over the car carefully, front bumper to back, leaning down to check the undercarriage and wheel wells. "Nothing," she said. "We'll check all our bags when we get back to the hotel, but the car is the most likely target because it's easiest to approach without much suspicion."

Back in Corpus, she repeated the process with everyone's luggage, and got the same results. Carlton didn't know whether to be disappointed or not. It would have been satisfying to learn how his movements were being monitored, but confirmation of his vulnerability would have been disquieting. After a short discussion, the group decided to put the problem out of mind, or at least on the back burner, for the remainder of the trip.

The next two days went by without incident, but despite the vow to avoid the problem, they learned on local TV news that the victim of multiple gunshots was not a Corpus Christi local, name and hometown being withheld. Not much information was given in the follow-up newspaper article, and nothing appeared the next day, so Carlton had no indication if the shooting was linked to the San Antonio and Houston murders. He hadn't received a call from Heather to grill him about his whereabouts, and he didn't know if that was good or bad, either.

Meanwhile, lacking any communication—positive or negative—with the DEA agent, Carlton turned his full attention to Diane. He found her company extremely pleasant once he became accustomed to the even, almost challenging, gaze with which she met every face-to-face encounter. During a particularly close moment, he admitted to his early apprehension upon coming under her "laser beam" look, prompting her to laugh and provide an explanation.

"I don't intend to make anyone uneasy," she laughed. "It comes from my upbringing, I suppose. I was always taught to look directly at someone when conversing, especially when listening. I've found that it helps me to remember everything in the conversation."

"Well, it removes all doubt about whom you're conversing with," he agreed. "It was just a little unsettling when we first met."

She snuggled in closer and began exploring with both hands. A seductive giggle followed. "It seems you've gotten over being unsettled."

CHAPTER 12

Back in San Antonio for the weekend, Carlton was still in limbo, undecided about what to do. Leave and stay gone while hoping another shooting took place here? Or stay and hope the next one to pop up was in another locale, but with identical earmarks of the FBI's on-the-loose serial killer? The decision was made for him on Friday evening, May 28, when he answered his door.

"Mr. Westerfield, I'm Jeffrey Bales, FBI." Agent Bales, about thirty-five, with sandy hair and fair complexion, thrust forward a shield and turned to his right to introduce his companion. "This is Agent Heather Colson of the Drug Enforcement Administration."

Agent Colson had her shield out and shoved it half-heartedly in Carlton's direction with a look of disdain on her face. Carlton made a production out of leaning forward to check out her shield, though he had barely glanced at the one Bales had proffered. He shifted his look from the badge to her face, narrowing his eyes with suspicion before going back to the badge, though it didn't have a photo to compare. Having had his fun for the moment, he smiled and looked back and forth between the two agents.

"What can I do for you?"

"Will you cut the crap, Carlton?" Agent Colson's impatient tone said she was tired of his comedy.

"May we come in?" Bales asked, undeterred by the interaction between them.

"Sure." Carlton stepped aside and flicked a hand toward the interior of his apartment. Upon his return from Corpus, he had gone over the apartment again, looking for anything out of the ordinary; not only a deposited weapon, but anything out of place or indicative of someone having been there in his absence. He wondered if allowing the agents inside might be a mistake, since they wouldn't need probable cause to look around casually, only to search other areas of his domicile. He hoped neither one wanted to use the bathroom; he hadn't bothered to check his own toilet tank.

Inside, he headed for his usual perch when entertaining guests, the single barstool at the breakfast bar. He gestured toward the small couch and recliner as he sat and hooked his feet over the lower frame of the barstool. Heather headed for the couch, and Bales reluctantly took a seat on the edge of the recliner. In the small apartment, it was going to be a cozy meeting.

"How can I help the FBI and DEA?" Carlton asked as the pair of agents were settling in.

"I was under the impression that you knew Agent Colson," Bales began doubtfully, his eyes traveling back and forth between her and Carlton.

"He does, he was just being a wiseass," Heather snapped by way of explanation.

"Yes, we know each other, but it's been a while," Carlton said. "I just wanted to make sure it was her, that's all. Can't be too careful these days."

"So I've noticed, especially with some people," Heather said tersely, skipping pleasantries and not even bothering with an eye-roll for his foolishness. "Which reminds me, how was Corpus?"

"Warm, breezy, and muggy," he answered, now wary of her showing up at his door with another agent in tow. Despite her recent helpful phone tips, she had just segued right into the most recent shooting by letting him know he had been observed at the coast by some means, reminding him that he was playing against the team with all the resources.

He chose to get the ball rolling with the new face by looking directly at Agent Jeffrey Bales. "Since y'all know I was there—and you obviously knew we were headed there beforehand—tell me what you need to know, and I'll tell you that I had nothing to do with the shooting that took place. Then I'll tell you where to find the three people I was with who can vouch for my whereabouts and my activities for every second of the day."

"Really? And how about the nights?" Heather asked pointedly, blue eyes boring into his.

"*Especially* the nights," came his immediate, testy response, leaving no doubt of its intent.

"Uh, Mr. Westerfield, we came to ask you questions in regard to your situation, so there's no need to get off-track here," Bales said, leaning forward on the edge of the recliner, and being more assertive with his follow-up remark, redundant as it was. "I think we need to keep this discussion on-subject."

His body language and tone said he was taking over, as did his sharp sidelong glance at Heather. Carlton wondered if he outranked her and what their respective positions in separate agencies meant during an inter-agency investigation. "That is, unless you know something unrelated that can add value to our efforts," he added, leaving Carlton to wonder what that meant.

Heather's next comment seemed to bear out Carlton's thought that he, Bales, was the senior partner for this, another informal chit-chat with the investigation's leading suspect. "Agent Bales is right, so let's get this back on point," she said, her tone still business-like, but minus the venom of the earlier exchange. "Actually, we think you may be able to help us, Carlton."

Carlton thought for a moment before responding. He hoped to learn something, but he wasn't willing to roll over and be overly nice to investigators who seemed hell-bent on indicting him under blatantly incorrect assumptions and slipshod investigative procedures. He took a deep breath and chose his words carefully.

"Let me get this straight. You think I can help—and *want* to help—with an investigation that is clearly aimed at one person, and one person only, despite the fact that he has *no motive*, *no need*, and *no more opportunity* to do these shootings than several million other citizens?" He kept his voice calm, but made a show of ticking off on his fingers the conflicting points he had already cited to Heather in their phone conversations. He hoped this guy Bales might see the obvious weakness in the investigation thus far and possibly have enough stroke in the affair to get the team off of Carlton Westerfield, and on to "some other dude," law enforcement's inside joke or not.

"That's why we're here," Heather said. "The inter-agency meetings aren't coming up with anything new, and after our conversation when you made those points, I decided to try something else.

"Jeffrey—Agent Bales—is on the FBI side, and he began noticing the lack of any alternative suspects, and all of the directives say to follow up on you. He and I met privately a few days ago and decided we needed to take an independent approach, but it has to be done in a way that we don't get any blowback." Her anxious tone at the end didn't go unnoticed.

She paused, and Carlton realized where this was going—or so he thought. Maybe the pair of younger agents had indeed seen the investigation turning into a personal vendetta against Carlton Westerfield and set out to check on it. Or this could be a ploy, an expanded version of "good cop, bad cop," sending in his former lover and a younger guy from the other agency to make nice and try to gain his confidence. He decided to test the water, see if he could confirm their motive by checking on their other players' whereabouts.

"So no blowback means not letting Moore or Fowler know we've talked."

"Right. Or Ikos."

"How do you know they're not checking up on the two of you? They may have someone in the parking lot right now, with binoculars on my front door, wondering why your car is parked by mine."

"We don't, not for sure." It was Bales stepping back in. "But Moore and Fowler are currently in California at a conference. And Stan Ikos is on vacation," he added, glancing toward Heather for verification.

"Yes, he's back home visiting family, so we think we have some leeway for a couple of days," Heather said. "I wanted Jeffrey to meet you and at least hear your side of the story. Until now, all he's heard is the stuff that makes you the prime suspect, same as everyone who attends Ikos' briefings."

Carlton nodded and looked directly at Agent Bales. "The stuff that makes me the prime—make that *only*—suspect is largely a figment of Stan Ikos' imagination and his desire to pin the shooting of his contract guy on someone. The FBI, for some reason, agrees with him about that. Plus, I think, a bit of jealousy on the part of Agent Darren Moore."

Bales didn't exhibit any surprise at the last part, and Carlton wondered how much, if any, of his and Heather's history she had shared with the young agent from the other service. From his lack of reaction, he figured Bales must know about their past romance…that, and Heather's use of his first name at least twice since they'd arrived. Maybe Bales was trying to make some history himself with the pretty DEA agent, he thought, and working against her current beau appealed to him.

In any case, hearing that another school of thought existed encouraged him and reminded him to be nicer to the only two law enforcement officers in the city who weren't waving handcuffs in his face. Without further prompting from Bales, he spent the next few minutes going over the same ground he had covered with Heather by phone, including the weapon hidden in his apartment. He finished by refuting the "unreliable witnesses'" tale of a man vaguely matching his description shooting three people in a *Nuevo Laredo* parking lot. And when Bales asked about it, he denied being responsible for sending the gory newspaper clipping to Ikos' office, the only outright lie.

He summarized his position by conceding to an understanding of the task force's initial findings, erroneous though they were. "I can see why I might look good for the Millstone shooting, but the evidence and witnesses are really weak. The *Nuevo Laredo* PD and the PFM still list the crime as open, unsolved. So to follow up by tagging me for these new shootings, based solely on that crime—*unsolved* at this point—is absurd."

Bales might have been in agreement with Agent Colson to some extent, but he wasn't entirely convinced. "You make some good points, Westerfield, but only because this task force hasn't come up with anything tying you directly to the shootings of Peters, Crenshaw, and Pembrooke. Not yet, anyway. And the investigation just began on the Corpus Christi victim. So far, you've been very near every single one of the shootings—"

"That little coincidence alone ought to tell you something!" Carlton interrupted. "If I were the slick hitman your task force is looking for, I'd have arranged a solid alibi for at least one or two shootings. As your bosses present it, the deck is being stacked against me to unbelievable levels. Surely you can see that I'm being framed."

"Agent Colson mentioned that in one of our task force meetings. She and I talked about it later, and that's why we're here right now, against my better judgement and against bureau policy.

"But Ikos and Dave Fowler, Moore's partner, have repeatedly pointed out your ability to talk your way through some dicey situations. And using this '*oh, poor me with no motive*' story fits right in with that. The missing motive is the oldest on record: *money*. And if it's there, we'll find it and find who's paying you, don't worry."

"Wait a minute," Carlton said, holding up his hands in a "halt" gesture. "If I've read and heard correctly about the three shooting victims, all of them were engaged at some level of criminal activity, but not a kingpin status. So who pays to have some mid-level, dirtbag scofflaw killed? Community Watchdogs? Crime Busters International?"

"That's a part of the puzzle that's still being studied," Bales answered, undeterred. "And like I said, we'll find it.

"Oh, and the information that's been gathered on you by the research agents on the force tells a different story about your professed lack of skill with a handgun. They found some information in your military files that disputes that bullshit story. In other words, you're just a little *too* slick…Slick."

Carlton shrugged, disappointed that the agent had just blown through everything he'd been offering in defense for the past ten minutes, but determined to keep his cool. "Well, it sounds like you've signed on with them without thinking it through. If so, there's not much I can do about it. But I appreciate your hearing my side of the story."

He stood, signaling an end to his willingness to talk and the end of the meeting, authorized or not by the heads of the joint task force. Both the agents stood also, although both had a slightly confused look. Noticing their looks, Carlton was able to claim a tiny psychological victory. If they had come with their claimed intentions, he'd given them all he had without ranting about it. What they did with it was beyond his purview. And if their impromptu pow-wow was a ploy to catch him off guard, then he'd done nothing to hurt himself or further their cause—beyond letting two agents earn some overtime pay.

He held the door as the pair walked out and shook each one's hand in turn, first Heather's then Bales'. The young FBI agent didn't seem fazed by Carlton's abrupt dismissal. Instead, he issued a professional smile with a firm handshake, one that looked a lot like a smirk, but without malice. Under different circumstances, Carlton might have started liking the guy.

On the landing, Heather turned back to face him. "I'm sure we'll be in touch."

"I hope so. And I wish y'all luck at finding the killer, I really do. Because when you do, you'll see it's not me."

Back inside, Carlton took a deep breath and sighed. He wondered about the stories one heard about law enforcement simply wearing out a suspect, grinding them into submission and, finally, the suspect making a confession when they couldn't stand it any longer. He wasn't anywhere near that point, but he'd had enough contact with law enforcement to last a lifetime. After thirty years of avoiding even a speeding ticket discussion with a traffic cop, the past three months or so had resulted in more verbal jousting with cocky, overbearing agents than Frank Nitti endured in a weekend of *Untouchables* reruns.

Plopping down on the couch, he smiled as he felt the warmth left by Heather Colson's pretty butt, and it took a minute to dispel that line of thinking and get back "on-subject," as Agent Bales would say.

The first order of business was to figure out why—for real—the pair had come by his apartment to visit and engage in another rambling conversation with their number-one suspect, with no pointed questions asked about the Corpus Christi murder and no order "not to leave town" when they left. Maybe that line was a figment of Hollywood's imagination, he thought. Were the younger agents really exploring and seeking facts beyond what the task force made available to them at weekly meetings? If so, why? It had to be Heather's straight-arrow dedication to her job, he figured, her propensity to do the job correctly, even if it meant going outside the box a bit.

If so, she had been able to convince Agent Jeffrey Bales (not hard for her to convince a man to do almost anything) to take a look with her, at least consider that there should be another suspect or two. And while Agent Bales had outwardly rejected Carlton's reasoning, maybe a seed of doubt had been planted, or so he hoped.

But if the agents had been assigned to approach him with their righteous-sounding spiel about finding other suspects, it meant he was being played; they hoped to trip him up, get him to say something inconsistent with previous statements. But again, they hadn't even *asked* anything specific, so how was that going to work?

Within a few minutes, he realized that further speculation was worthless at this point. He had no way to know the pair's real agenda, and until something else happened, he was spinning his wheels needlessly. The idle thought reminded him of the Eagles' advice in *Take It Easy,* something about not letting the sound of one's own wheels drive oneself whacky.

Good advice, think I'll heed it.

CHAPTER 13

Saturday turned out to be another nice day, warm and breezy, a typical mid-spring day in South Texas. Right after breakfast, Carlton launched into his Saturday routine, but having been gone for most of the week, nothing required much attention. While the final load of laundry was drying, his phone, the older one he'd dubbed "Heather," rang. He checked the number; it was her most recent one, so it indicated she had probably dedicated the phone solely to calling him, at least for a few more calls. She may have discarded the previous one, he thought, but maybe not, so he'd keep that number on hand, too. The mental gymnastics regarding burner phones reminded him that leaving a life of crime wasn't as simple as just ceasing to do anything illegal.

"Good morning."

"If you say so. I'll bet you're cleaning house and doing laundry."

"You'd win that bet. As I'm first to point out, man works from sun to sun, but a woman's work is never done. And what are you up to this fine day?"

"Not laundry, that's for sure. And no other 'woman's work' as you call it, you sexist pig.

"I got the ID on the Corpus vic. His name was Gabriel Mason, local doper and drug runner of the dime-bag variety."

Carlton sighed. *"At the risk of sounding like a broken record, I'll say I've never heard of him. And no one would pay fifteen cents to have him killed. But he was another stellar citizen, right?"*

"The mayor was going to award him a medal next week for his civic service to this community over the past thirty-some-odd years, but his untimely death got the ceremony cancelled."

"Is it possible your task force will start seeing these hits as some kind of vigilante justice?"

"As of this morning, Jeffrey Bales is starting to lean that way. However, he doesn't conclude that it takes the heat off of you. In fact, he thinks you'd make a good vigilante."

Carlton had to laugh at that. *"You know better, so maybe you can enlighten him about my missing sense of civic concern."*

"I do know better, but the profile of several serial and ritual killers included a bias toward taking out what they perceived as threats to society, ironic as that seems."

Carlton thought it over for a moment. *"Not really, I guess. A nice, clean-cut mechanic might think of himself as far superior to slimeball dope runners who peddle smack to school kids."*

"Point taken, but our justice code doesn't quite differentiate crimes that way. So your observation makes you look better for the shootings every time another dirtbag turns up dead and maimed."

Carlton sighed again, long and loud. *"I get it, I understand big task forces operate with mountains of statistics and psychological profiles instead of—"*

"Heather stopped him in mid-sentence. *"There's your first misperception. This isn't a big task force, it's only about eight people, including the research guys and gals. A big task force might be a hundred or more, working from multiple offices."*

"Thank God I have a smaller fan base."

"Well, before I forget, you should know that your small fan base may want to question you again."

"Fine by me. I was never out of sight from my companions the entire time, and all three of them will be more than willing to say so."

"They'll be questioned separately," she warned. *"And I'd advise you not to coach them beforehand, since stories that match too well might look like somebody was warning you."*

"Don't worry, I don't have to. I just hope someone in your cozy little force listens to what they say and starts realizing I didn't do this one, nor did I do any of the others."

"If you say so. Personally, I hope you didn't. Oh, go check your laundry; your clothes are probably dry by now."

The connection went silent long enough to make Carlton to look at his screen. She had, as usual, ended the call without fanfare. He sighed and snapped his phone shut, then realized the silence in the laundry alcove meant the dryer had finished, just as Agent Heather Colson had suggested. Then he wondered why all the women in his life seemed to know so much more than he did.

Just before noon, Reynaldo returned from his ranch with Paula and Diane, all claiming to be hungry. Three days of seafood and steaks, plus no breakfast put them all in a mood for something different, and burgers became the unanimous choice. Carlton suggested Chis Madrid's on Blanco Road, a long-time favorite in the city.

During the meal, he told them about his visit with Heather and Agent Jeffrey Bales, along with her follow-up phone call and the identification of the latest victim. He also made the trio aware of the likelihood of their upcoming session with someone on the task force.

Reynaldo and Paula nodded their affirmation, secure in their knowledge that the plain truth would work best in this case, and no prior discussion would be necessary, which was exactly what Carlton wanted to happen. With Diane, it was a different story.

"How do you think we should play it?" she asked, tipping Carlton off that she had been questioned before while "exploring both sides of the law."

"She warned me not to give y'all any coaching for the session, which makes good sense. They'll probably question you separately, and if your stories start coming up *too* closely matched, it will appear coached, so I'd say just play it straight up. It's the first time in this mess I've had a firm alibi, much less three people vouching for me, so it would be best to have it sound as natural and unrehearsed as possible, even if a couple of details don't match exactly. What's important is that we were all in one car, and I wasn't out of anyone's sight long enough to cap that guy and dump his body in an alley.

"Maybe I'm about to get a change of luck," he added hopefully.

"I certainly hope so," she agreed. "And you're right about the three of us simply giving our own take, no coordinating of stories. It was my first time in that city, so I'll have a good tourist's viewpoint to throw in about all the places you showed me. Reynaldo and Paula's viewpoints will be slightly different and the combination should make it sound right, just as it occurred."

"How did Heather sound otherwise?" Reynaldo asked. "She must be seeing by now that you're not the shooter if she's having private meetings with a co-worker and bringing him to your apartment for an interview."

"I can only hope their little visit was on the up-and-up, and they weren't assigned to grill me as the 'good cops,' so the 'bad cops' can keep up their tunnel-vision efforts. But I don't know, just couldn't tell about that guy Bales.

"Anyway, if I was hoping for a break in the shooter's action, it hasn't happened yet. Just as we thought possible, the vic was from San Antonio, not Corpus, making it theoretically possible for me to have known him, and had a grudge or some reason to pop him."

Paula, who had remained quiet for the past several minutes, spoke up. "Without coaching us, what should we say—or not say—about Bert Morris?"

Carlton thought for a moment, then looked at each of his companions in turn. "I think play it right down the center. Tell exactly what each of you saw and heard of the exchange. And Paula, give the background about your meeting him years ago, and your impression of him at that time. Anybody have a different thought?"

"Maybe his shady activity and lurking around your car will give them something else to study," Diane offered. "It can't hurt to have them looking somewhere else.

"And I'm going to keep on looking at Bert Morris and try to find a thread between him and anyone else we've heard of."

Looks were exchanged around the table, but no one had a differing viewpoint. Diane proposed a toast, "to the truth, as rare as my hamburger patty." Touching iced tea glasses all around, the group fell back into a discussion of the Corpus Christi trip that turned into a fit of giggles between the women. Reynaldo and Carlton just looked at each other and worked on their burgers, hoping they weren't the butt of some inside joke.

After enjoying the meal, all agreed to a sufficiency of food for one day and agreed to meet for a late breakfast the next day. Reynaldo, Paula, and Diane were headed back to Wichita Falls on Tuesday for what promised to be a busy week of construction business. When they dropped Carlton off, he told them he would try to reach Heather with their schedule, so she could advise whoever was going to question them. All three agreed that making themselves readily available for the questioning session would look best to the investigators. They were anxious to help their friend, and this seemed to be the first and best opportunity to do so.

Carlton hoped they were right and was feeling better about his prospects...for about two minutes. As he climbed the stairs to his apartment, he heard voices on the landing above him, sounding like two or three men speaking in hushed tones. Going up the final flight quietly, he turned the corner toward his apartment and saw that he had company for the afternoon. Agents Moore and Fowler had been joined by Agent Jeffrey Bales, all three congregating around his front door.

"Gentlemen!" he called out cheerfully, trying to mask the apprehension he felt. Even with Heather's forewarning, he couldn't dispel the dread creeping into his mood upon seeing this unfold. "So glad you could make it on such short notice!"

If the smart-assed greeting affected anyone, it didn't show on their faces. Instead, Fowler produced a piece of folded paper and handed it over as Carlton approached, key in hand. He took the paper, but left it folded and raised his eyes in a questioning look at the agents.

"It's a search warrant, Mr. Westerfield," Fowler explained without emotion.

Carlton shrugged and opened the paper, glanced at it, then re-folded it and stepped forcefully between the men to open his door. "Come in, then," he said, mimicking Fowler by not bothering to invoke the slightest tone of invitation.

He stepped inside first. As the three agents filed in behind him, he took his usual seat on the single barstool, a move that didn't go unnoticed by Agent Bales.

"That your usual spot, Westerfield?" he asked, obviously recalling the psychological high-ground advantage it inferred while he and Heather had sat across from him less than twenty-four hours earlier.

"Only when I have unwelcome guests," came the reply. "As most of my guests seem to be lately."

"That's not very accommodating of you, Westerfield," Darren Moore replied, trying out a hurt tone that didn't match the smirk on his face.

"I didn't intend it to be," he retorted. He was becoming aggravated at his own smart mouth, but the demeanor of the agents was making it difficult to restrain himself, especially when their comments left them open to easy pot shots.

He decided to change gears a bit and ease up on the tension building in the room. He opened the warrant and skimmed through the contents. "I don't see anything in here that prohibits my watching this process," he said, looking at Fowler while holding the paper out as though Fowler might want to look for himself.

"Not at all, Westerfield. Make yourself at home. Oh, I forgot, you *are* at home."

Agent Fowler's accompanying smirk was such a good imitation of the others' Carlton figured the facial expression must be a government-agency issue item handed out at graduation, like their badges. He had at least two good comebacks, but decided to leave them unsaid for the moment. With this trio, he'd have plenty of opportunity in the next hour or so.

The search didn't take long. The most interesting part was, of course, the closet ceiling panel. From his vantage point in the living room, Carlton watched as Jeffrey Bales opened the coat closet door and peered in, looking for a light switch that didn't exist, a victim of cost-conscious apartment construction. The agent produced a small flashlight and shined it needlessly around all four tiny walls and into the already-visible corners before turning it up to the ceiling and stopping on the sheetrock panel. He held the beam on the panel for several seconds, as though deciding whether or not to check it out.

Watching the charade, Carlton nearly laughed. After disposing of the gun, he had cleaned up the ceiling area, wiping the dust from the entire perimeter with a damp cloth. Then he vacuumed the carpet thoroughly, searching with a flashlight to make sure he had gotten every flake of the dislodged paint. He put a new bag in the vacuum cleaner and tossed the used one in a carwash dumpster. Now, seeing the guy considering how to get up there—and make a mess again—he realized his extreme efforts that day had been overkill. He could have vacuumed up the flakes and left it at that, but he'd gotten so much satisfaction from foiling whomever had deposited the damning evidence, he'd relished the task.

"You'll need something to stand on," he said, trying—not very hard—to suppress a grin. He stood from his barstool, picked it up, and carried it over to the closet, while his actions got the attention of the other two agents. Moore and Fowler crowded in behind Carlton as he placed the stool on the closet floor, then had to move aside when he stepped back to let the young agent deal with the tricky substitute for a ladder.

As with anyone who has used a swivel-chair platform for elevation from a carpeted floor, Bales didn't look very agile climbing on the stool and trying to get both feet planted on the cushion without it rotating on him. The other two did nothing to help in the way of steadying the chair, so Carlton stepped forward and grasped it firmly. "I don't have renter's liability insurance, so don't get hurt in here," he said, not entirely joking.

When standing, Bales was in the wrong position to move the panel, but he finally managed to push it into the ceiling and off to the side. Holding the light above him, he awkwardly extended his torso into the opening and shined the light around. The search went on long enough to tell Carlton that his suspicions were correct, and he cleared his throat to get their attention, then waited another three seconds for dramatic effect.

"It's not there," he said simply.

Carlton felt the other two men shift behind him as Bales jerked his arm back from the opening, banging his elbow on the frame as he withdrew. Their response to his remark confirmed what he had thought from the previous Thursday, when the sticking door lock had alerted him to an uninvited visitor. Leaving the barstool and its half-crouched occupant in the closet, he stepped back into the hallway and turned to look at Moore and Fowler, but said nothing. He kept his peripheral vision on Bales to make sure the agent didn't get a hand in his pocket to withdraw anything else to plant in the currently vacant spot.

Fowler, the veteran agent, spoke first. "You think you're pretty fucking smart, don't you? Maybe you're *too* smart." By the end of his statement, his voice was a snarl.

Carlton shrugged and concentrated on keeping his voice even and non-confrontational, even if his words might be taken as a bit contentious. "You're the second one to tell me that this week, so I'll have to say guilty as charged."

Though younger than his partner, Darren Moore exhibited his status as the senior agent when he spoke. "What'd you do with it?" he asked quietly, clearly slipping into the good-cop mode of accepting defeat while imparting a polite request for help in finding a lost item.

Carlton smiled inwardly at the ploy and was unable to stop himself from asking innocently, "What'd I do with *what*?"

He had to hand it to the agents; professionalism took over while the three made a final cursory sweep around his small apartment. None said anything and facial expressions remained neutral as the trio trooped out the door with only a terse "thank you, Mr. Westerfield" from Moore as they departed.

CHAPTER 14

Carlton's friends didn't have to try hard to make themselves available for questioning. Five minutes after dropping him off, an SAPD patrol car lit up Reynaldo's Lexus on Military Highway, just before reaching Loop 410. Then a Castle Hills PD car appeared with lights flashing, and pulled in front of Reynaldo, effectively blocking him in. In addition to the SAPD uniform that emerged, two plainclothes, a man and a woman, popped out of the back doors and approached in the uniform's wake, while a third plainclothes man stayed put and spoke into his phone.

"Good afternoon, Sir," the patrolman said politely. "May I see your license and proof of insurance?"

Reynaldo complied, handing over his Concealed Handgun License also, as required by law, then placed both hands high on the steering wheel, in plain sight.

The cop, wary at first, looked at the two licenses, comparing the information on both with the man seated in the car. Every few seconds his eyes drifted back to Reynaldo, who kept still, his hands staying on the steering wheel. Finding everything in order, the patrolman visibly relaxed, but held on to the licenses. "Are you presently carrying a weapon, Mr. Gomez?"

"Yes, a .38 Special revolver is in the glove box. It's loaded."

The patrolman nodded and leaned down to look inside the car, shifting his eyes from Paula in the passenger seat to Diane in the back. "Are you ladies carrying?"

Both answered no while shaking their heads. The patrolman stepped back to allow room for the plainclothes at the driver's window. Each of them produced a badge wallet, flipped them open simultaneously and proffered them toward Reynaldo in a move that looked practiced. The pair of agents had done their routine before. He looked at the badges, then up to the agents' faces in turn and nodded, but said nothing.

"I'm Agent Nancy Ferguson of the Federal Bureau of Investigation, and this is Agent Philip Maris of the Drug Enforcement Administration. We'd like to ask you a few questions. Would you be willing to follow us to our office?"

Reynaldo turned to his passengers, still saying nothing, but getting nods of approval from both women. He turned back to the agent. "Okay, sure."

It didn't take long to get from Castle Hills to the Federal Building near the UTSA campus. The SAPD car dropped off the agents, and Reynaldo parked near the entrance. Both groups merged at the front door where each of the "guests" was escorted inside by an agent. Again, the move seemed structured and practiced for just the right amount of intimidation without being overbearing. Walking side by side, the group looked oddly like a wedding procession strolling through the lobby, eliciting a faint smile from Diane. Paula, on the other hand, looked terrified while Reynaldo, having recently undergone a battery of questioning from both cartel enforcement thugs and law enforcement agents, looked apprehensive.

Delivered to separate rooms, their escorts left and reshuffled elsewhere, then entered the rooms again with additional agents, two per room, giving the impression that each agent partnered with a specific individual for such sessions; however, their look-alike dress, style, and demeanor made that assumption a pure guess on the part of the three cooperative "guests," now feeling very much like detainees.

"I'm Agent Martinez and this is Agent Jameson. Would you state your name for the record, please?"

"Diane Martin."

"Where do you live, Ms. Martin?"

"Wichita Falls."

"That's Texas?"

"Yes."

A few questions regarding contact information followed, along with repeated numbers and alternative methods for Diane to be reached, twenty-four/seven.

"What do you do for living, Ms. Martin?"

"I work for Gomez Construction in Wichita Falls as a personnel consultant and client verification specialist."

More contact information dialogue followed, the other agent writing all of it down.

Martinez scribbled quickly on her own pad, then looked up. "Gomez Construction. You work for Reynaldo Gomez?"

"Yes."

"And what does a"—Agent Martinez looked down at her notes—"a personnel verification consultant and client consultant do, exactly?"

"I run background checks on prospective workers and clients to make sure Mr. Gomez wants to hire them or do business with them," Diane answered, ignoring the agent's incorrect note wording.

A nod from Martinez and more scribbling, this time from both agents. Agent Jameson, a solidly built, short-haired blonde with brown eyes, zero makeup, and a humorless look took a breath and looked up from her notes, preparing to start her shift.

The easy part's over, Diane thought. She was right.

"How did you meet Carlton Westerfield?"

"Through Mr. Gomez, about two weeks ago."

"Does your specialty include researching targets for Mr. Westerfield to kill?"

Diane had been ready for the intensity to ratchet up, but the question was still a surprise coming this soon in the session. "No," she replied, keeping her laser look locked onto Jameson's expressionless face. In her peripheral vision, she saw Martinez scribbling away. Of the two, Jameson was obviously the lead. Martinez, petite and dark, seemed the junior of the pair, and she knew the blonde would have her own take on the one-word response, no matter what Martinez wrote.

"What do you know about Bert Morris?"

"Nothing."

Jameson looked at her impatiently, with just a touch of disdain in the set of her mouth. "That answer came pretty quick. Do you even know who Bert Morris is?"

"Yes."

"Care to elaborate, Ms. Martin?" The sarcasm was hard to miss.

Diane mentally sifted through a few responses as quickly as possible, settling on "Okay."

"Well, how did you meet Bert Morris?" the agent said a little too loudly, her impatience at having to pry answers from the detainee starting to show through the professional veneer.

"I didn't meet him. I saw him from about twenty feet away while he and Mr. Westerfield talked."

"When was this?"

Hearing the building rancor in the agent's voice, Diane gave a brief narrative of the circumstances surrounding her non-introduction to Bert Morris, hitting the high points enough to keep the agent's frustration at bay, though barely. Meanwhile, Agent Martinez scribbled some more, flipping to a new page before Diane had finished.

"So you caught his name in the conversation, but weren't introduced to him?"

"Yes."

Seven questions and seven sparse, but concise, answers later, Jameson threw in the towel. "You're really full of good information, aren't you Ms. Martin. And delighted to give it to us, right?'

Diane considered the questions and decided on answers quickly. "No and no."

Those answers didn't make her any more popular with Jameson. She glanced over at her partner, then looked back sharply at Diane. "You think you're smarter than we are?" The question was a goading technique, but Diane saw it coming and didn't say what she felt.

"I hadn't thought about it at all."

The response clearly wasn't what Jameson expected or wanted. She narrowed her eyes, but let good training take over and gave an unseen signal for Martinez to come back into the fray for a few questions. She reached for Martinez' tablet and leaned back, trying to project her disdain and superiority over the detainee, but Diane's unrelenting eye contact made the effort look pointless.

From there, the questions turned to the trip to Corpus, easy for Diane to give answers geared to match anyone's first visit to a picturesque seaside city. It didn't matter if she got a detail or two wrong. Only when the talk progressed to Carlton's activities did the mood grow tense again.

"Where did you stay in Corpus?" Agent Martinez continued the session with a couple of easy ones.

"Um, a Radisson. It was near the ship, the aircraft carrier museum."

"Separate rooms?"

"We had two suites, next door to each other."

"Women in one, men in the other?"

Diane was growing tired of this useless, harassing line of questioning and decided to bite back. "That wouldn't have been much of a fun trip, would it?" she replied tartly, staring down Martinez before shifting the laser to Jameson, who glared at her. "Oh, sorry, not for me, anyway," she added, clearly not sorry at all for the implication or the look it elicited from Jameson.

The barb rattled the pretty, feminine Martinez too, and she fumbled the next stage of questions. "So you stayed with Carlton, and Ms. Hendricks and Mr. Gomez stayed together?"

"I stayed with Carlton. I can't say about Ms. Hendricks and Mr. Gomez."

"But you're all *friends*, right? I mean if all four—"

"Not *that* close of friends." The laser beam increased intensity with that answer.

"Are you sure?" The question came from left field, where Agent Jameson was standing, gloves on, and itching for a fight.

A rare smile from Diane punctuated the laser beam. "Not yet, anyway. But hey, we just met."

"And how can you be sure Mr. Westerfield didn't leave the room without your knowledge?" Martinez asked after a sharp look at her partner for the uncalled-for question.

Diane didn't hesitate. "Because he was too occupied to leave. And later, he was too tired."

Over an hour and four tablet pages later, Jameson stood abruptly and signaled the end of the session. Turning to open the door, she looked at Diane with what appeared to be pure hate, tempered only by training and professionalism. "Thank you for your time, Ms. Martin," she said curtly, handing her a pair of business cards. "Call one of us if you think of anything useful. That is, if you can define *useful*," she added with a smirk. "We'll be in touch."

Diane left the room accompanied by Martinez, who led her to the lobby and instructed her to wait for her companions. As she sat down, Diane noticed her hands were on the verge of shaking and her heart rate was a bit elevated. Still, she felt she had weathered the Jameson/Martinez storm pretty well. She couldn't recall a single exchange that should have made the law agency more interested in Carlton Westerfield…or anything else. However, neither had anything transpired to make them back off, she realized. Ten minutes later, she had calmed down considerably and was wondering what was going on in the other two questioning sessions.

"Ms. Hendricks, my name is Steven Belk, FBI. This is Agent Philip Maris. He's with the Drug Enforcement Administration. Would you state your full name for the record?"

"Paula Faye Hendricks."

The next five minutes duplicated Diane's experience and probably every single session held in the fabled agency's hallowed halls all over the nation. For Paula, the preliminary inquiries settled her down from her previous nervous state, a process she didn't notice until later, when she realized it was done that way by design. What was *not* by design was the opportunity for Paula to settle down and use her own strategy, a combination of good genes and the resulting natural ability of attractive people—a strategy at which she was an expert. Along with superb acting skills, it was going to be a long afternoon for Agents Belk and Maris, though neither one knew it or would mind in the least.

"How long have you known Reynaldo Gomez?" Agent Maris asked, taking the first shift of the real questions.

"About fifteen years," she answered after thinking it over.

"Are you involved in Mr. Gomez' drug smuggling operation?"

"No."

"Do you know Clive Millstone, sometimes known as Cletus Miller?"

"Yes. He shot my half-brother."

"And were you involved in setting him up to get shot himself? In retaliation for killing your brother?"

"No."

"You didn't help Carlton Westerfield and Reynaldo Gomez shoot him?"

"No."

"You currently have a relationship with Mr. Gomez, right?"

"Yes."

"Would you tell us the nature of your relationship?"

"Well…we spend a lot of time together, if that's what you mean."

"Have you spent a lot of time together for the last fifteen years?"

Paula didn't flinch. "Enough time to have a child together, a daughter who lives in Mexico City."

"I see," Maris said, obviously not seeing at all from what he had just heard.

Paula took the moment to lean in a bit and expound on the events that had resulted in Celia's living in Mexico. The explanation was thorough, and Paula became animated while telling the story, cocking her head to one side or the other and smiling to make a particular point, then leaning back and spreading her arms when describing her daughter meaning "the entire world to her and Reynaldo." By the end of the long narrative, Agent Maris was lost in dark brown eyes and hoped Belk was getting it all down on paper. If not, they would have to spend time listening to the recorder to straighten out their notes, a practice frowned on by supervisors.

"Okay, what about Bert Morris? How do you know Bert Morris?"

"I met him while I worked at his brother's pawnshop, here in San Antonio. That was um, five or six years ago, I think."

"Do you see him very often now?"

"I saw him the other day at Carlton's apartment. He was in the parking lot, doing something to Carlton's car, and they were having a discussion."

"Did you get in on the discussion?"

"Um, no. I just saw it was him and asked what he was doing there, or something like that, it was such a shock to see him after all this time."

"But you didn't interact with him?"

"No, he and Carlton were too busy interacting."

The answer got a smile from both agents, which allowed Paula to try out one of her own, resulting in several more unnecessary questions, all designed to get another smile from her. A few of them worked, and Paula was in her element.

Forty or fifty questions later, many about Big Mo and Carlton, and the session wound down. Both agents' tablets were full of notes, and both of them felt they had charmed the attractive woman out of truthful answers, which, basically, was correct. However, in the scope of finding out who was shooting local outlaws in a ritualistic manner, not much was added to the file except a bit of additional information regarding the now-deceased gangster, Randall Morris, and his shifty brother, Bert.

Standing up, both Maris and Belk handed her a business card. Maris scribbled his cell number on his, getting a smile from Paula and a promise to call if she thought of anything else related to their questions. Maris smiled back, but it was Agent Belk who escorted her to the lobby.

Oddly, Carlton Westerfield, the supposed target of this entire exercise, remained a mystery, with nothing added to point to him as the shooter.

Reynaldo's session went smoother than he had expected, with early questions related to his current business relationship with Carlton (none) and his current relationship with Ms. Hendricks (considerable). The lead agent, Nancy Ferguson, asked a few pointed questions about his past activities with Faustino Perez, now deceased, and his dealings with the *Golfo* Cartel before moving on to his current business in Wichita Falls, a subject that got considerable coverage by Agent Ferguson.

Her partner for the session was Barry Ginsburg of the DEA. He spent fifteen minutes re-visiting the *Golfo* Cartel business, with Reynaldo answering the same questions, giving the same answers regarding a failed attempt to do business with the group due to "a misunderstanding with the Benavides brothers."

The switch to Clive Millstone followed; Reynaldo related how he had shot Tino Perez in the face, then forced him and Carlton, at gunpoint, to the Laredo warehouse. After a brief telling of their escape and subsequent capture by Heather Colson, Stan Ikos, and other DEA agents, Ginsburg seemed satisfied with that area. The agent seemed disappointed that Reynaldo knew nothing about the fate of Clive Millstone aka Cletus Miller. In fact, Reynaldo was "very surprised" to learn that someone had shot and severely wounded the Brit soon after the Border skirmish.

Then, back to Agent Ferguson for a quick visit to the Bert Morris encounter and the Corpus trip, and the session was pretty much done, although Reynaldo was kept in the room for a while awaiting the end of the women's sessions. Finally, he was handed two business cards and led to the lobby.

As it occurred, all three were in the front lobby within fifteen minutes of each other, and the long Saturday afternoon had turned to evening. It was safe to assume everyone involved was glad to be finished—that is, except Agents Belk and Maris.

CHAPTER 15

Max and Louie's New York style diner near Highway 281 was the choice for the late breakfast. Reynaldo griped about having to drive "across the city" to eat breakfast, but the others ribbed him until he gave up and smiled. After ordering, the talk briefly turned to comparisons of each one's questions, an exercise Carlton's three friends had already performed the previous night after leaving the federal building. Now, he wanted to be brought up to speed and began by quietly telling the highlights of his encounter, including the critical moment when Agent Bales failed to find the gun.

Reynaldo and Paula gave him quick summaries of their sessions, speaking quietly, although the din around them made it unnecessary. Though differences were apparent in the agent teams' styles, all agreed the sessions couldn't have been much help, not if they were looking to bag Carlton Westerfield.

"Which pleases me beyond belief," he declared, eyeing the oversize breakfast platter coming his way. "Maybe when they compare notes on the Corpus job, they'll discover I wasn't such a good pick for the other three either."

"My team seemed more intent on matching my job description with finding targets for Carlton," Diane said, "at least at first. Then they switched to checking my knowledge of Corpus Christi before getting way too personal about our weekend activities.

"And you're right, nothing in particular seemed focused on pinning the shootings on Carlton. It's as though they're just spinning their wheels, going through the motions, and putting in the necessary hours to say it's an investigation.

"But we accomplished something, even if they didn't," she announced, digging in her purse for the business cards she had collected from everyone.

"I can check all these names against the victims and the Morris brothers and see if I can find anywhere their paths crossed."

The discussion ended for the next half hour while all four enjoyed the food and commented about the portions being too large; however, at the end of the commentary period, not much was left on their plates. Now able to complain about overeating, the four made their way to the parking lot, where Reynaldo resumed his tirade—now about having to drive "*back* across the city."

"Which reminds me," he said, "Paula and I decided to go to Wichita Falls today, and Diane is going to stay over and work on her stuff from the ranch. You want to go with us, pick up your car, and stay out there?"

"Sure. On Monday, I want to rent a garage at my apartment. I've thought about Bert's unsubtle mention of his bomb-building skills, and I'd like to make it harder for him to find."

"You're welcome to one of the ranch trucks."

"Thanks, I'll think about it. If I do, I'll leave the Caddy at the ranch."

At Reynaldo's ranch house, Diane fired up her laptop and started to work, cross-referencing every agent's name with the victims, plus both Morris brothers. Another two hours of digital sleuthing produced nothing of interest. Carlton stretched and leaned back in the recliner, disappointed with another fruitless effort.

Outside, the sound of cows being fed drew Diane to the window to watch as the ranch hands broke open fresh hay bales and tossed big chunks over the fence where the small herd jostled and lowed, butting heads to get at the food. It was a scene that had entertained Diane earlier in her visit, and she claimed to be just as delighted now as the first time she'd witnessed it.

"Well, you're easily entertained," Carlton laughed. "Reynaldo really likes his cows, but I think the key to his—" He stopped and turned toward the window where Diane was still watching the cow-feeding activity. He opened his mouth to say more, but thought better of it.

Noticing his pause, she turned to see the odd look on his face as he debated whether or not to say more. She watched him, the laser beam powering up, but she said nothing.

Carlton knew he had to do better to fool the perceptive woman and be able to keep his thoughts to himself. He explained his momentary pause. "I was going to say the *key* to Reynaldo's success is the construction business, not those silly cows. They cost him money, but it's his pastime, he really likes fooling with this stuff.

"And when I said the word 'key,' it reminded me that I still haven't found the other key to my apartment. I was going to try it out on my front door and see if it worked any better than the one I carry, the one that doesn't make the deadbolt seat fully."

"Maybe the office will have you a new one made that works better."

"Oh, they will—for twenty bucks! That's why I was hoping to find my other one."

Diane continued watching him for a few seconds before returning her attention to the window and the cows outside. Carlton breathed an inward sigh of relief at the apparent success of his impromptu excuse. The word "key" had indeed reminded him of the missing key to his apartment, but not as he had told Diane. He knew exactly what had happened to the key, the key he hadn't had since the day he moved in. Reynaldo and Paula had helped him by moving one load of stuff while he cleaned his old digs. He had given the spare key to Paula that day, and she'd never returned it. Just now, his mental gymnastics had instantly connected Paula and the key to the easy access *someone* had employed to hide a weapon.

In his recent brush with the FBI, the agents had clearly been rattled when he informed them: *"It's not there."* At the time, he took their response as strong indication that one of them had planted the auto-pistol in his apartment, but their chagrin may have simply been anger at his tacit admission that something incriminating *had* been there, but was no longer, and he was rubbing their noses in the dirt.

When Paula recognized Bert Morris lurking in his parking lot, then later told of meeting him years earlier for a brief time, Carlton had wished he could grill her about the two events, and see how she could reconcile them. However, riding in the car with Reynaldo and Diane didn't seem like the right time to ask some very direct questions, regardless of Paula's history of unexplained discrepancies, several of which had involved Carlton. In the three or more years he'd known her, Paula Hendricks and the truth were sometimes complete strangers.

Diane worked for a while on Reynaldo's business, then went back to feeding names into data bases, trying to find a connection between any of the parties involved in "the mess," as it had become known. Carlton watched for a while, trying to make sense of the keyboard and mouse machinations. Just when he thought he perceived a pattern to her research, she launched off in another direction, leaving him bewildered—and secretly surprised she was not having success. He decided to suggest—diplomatically, he hoped—a change in the type of connections that might exist between the players.

"We keep looking for times and places their paths might have crossed," he began. "What if the common denominator isn't a time or place, but an event? Or maybe just an experience that happened to each of them, putting them all in the same basket, a basket that's getting shot and killed."

"Okay, like what?" she asked. "What event or experience would those four criminal types have in common—except being criminals?"

Carlton didn't have a ready answer. "Could the net be too big, the search criteria too general? Let's break it down to the type of crimes each one pulled, and match that with the law agency. You know, Vince Peters was boosting cars and selling them across state lines, so the FBI got involved. Also, by crossing state lines, he came under the RICO statutes, so that automatically calls out the feds and gets longer sentences. They may get some legwork from local PD or Sheriff's Department, but I think the federal jurisdiction takes precedence when it comes down to the bust."

Diane nodded, seeing where he was going with this. A crime prosecuted under the Racketeer Influenced and Corrupt Organizations Act would get a lot more attention than, say, a dime-bag slinger like Gabriel Mason. And he'd get the DEA on his back only if he dealt in bigger numbers than his rap sheet suggested. Otherwise, local police drug units would be rousting him, not feds.

"So my search has been with too broad a brush, you think?" she asked.

Carlton shook his head, afraid his suggestion may have been taken as criticism. "I don't know enough to judge that, obviously. To me, your research has been phenomenal, but a confusing process to watch. So much information, I have no idea how you sift through all of it. That's what made me think we might need to focus on a narrower path, maybe try to put two of the dirtbags together with the law agency that would have prosecuted them. If you find something, then plug in the other two with their respective agencies."

"Like Vince Peters and Raquel Pembrooke? From what we know, neither was into the drug business, so the FBI would have been the one to chase them instead of the DEA, right?"

"Yes. In fact, Heather told me the FBI was running a mole at Peters' organization when he got hit, that's how they were onto the method of his murder so quickly."

"But she know about it the day after it happened, didn't she?"

"That's when she made me aware of this "joint task force" thing," he replied, making quote marks in the air. "But remember, Darren Moore of the FBI is her new squeeze, plus her POC for task force business."

Diane smile at that. "So maybe business talk, maybe pillow talk? And if I were doing this research thing a year from now, the available data might be linked up between all the victims?"

"Right, but for now, probably not. Maybe the four victims don't have a common denominator except crime."

"And whoever's busting them."

"It's just a wild guess, but I think it's a possibility."

Diane looked pensive for a minute, the laser look actually softening. Carlton wondered if she looked that way when he hadn't been able to scrutinize her facial expression—like when her face was too close for his eyes to focus on, during those nights in Corpus... Her next remark brought him back to the present, making him abandon the pleasant thought.

She leaned forward quickly, the intensity back. "I've already checked to see if the victims used the same lawyer during their brushes with the law. That was a no-go."

"Maybe the lawyers swapped firms. Or some type of law firm referral is a common thread."

"Or maybe the outcome of their trials is the common denominator for all four. Each of the victims has been in trouble, but all four were out running loose this past three weeks or so."

"Yeah, out running loose and getting killed—but not by me. What are you thinking?"

"All of them were acquitted? Only Pembrooke and Peters were heard by the same judge, but years apart, so that's a pretty iffy link."

"All plea bargained?" Carlton suggested. "I don't know enough about how that works, which suits me just fine," he added, smiling "The less I know about that, the more fortunate I feel."

She sighed. Their ideas weren't leading to anything worth pursuing. An entirely different search criteria was needed. She looked at Carlton to bounce another thought around. "Maybe I have to track each one through the justice system individually, making notes of everything of significance. After compiling a crime bio of all four, we can look for commonalities between them."

Carlton shrugged and looked doubtful. "Sounds like a lot of effort for what might be a slim connection."

"Well, I'm open to Plan B," she countered. "We're not making progress as it is, so something else needs to be tried."

"It's your time and effort at play here. By the way, I can never thank you enough for doing all of this, no matter the outcome."

It was Diane's turn to shrug. "I appreciate that, but I'm getting paid to do this. As well as wanting to help you," she added quickly, embarrassed at how the admission of being paid sounded to her own ears.

Carlton thought about her remark. "You're on the clock then? I mean, I certainly hope so, but you'd better tell me your hourly rate," he said, grinning at her. "I'll gladly pay all I can."

She smiled, shaking her head. "Reynaldo Gomez is paying me, and quite well, by the way. He's very fond of you and feels far in your debt for what you did for him and Paula. Plus what you did for him with Cletus Miller in retaliation for Tino's death. He told me so himself, *'those are the kind of debts that can be addressed, but never fully repaid.'"*

Carlton was moved by the revelation. "Yeah, well, as I told you earlier, that's the kind of relationship the three of us had—I guess a result of going through a lot of stuff together." Now he was embarrassed and looked away, wishing the subject would change.

Seeing his discomfort, Diane turned back to her laptop. "Okay, let's start with the first victim, Vincent Alan Peters. I have something on his early life to get started...here it is. Born in St. Louis in 1969." She looked around for something and pointed to a legal pad on the coffee table. "Write down this stuff as I find it, and leave a line between each item. Be sure to put the date first."

By her tone, Carlton could tell the task was on, the laser beam powered up.

Over two hours later, he had four pages, one for each of the victims, more or less filled with one-line snippets of information regarding events in their lives: birth dates, graduations, marriages, divorces, arrests, trials, and convictions. By laying the papers side by side, the dates were easy to compare, and it was obvious why she hadn't found crossing paths by the disparity of trial and conviction or acquittal dates—none matched up year-for-year, although a couple fell close. And when the victims' sheets were separated by the likely agency to have caught their cases, the dates didn't come close. As she had found earlier, Peters' and Pembrooke's previous encounters with the legal system were years apart, with Peters busted by the FBI on a stolen goods charge in 2012 that was overturned by an evidentiary procedure snafu, while Pembrooke had not even been looked at by the feds until a year ago, when her case was referred by the SAPD Vice Squad for possible interstate child pornography. Diane could find no information on the status of the ensuing investigation, though.

With Crenshaw and Mason, victims number two and four respectively, the dates for trials and convictions of each of the repeat offenders came within a year, but no reason to make the "life events" thread helpful. Plus, the FBI and the DEA had both been involved on Crenshaw, as well as Houston PD Vice Squad. Poring over the sheets, Diane pointed out the fallibility of the exercise. "This is just a more thorough way to check for path crossing than throwing all of them into the mix and hoping for hits, like I did earlier. There has to be some other common factor for these jailbirds to have roosted in the same place."

Carlton thought for a moment. "Or *not*. *Not* roosted, that is. Maybe the common event thread is failures of law enforcement agencies, not convictions, or even trials and acquittals."

"You mean the time—or times—they got away, for some reason or another. Like bad busts, or the bad evidence beef that got Peters off nearly a decade ago."

"Right. But the agency or individual handling the case knew for certain it was a good bust."

"So, retaliation for making the agency look bad?"

"Or the individual," Carlton said. "More likely an individual or a couple of partners who worked hard to get the bust, but were overturned by some legal quirk."

"That works," Diane agreed, "but not when we're looking at two different agencies, plus the legwork done by local PDs. And that guy Peters was even chased around the block by ATF in 2015, so that's *three* different agencies."

Carlton nodded. It was hard to reconcile their theory with the thin possibility of three separate agencies—often competing for jurisdiction—teaming up to play judge, jury, and hangman for the four criminals. He leaned back and rubbed his tired eyes. "This gets us back to the possibility of a vigilante pulling these shootings—but putting my signature on them."

Diane agreed. "It does point to that, but still, the various agencies all involved in these...assassinations?"

"It would mean they have this common labor pool of bad guys to choose from—"

"Like the contractors federal agencies use," she interrupted. "Like Cletus Miller. We're back to him, but it's not him personally, so who?"

"His trainee, his protégé," Carlton mumbled absently, suddenly realizing how brain-tired the exercise had made him.

"I hate to admit defeat," Diane sighed, her voice tired and the laser beam on low. "But these four victims just don't seem to present anything that ties them together. Not that I can find.

"I've still got the agents' names to try in some different places, but I'm not real optimistic after they didn't match up with any of the victims as arresting officer. I think they may have just been handed a list of questions and assigned to ask them and record our answers. They may have no connection whatsoever with the vics.

"And I did a couple of runs plugging Bert and Randall Morris into the mix with the vics and got zip. All I learned was Bert had a pawnshop, too, and had a few minor dings with fencing goods, but no convictions. Guess the pawn business runs in the family."

That got Carlton's interest. "Where did he operate?"

"Solely in Minnesota. And one of the vics has a connection to that area; Raquel Pembrooke lived in St. Paul for two years. But no brushes with the law happened, not anything that made it onto a data base."

"Well, maybe the next victim will have the decency to be more helpful," Carlton said. "I just hope he or she doesn't turn up dead here on Reynaldo's ranch."

Diane laughed. "Even if that happens, I can provide you with an alibi for tonight," she said, leaving her chair and moving close to Carlton's. Her hands worked as well on his neck as they did on a computer keyboard.

He reached for her hand and made an exaggerated show of pulling himself from his seat. "I like that plan, tired as I am. I feel like a horse that's been ridden hard and put away wet."

Diane thought about what he'd said, guessing it was some old Texas expression, then shook her head. "I don't know anything about horses, but that's better than the other way around, isn't it?"

CHAPTER 16

Carlton's cynical remark would have been funny under different circumstances. Not the one about being put away wet, but the one about the next victim showing up on Reynaldo's ranch. It wasn't quite that bad, but bad enough, as he learned the next morning.

It was Memorial Day, and it had fallen on this, a Monday, so no one was getting an extra day off this year—certainly not the ranch hands, who were already banging around on something in the pens. To Carlton and Diane it made no difference; neither even remembered nine-to-five workdays, no matter what day the calendar indicated. Still, Carlton was up just after sunrise, in the kitchen trying to figure out the coffeemaker. After rifling through cabinets for coffee, filters, and cups, he was squinting at the can, trying to read instructions for how much coffee to put in the filter thing and how much water would be sufficient for four cups—since there was no such line on the pot. Intent on his quest, he didn't hear Diane when she padded in, feet bare and body only slightly less so.

"You're up early," she murmured by way of greeting, the trace of irritation in her voice giving away the intended verbiage: *"What the hell are you doing up at this hour?"*

"Good morning!" he proclaimed, hoping it was true. "Do you know how to make coffee?"

"*Huh?* Make coffee?" she asked, rubbing her eyes, then squinting at him leaned over the counter trying to decipher the coffee can label. "You don't know how to make coffee?" she asked, not bothering to mask the incredulity in her voice.

"Uh, no," he said meekly. "I only know how to *get* coffee. I *get* in my car and go *get* coffee."

That did the trick, as he hoped it would. She burst out laughing and shoved him aside with her hip as she reached for the coffee can with one hand while digging in a drawer for a spoon with the other. Carlton watched as she went through the motions methodically and stepped back from the counter with a smirk. As best he could judge, it had taken her nineteen seconds, including filling the pot with water and pouring it into the top before beating the trickling brew to the warmer with it. Not a drop was spilled.

"Unbelievable," he remarked, meaning it and watching the process work flawlessly. The few times in his life he had finally managed to get all the water poured in, scalding coffee was already running out onto the warming base, splashing the brew and steam all over the place...something to do with failing to get the pot in place quickly enough. The experience had convinced him to *get* coffee, not *make* it. Carlton Westerfield was a man of some talents, but none of them in the kitchen.

He turned toward Diane to see the smirk still in place and shrugged, an embarrassed grin on his own face. He was trying to come up with something to excuse his absence of kitchen smarts when he heard his burner ringing on the table where he'd left it. Glad to escape the laser beam smirk, he almost dashed for it.

"Good morning," he started cheerfully. "How are you?"

"I'll know after we talk. Where are you?"

"Near Sabinal, at Reynaldo's ranch? Why? Where are you?"

A groan at the other end warned him of bad news coming. *"Oh, my God, Carlton! You're making it really hard to believe in you, you know it?"*

"Huh? Why? What are you talking about?"

"I'm talking about the shooting victim found in Sabinal this morning at four twenty-seven a.m. by a Uvalde County Sheriff's patrol."

Carlton was stunned beyond words, recalling his weak attempt at levity the previous night. The body hadn't been found on Reynaldo's ranch, but the tiny town was only about ten miles from the ranch gate. He felt his stomach lurch as he processed the information, the impact of another victim turning up absurdly close to where he had spent the past twenty or so hours. A dozen questions flooded his mind, but he had only opened his mouth to ask the important one when Heather Colson delivered the worst news possible.

"Four small-caliber rounds to the head, one big slug to each knee—correction, make that one kneecap and one upper leg. Someone's getting sloppy, or someone needs some target practice. You getting enough range time?"

Carlton ignored the remark. *"They ID the vic yet?"*

"Nope. A portly Hispanic male, mid to late forties, five-eight, but about two-ten on the scales. Found on the railroad tracks that run beside Highway 90."

Carlton went silent, not knowing what he could ask or say that would change things or mitigate the obvious thoughts going through the DEA agent's mind. After almost a full minute, it was her turn to think the connection had been broken.

"Are you still there?" she asked.

A big exhalation. *"Yes, I'm here. But I wish I were somewhere else. Anywhere else, but far away."*

"Are you alone? More importantly, have you been alone for any period of time while you've been at the ranch?"

Hearing the questions hit him with a minor flood of relief. Incredibly, he had not even thought through his exact circumstances during the previous twenty-odd hours, nearly a full day and night that he'd scarcely been out of Reynaldo's, Paula's, or Diane Martin's sight.

"Yes. I mean no! No, I'm not alone and haven't been for, oh, twenty hours or so."

"What, exactly do you mean by 'yes, I mean no?'" Her tone was migrating from exasperation to suspicion by the end of the question.

"I mean yes, I have an alibi, because no, I'm not alone, and haven't been for the past twenty hours. They fix a TOD yet?"

"No time of death yet. Autopsy probably won't happen until tomorrow, but it looks like the guy was shot elsewhere and dumped in Sabinal, since the bullet holes had quit leaking.

"Oh, and one more thing: he was hit by a train, post-mortem. That's going to complicate the autopsy."

"I think I know how he feels."

"Well, as they say: you ain't seen nothin' yet. Uvalde Sheriff's Department caught the call, but I'll bet you're going to have visitors real soon after our briefing tomorrow."

Carlton thought about that for a few seconds before thanking her for the heads-up, but the call had already ended.

He snapped his phone shut and slumped over the counter, shaking his head. Diane handed him a cup of coffee and said nothing. Having heard his end of the conversation, it wasn't hard to figure out that his worst nightmare, an event he'd sarcastically joked about, had occurred. She could wait until he felt like talking about it. What else could she—or anyone—do? Not having an answer, she sipped her coffee.

Diane worked through the morning on Reynaldo's business, texting and e-mailing as she scrolled through pages and pages of something Carlton couldn't see from his position. Sitting on the couch, Carlton studied her multi-tasking skills for a while before leaning back to brood over the bad news. Having spent hours on it already, he didn't think it would accomplish anything to analyze the overall problem. But if he could break it down into segments, one part or another might present a plan of action...

He wished he had the identification of the newest victim, and what type of illegal activity he'd been involved in. Maybe the added victim would finally provide some kind of pattern for the string of shootings, something that would enable Diane to find the connecting link—if there was one, he thought dejectedly. Without being able to spot it in four shootings, he had little faith that five was the magic number.

So far, despite taking precautions, the lucky break of ridding his house of incriminating evidence, and clearly presenting his case to Heather and Jeffrey Bales, nothing had changed to get the federal agents off his trail. Leaving town hadn't worked; this was the third shooting that had occurred while he was far from San Antonio, but within scant miles of the murders. That meant he was being tracked, but how? Diane's new gadget hadn't picked up anything, narrowing it down to some robust physical surveillance...or one of his three companions, whether unwittingly or not, was leaving cookie crumbs. The thought was not one he wanted to dwell on, but the possibilities were thinning out, and the odds of an outside watcher being able to nail down his whereabouts, get the job done, then get the victim in place, were beyond slim—try non-existent.

Not that he had any reason to mistrust his friends, not yet; they had tried to keep him occupied and away from the city, hoping to learn of shootings that Carlton could not have performed under any circumstances.

In theory, that plan could have exonerated him fully from the role of serial killer. However, it had only worked up to a point; he'd been too busy for the Houston job, if anyone wanted to check with rental car bosses. Shortly thereafter, he'd had three witnesses to alibi him for the Corpus victim, and now, Diane could provide the same when the Sabinal shooting was investigated. The problem was, Carlton Westerfield had been in the vicinity of all three shootings that had left bodies strewn across southeast Texas, and at the time they occurred. That put *opportunity*, one of law enforcement's investigative cornerstones, at the top of their favorites' list, because Carlton's alibi witnesses surely weren't. Though he hadn't voiced it, his three friends had endured an extended grilling due, in part, to their personal histories.

While Carlton wasn't sure about Diane's history in law enforcement's files, she had alluded to activities "on both sides of the law." If anything was documented, it would make her a lot less reliable as an alibi witness, and subject to the semi-rough verbal treatment she had described at the hands of Agents Martinez and Jameson. As for Reynaldo, the federal task force had a lot of first-hand information about Reynaldo Gomez, all of it unfavorable. And Paula Hendricks was the sister of deceased drug distributor Tino Perez. Also, she had worked for Randall "Big Mo" Morris for years—until he was murdered in his pawn shop, a crime still unsolved. That history wouldn't get her a passing grade from law enforcement, regardless of what was on file.

He sighed, realizing his thought process wasn't producing anything useful. So far, nothing pointed to a way out, and the main problem remained the unshakeable surveillance, his inability to avoid the scene of the shootings. As long as that continued, he would stay in the sights of two or three law enforcement agencies. Discovering the party behind that would go a long way toward solving the problem, but a different plan was needed, something far removed from anything they had tried. Whatever it was, it had to exclude everyone—except the one responsible for tracking him. That meant a process of elimination, and that meant lying—or at best, not telling the entire truth. It wasn't his strong suit, and just thinking about it made him uncomfortable, almost physically ill. But something had to happen—and soon.

Diane was finishing up on her work, shuffling papers and shutting down her laptop. It was almost noon, and Carlton realized they'd skipped breakfast. He was hungry and knew Diane was too, but it was time to get started on his plan, here and now. Pulling his phone, he stepped in front of her work area and headed out the door, holding the phone to his ear and waiting for Ralph Lopez at Superior Auto Leasing to answer. Within three minutes, he came back inside, smiling.

"You hungry?" he asked, knowing the answer.

"Thought you'd never ask." She nodded toward his phone in his hand. "No more bad news, I hope."

"Nope. Good news, in fact. Some cars need to be shifted around, and I'm the man for the job."

"I hope we have time to eat first. Reynaldo wants me to come back to the office when I can, so if you're leaving town anyway, I'll head back to Wichita Falls this afternoon."

"Okay. When will you be back?"

"Probably this weekend. You?"

"It's Houston, then New Orleans for me, so probably two or three days at most, unless something changes while I'm on the road, like a side trip to Little Rock. I'll be back by the weekend for sure."

"Didn't your friend tell you to expect visitors? What are you going to do about them?"

"Nothing at all. I've made myself available for them and answered all their questions two or three times. Look where it got me. They want me, they can track me down, I'm sure."

"I'll have to agree it can't get much worse, whatever you do. And they've not used the TV cop line 'don't leave town.'"

Carlton smiled. "Exactly. But what I'm *not* going to do is leave my car where it can get the wrong accessories added. I don't have time to get a garage rented at my apartment, so I'm going to take Reynaldo up on his offer to use one of his pickups and leave the Caddy in the ranch maintenance shop, unless you want to drive it to Wichita Falls."

She thought briefly before shaking her head. "No, why don't you drop me at the airport? After we eat, of course," she added, her laser beam reminding him of a human lie detector in a sci-fi movie.

"Yes ma'am, S. A. International it is," he said with a mock salute. "But after lunch at Bill Miller Barbeque."

Plan initiated, he hoped the woman's lie detector didn't work.

The killer had finished the job fairly early in the night. Popping the unsuspecting guy hadn't been a problem; the problem was toting his big ass into another stolen car and driving west, out Highway 90, to the small town of Sabinal. Arriving there at 1:00 a.m., the little town was already shut down for the night, the only sign of life being occasional cars catching the single traffic light on their way to or from San Antonio or Del Rio, some one hundred and sixty miles away on the Border.

Turning off the highway, it was only a block or so to the railroad track, just as Google Maps had promised. What Google hadn't promised was how hard it would be to get the stiffening body out of the tiny trunk of the boosted Kia and onto the tracks before anyone out at that time of night saw what was going on.

The killer needn't have worried, no one was out for the five or six minutes it took to drag the dead man from the car and flip him three complete rolls, until his torso flopped unceremoniously over one rail, just a few feet from the edge of the street where the Kia sat idling. Sweating profusely, the killer jumped back in the butt-beater car and drove away. That will have to do, he thought, completing another strange ritual and wondering why his own peripheral plans had not come to fruition. They would have eased the burden on the killer, made the ongoing project a lot easier, and the frame-up more of a sure thing. But no, that bastard who had his balls in a vice wasn't really on board and didn't give a damn whether he, the one doing the job, had anything working in his favor or not.

One good point about last night's job: it was the fifth, and that meant he was almost finished with the project, if the maniac bastard running this show lived up to his promise of "seven or eight" jobs. He had promised him that much, anyway, explaining that "it cleaned up his list," whatever that meant. For the killer, it meant almost to home plate and getting this unpleasant business behind him, once and for all. Because there wouldn't be another time when he'd be over a barrel and forced to do jobs for free. He had a plan that would make certain of that…in fact, it would put the icing on the cake.

And the frame-up target? Well, he wouldn't like it either.

CHAPTER 17

After dropping Diane off at the airport, Carlton turned off both phones and drove to Superior Auto Leasing. Ralph Lopez was behind his desk, peering at two sheets of paper plucked from the disarray on his desk. Holding them side by side, he was apparently comparing something and, judging by the expression on his face, it was disagreeable.

"Hey, Ralph, how's it going?" Carlton asked, breaking the lot manager's concentration.

"Oh, yeah, fine, fine. What's up with you?" He pushed the papers onto the pile, a move that Carlton thought would eliminate them forever.

"I need a favor. I want to leave my buddy's pickup here at the back of the lot and rent a car from you."

Ralph was nodding approval before Carlton finished speaking. "Sure, Carlton, no prob. You got girlfriend problems again?"

It was a recurring event between Ralph and Carlton, a long-time driver, and the most dependable of Superior's bunch of oddball retirees. The others were unemployed, and under-employed drivers, bored to death of staying home with a wife and listening to her nag about mowing the yard or cleaning the garage. Not Carlton Westerfield.

He had rented an undercover vehicle a few times in the past and left his car hidden, claiming to be dodging some woman or another, and Ralph liked being part of the subterfuge. After years of Carlton's dependable driving, Superior's owner, Phil Barnett, had even told Ralph to hand over the key to his Jaguar if their top driver needed it. It seemed that Phil, though a wealthy man, still caught heat about mowing the yard and cleaning out the garage, according to Ralph. Carlton figured he liked accommodating a fellow womanizer, though he had no proof of Phil's habits.

Smiling, Carlton hedged on his answer. "Yeah, I need to move around incognito for the rest of this week, Ralph, and I want to rent your least-desired car. Or do you need anything taken somewhere to swap out? Anywhere but Houston, that is?"

Lopez turned to study the board behind his desk. "How about El Paso? Or Amarillo? Either of those places get you out of sight long enough?"

"Yep, I like both of those. But nobody, and I mean *nobody* can know where I've gone, Ralph."

Ralph looked at Carlton and grinned. "Not a problem. Anybody gets curious, I'll tell them to find out by looking at the board. Or on my desk."

"Perfect. That would throw them off until Christmas. I appreciate it."

"Sure, Carlton. Oh, and the best part might be this: I need a gold Hyundai taken to Amarillo and swapped for the white RAV 4 they have. And I also need a blue Camry traded for a red RAV 4 in El Paso. You choose off the key board, I don't care which. And I'll figure it out later, but for a day or two, I don't even *know* which car you left in, or where you went." The grin widened as he laid out the ruse.

"That's better than perfect, Ralph. I'll park the pickup in back and leave the key on your desk. And one of your cars will get swapped out in the next three days or so."

The gold Elantra purred along IH-10 in the afternoon heat until reaching Exit 456 at the truck stop mecca, Junction, Texas. Turning north from there, Carlton knew he could easily accomplish what the popular country and western song presented as some kind of rodeo Holy Grail, arriving at Amarillo by morning after leaving San Antonio, presumably the night before.

He had chosen the Amarillo gig over El Paso in order to maintain better phone service in the event Heather texted him with breaking news he could retrieve later, since his burner phones would both be turned off, batteries removed. Indeed, he intended to stay below everyone's radar: friends, enemies, DEA, FBI, Texas Rangers…and anyone else who might have an interest in his whereabouts.

He knew the car delivery lie was pretty thin, especially if someone like the FBI really wanted to lean on Diane, then Ralph Lopez, to unravel his cover story. Still, it might be enough time for something to happen while he was five hundred miles from the scene, with motel, restaurant, and gasoline receipts accumulating in his wallet. His lie had barely mentioned the job's destinations, and the possible side trip he'd tossed in should obscure his true whereabouts for the next few days. The trap was set well enough, he thought, but he hoped it didn't catch anyone, not this time.

He gave up the pavement battle about nine that evening, stopping for the night in Lubbock. Just over a hundred miles remained to reach Amarillo, so he would have the car delivered and be in the RAV 4 well before noon. He realized that would put him ahead of the schedule in his mind, in which he wanted to stay gone for at least three days. Going over his route mentally, he decided on a delay at Palo Duro Canyon State Park, just south of Amarillo. It had been years since he had visited the magnificent canyon, the second-largest in the U. S.

Carved by a fork of the Red River as it flowed off the *Llano Estacado* to the Caprock Escarpment, the canyon was an astonishing sight to first-time visitors, and no less surprising to Carlton after decades since his last time there. The huge, multi-colored gash appeared suddenly in the middle of what had appeared to be miles of endless grassland prairie, and extending for over a hundred miles through the expanse of North Texas. The park was a popular tourist area, and Carlton's entry was a paid and documented stop, over six hundred miles from Houston. It was exactly the type of proof he wanted to eliminate him from a shooting in the other end of Texas.

Without any camping gear, he spent the entire day in the park, sight-seeing and taking short hikes, interrupted by lunch in the Trading Post. He left soon after sunset to spend the night in the nearby town of—where else?—Canyon. After checking into the overpriced motel, he ate at the nearest diner and headed back to the room for an evening of TV wasteland. Once in the room, he replaced the phone batteries and turned both of them on, expecting to have a terse message from Heather scolding him for avoiding her or missing a meeting with the goons from her task force. There were a few missed calls from a number he didn't recognize, which he attributed to marketers, but nothing from Agent Colson. Nothing, *nada*. He decided to leave the phones on until bedtime.

The classic western channel was available, but watching Clint being hung high for the twentieth time didn't sound too entertaining, so he opted for a wildlife documentary on the mating rituals of spiders. It reminded him too much of his own personal life, so he switched to baseball and watched the Yankees beat the White Sox unmercifully.

Hanging a guy from a tree limb, devouring your partner after sex, using a bat to demolish your opponent—what's this world coming to?

He turned off the TV and leaned back to contemplate what to do after returning to San Antonio; first, if a shooting had occurred, and where; second, if nothing at all had happened. At first, the act of having to undergo this mental exercise angered him; he shouldn't have to be coming up with a defense for something he couldn't *possibly* have done, not this time. After the brief angry spell, he calmed down and wondered if he could channel his ire in a helpful direction. After all, being cooperative, low-key, and quiet hadn't been serving him well lately, as it had earlier in his career. He returned to the mental homework with a different attitude. Grinding through the scenarios, he began to have inklings of an approach he could take during his next encounter with the FBI, the task force guys/gals, or Heather. He tried to anticipate questions he might be asked and answers that would work best, instead of shooting off his mouth with a clever quip. Plus, he had a few questions of his own that might be answered if he played it right. Short of hiring a lawyer to force their hand—*arrest, or leave my client alone*—it seemed a reasonable way to proceed. A little before midnight, he gave up, thinking he at least had a feel for how to handle his next visit with law enforcement representatives.

As he reached for the phones to dismantle them, the one he'd tagged "Heather" rang, startling him enough to jerk his hand back. Laughing at his jumpiness, he hoped this would be a better call than previous ones from the DEA agent. Maybe he wouldn't have to be such a jerk after all.

"Hi, there."
"Hi to you. Where are you?"
"Out of town, way out of town.
"So you're not going to tell me?"
"Why? So I can hear you tell me that another body has been found about a hundred feet from me?"
"Okay, Can't say I blame you."

With that subject closed, Carlton changed gears, hoping to stay civil. *"How was your task force meeting today?"*

"Same as the others. The vic was a guy named Humberto Ruiz, a mid-level dope peddler who supplied slingers on the West Side and even into the northwest part of the city. The MO was discussed again, and guess whose name came up?"

Ignoring her last remark, Carlton started to make his point. *"So just like the others, a miscreant, a criminal. Being a dope peddler, your team was after him, not the FBI, right?"*

"We were acquainted with Mr. Ruiz," she answered cautiously. *"What are you getting at?"*

"Come on, Heather. A mid-level guy in a city this size has the full force of a federal agency on him? He's more like somebody SAPD would know all about, put a drug unit on him, try to squeeze his street slingers into giving him up."

"That's basically right, but we can get called in to help, even with a low-profile case. We aren't called Drug Enforcement because we investigate barking dogs, you know. Besides, the task force is investigating the serial killer aspect, not the victims' livelihood." By now, her tone was verging on irritation, not caution. *"Look, what are you trying to find out?"*

Carlton took a deep breath and started to count. Maybe a thousand would have worked, but at three, he gave up and exploded. *"I'm trying to find out why a bigshot agency—make that two bigshot agencies—are running the shoddiest investigation ever undertaken in history, trying to railroad me for some bizarre shootings of people I don't know, have no interest in, and no possible connection to!*

"I'm trying to figure out who is tracking me and pulling off these shootings very near me, even when I'm out of town without telling anyone where I'm going. Three of them, Heather! That's way beyond coincidence, and way beyond the doer's ability to pull off by himself. If you brilliant cops can't figure that much out, you don't have the ability to quell the neighborhood barking dog, so don't pat your team on the back just yet.

"I have a friend who's been trying to figure out a connection between all the victims and any connection to me. It's not there, Heather. Instead, the connection lies with the DEA and the FBI. All the victims are slimeballs that your famous federal agencies haven't been able to indict, much less convict. So am I supposed to be the substitute collar for them?" Tirade over, he took a deep breath to calm down.

Heather took the slight pause to respond. *"As I told you before, there's a reason the DA isn't willing to accept the felony report of first degree murder and put the case before a grand jury. You know how that works, Carlton, those guys don't want to back a loser, because it looks bad at election time."*

Carlton saw where this was going and set the verbal trap. *"Oh? And why doesn't he think a grand jury would vote to indict?"*

"Because he doesn't think there's enough evidence for them to bring an indictment against you to meet the state's requirements," she explained patiently, as though to a child. *"Remember, murder is usually a state crime, even though federal agencies are investigating the shootings due to the serial killer status—"*

"Wait! He doesn't think there's enough evidence? Is there an echo on this phone call, or isn't that what I've been telling you and your buddies?"

She ignored his sarcastic interruption. *"—and then there's the line of reasoning Jeffrey Bales and I discussed privately."*

"Well, gosh, Heather! And what line of reasoning would that be?"

"The same thing that took you and your friend so long to figure out—that the connection isn't with you. It's with the FBI and the DEA. You're right, all of the victims have been busted, but not a single indictment has come down on those four—make that five dirtbags."

"Does that ever get mentioned at one of your meetings?"

The pause told him more than her words. *"Yes, but it keeps coming back to MO and proximity to the crime."*

"I just explained how that doesn't wash, Heather. Let me expound on that a little: I'm five-eleven, weigh about a buck-seventy. I'm in pretty good shape, but I can draw Social Security if I want to. I'd have a hard time shooting Ruiz in San Antonio and loading his two-ten butt in a car, hauling it to Sabinal and tossing him out on the railroad tracks.

"I don't know how many of the other vics were shot here and hauled elsewhere, but that kind of job requires two strong guys, at least. And Inspector Clouseau still has only one suspect?"

"Maybe you'd like to explain that to Ikos, but he would point out that the victim was shot with two different caliber weapons, so maybe you had a helper."

Carton groaned. *"You're probably right, but I'd like to discuss it with him anyway. When's the next meeting? Next Tuesday?"* When she didn't respond, he continued. *"And the tracking of Carlton Westerfield that's going on to accomplish that proximity crap? The bodies showing up at my feet, no matter where I happen to be? Who's doing that?"*

"Carlton, why haven't you just hired a lawyer?" she asked, exasperation heavy in her voice.

The subject change took him by surprise, and he answered poorly. *"Because I haven't done anything wrong, so why should I have to spend the money? But if I'm arrested, I'll scream for a public defender before y'all get done Mirandizing me."*

That got a brittle laugh from Heather. *"You used the word 'y'all,' which reminds me of the first time you met Stan Ikos. He started out disliking you because you gave him a pretty good grammar lesson on its usage. He told the story again when Darren and Dave gave him your response to their offer of a ride. They even asked me if you ever taught school."*

"No, I didn't, but I wonder if those guys ever attended one that had a grammar course. Oh, and where did your boss come from? I had him pegged for Upper Mid-west, but if you told me where he transferred from, I don't remember."

"He came here from the Minneapolis office.

"Anyway, I was thinking a lawyer might be able to get answers to your questions. At least, he or she could get some relief from the questioning sessions. Which you missed today, by the way."

"Too bad. They haven't proven very productive in the past. I keep telling the truth, and your boyfriend keeps after me."

"Maybe not for long."

"You mean he's seeing the light? I'm not going to be harassed any longer?"

"No, I mean he may not be my boyfriend for long."

"Oh!" The useless, one-word response was all Carlton had to say—and just as well; it was the final word of the conversation.

Again, Carlton stared at his phone, then cursed himself for the silly habit of looking at his phone's screen when the maddeningly helpful agent abruptly ended their conversations. This time, though, he could blame his quirk on his astonishment at hearing Agent Colson say exactly what he'd been trying to get through to her since their dinner date two weeks ago—he wasn't the doer because he had absolutely no reason to be; no incentive, no connection to the victims, and certainly, no interest in being a vigilante, as the shootings were shaping up to be—and no evidence to the contrary existed.

He groaned with frustration and lay back on the uncomfortable bed. He had just closed his eyes when he remembered the live phones and got up to turn them off and remove the batteries. The one he'd just used had a blinking light signaling a text message. When he opened the text, the short message stared back at him, as though daring him to do anything about it.

Moore and Ikos

He finished dismantling the phones and decided to get some sleep. However, it was not to be, not for a while. He lay thinking about the text, putting the two SACs' names into context with everyone involved in the investigation, including the victims. He was already familiar with Darren Moore's part in the investigation: lead guy for the FBI; a smarmy, but competent interrogator, along with his partner. Oh, and the POC for DEA agent Heather Colson. Maybe she was warning him of another pending question session with her soon-to-be-dropped beau. But how did Stan Ikos connect, other than the desk jockey head of the DEA and chief antagonist of Carlton Westerfield?

He went over the first time he'd met Special Agent Ikos at a lunch meeting arranged by Agent Colson, during which he'd made it clear that his position was running things, not doing grunt field work like meeting with a mere confidential informant. It was a contentious occasion, with both Ikos and Carlton tossing barbs back and forth, almost from the minute they laid eyes on each other. In addition to the man's dismissive rudeness, his clipped tone of voice grated on Carlton from the moment they'd first spoken and he'd mentally tried to place his background…then it hit him.

There were still plenty of mysteries, and he needed Google Maps to make sure. However, with two big dots almost connected he had no trouble going to sleep.

CHAPTER 18

The next day, Wednesday was the second day of June. Carlton swapped vehicles at Superior's Amarillo location and headed the SUV for home. In no particular hurry, he rolled into San Antonio in the wee hours of Thursday, far too late to deliver the car. A quick shower and bed awaited him at his apartment, and he enjoyed a full eight hours' sleep for the first time in weeks. It was almost noon when he awoke, hungry and disoriented, having not slept that late in years. Unable to pick a good place for lunch, he settled for a quick burger stop on the way to Superior. Somehow, missing breakfast just wasn't right, and it was mid-afternoon before he started to feel better.

The long drive, covering miles of open highway with little traffic, had given him ample time to ponder the short, cryptic message he'd gotten from Heather after an interesting conversation. He'd known from the beginning that Stan Ikos was the driving force behind the investigation, but he couldn't fathom how seeing his name and Moore's in a text was supposed to help him—or if Heather had intended it to. That led to wondering if any new shootings had taken place and, if so, where. Maybe later...

Ralph Lopez was gone for lunch, so he left the RAV 4 with a porter and retrieved Reynaldo's pickup. Exiting the lot, he decided to keep the undercover vehicle for a while. The Caddy was safely locked in the ranch's repair shop in Sabinal, and it wouldn't hurt to carry on without wondering about a tracking device—or worse—being added to his transportation.

The rest of the afternoon went by quietly, with no news from anyone, and Carlton didn't want to check the news for another serial killing. He had set the trap for Diane by lying about the car delivery job, and he hoped she didn't turn out to be the leak. Though he recalled she had seemed in a hurry to get to her real job in Wichita Falls by flying, that fact told him nothing. He had no reason to think she was involved in disclosing his whereabouts to the killer, but he'd had to start with someone and eliminate every person who had access to him. A fine plan, a solid plan…but he'd found himself thinking about her a lot during the drive—not a good sign in his quest to revive his loner lifestyle. And a really bad one if some poor dolt had been found in Houston with his or her kneecaps shot to pieces.

Also, he realized while driving that Diane would likely see Paula in Wichita Falls, and his supposed trip to Houston and New Orleans might be mentioned. That meant his singular elimination of Diane wasn't foolproof. Paula wasn't exactly a suspect, but Carlton had valid reasons to question the extent of her relationship with Bert Morris, who was the oddest piece of the puzzle, and one for which he had recently located a spot on the board. It remained to be seen if his former lover was the link to that spot. After three-plus years of dealing with Paula Hendricks on many levels, Carlton wouldn't have been surprised by anything. The thought made him worry about his friend Reynaldo, who was permanently attached to the woman via their daughter.

The call came at eight-thirty that evening. Not a phone call, but a *caller*, two of them, arrived at Carlton's door and gave three quick rings on the doorbell. He checked the peephole and saw two suits standing too near to see the faces, not surprising when he considered the possibilities. Nor were the faces on top of the suits, but he wondered why Heather couldn't have pecked a few more words into her text.

"Agent Moore, what a surprise! And you've brought your friend, Agent Ikos! Come in."

The two senior agents walked in silently, looking around the apartment without speaking a word, as though they expected something to be going on. Carlton didn't know if that was from their training, but he suspected that is was another intimidation tactic the pair had picked up in years of in-person interviews. And it probably worked on some guy who had something to hide; however, Carlton had spent a fruitless half-hour scouring his apartment, checking every possible place for an unwanted object. Comfortable that his place was clean made their grim, furtive appraisal of his small apartment almost comedic.

Despite his internal promise to do better, Carlton couldn't stop himself. "Can I offer y'all something? A glass of tepid tap water? A cup of hemlock?"

"Thank you, no, you wiseass Texas hillbilly," Ikos answered for both of them, anger mottling his face.

Clearly, Carlton's usage of the southern-based, second-person plural pronoun still grated on the DEA guy's nerves, but a sharp glance from Moore made him refrain from whatever he was about to add.

The FBI man took over. "We'd like to ask you some questions about where you've been the past seventy-two hours."

Carlton shrugged and took his perch on the bar stool while motioning the agents to the couch. "Ask away."

"Well, where have you been? And don't say 'out of town.'" We'd like something more specific."

"Amarillo."

"Like I said, more specific. When did you leave, and when did you return?"

"I left Monday afternoon and got back about four this morning."

"How convenient," Ikos said, horning his way back in. "I guess you can prove that ridiculous story?"

"Yes, but why do I need to?" Carlton asked, an uneasy feeling starting to form in the pit of his stomach.

"Because a man named Masra Ali Mohammed of San Antonio was found in a ditch near Katy with his knees shot to shit and a big hole in his forehead to boot," Darren Moore explained with another warning glance at his cohort. "And it looks a lot like the other recent murders of this serial killing spree," he said as an unneeded afterthought.

"Which all look like the job you did on Cletus Miller," Ikos threw in, ignoring his partner's signals.

The news didn't shock Carlton, but it upset him that his lie about going to Houston had apparently been passed along to the killer, a lie that almost certainly was passed along by Diane Martin or Paula Hendricks.

Hiding his dismay, he waved off their story. "As I've explained a dozen times, I didn't do a job on Cletus Miller. I should have, but I guess somebody beat me to it. And I didn't do jobs on anybody else, so you're wasting time talking to me about it.

"It sounds like this guy was hauled to Katy and dumped like the last guy. What was his name? Ruiz? Dumped in Sabinal? Well, I'm not big enough or young enough to load bodies, haul them around, and pull them out of a trunk to dump them elsewhere."

"Oh, sure," Moore continued, using the same offhand wave of his hand Carlton had tried on him. "But why don't you tell us all about where you were and what you did anyway."

"I already did. I drove to Amarillo, then back here."

"The entire time? No quick trips back this direction to pick up a strong accomplice and murder Mr. Mohammed?"

He shook his head, while a growing sense of despair at having been fooled and Moore's inane question made it difficult to keep his breathing slow and steady. "It's about five hundred miles to Amarillo, so I've been on the road a lot. I even took a side trip to a state park in the Panhandle, for which I have my ticket stub. My photo is probably on a security camera there, too, plus at a couple of motels I stayed in."

"And no quick back-tracking, because there's no such thing, unless you fly. You did check the airlines, right?"

"What was the purpose of your trip to Amarillo?" Moore asked, ignoring the airlines question.

"I delivered a car to a leasing company lot in Amarillo and drove another car back. It's what I do for a living, remember?"

"I remember. There's not much dependability in your driving schedule, is there?"

Another shrug. "Ask your source. I'm sure she will agree with you on that now that she passed along the wrong information."

If the gender-specific suggestion had an effect on the two agents, it didn't show on their faces, even when they exchanged a look. Instead, both looked blankly at each other as though trying to decipher the comment. Either extremely good acting, or the two really hadn't been informed of his fake Houston job, meaning the killer wasn't connected to the agencies' lead guys. The pause lasted about ten seconds, a long time of dead silence during a back-and-forth exchange between law enforcement and suspect. Carlton waited them out, guessing Moore would continue the session. He was wrong.

"Like most things that come out of your mouth, I don't know what you're saying, Westerfield," Ikos began. "But you'd better come up with plenty of time-stamped receipts and camera shots putting you somewhere besides Katy during the entire three days. Or San Antonio, for that matter."

The agent's last remark told Carlton the murder might have been done here and the body transported, as were the previous two victims. Katy was a suburb of Houston, on its west side, so a two-hour drive to ditch a body from San Antonio made sense. He decided to change gears and try to learn something. That meant being cooperative, so he nodded agreeably and reached for his wallet. He extracted a small sheaf of receipts for gasoline, food, and motel stays, along with a windshield ticket from Palo Duro State Park. He stood and walked toward the computer alcove in the wall next to the kitchen behind him.

"What are you doing?" Ikos asked, nervous at the unexpected move.

Carlton ignored him and turned on the printer-copier. As it went through the series of clicks, clacks and machinations, he turned to the DEA man. "I'm making copies of all this so you can have it and study the times and mileages between these points. Then you can compare it to the victim's time of death, and you'll find I was hundreds of miles away."

"We want the originals of those receipts, Westerfield."

Carlton was shaking his head before the sentence ended. "Nope. Y'all have a way of losing evidence, so both of you watching me make these copies will have to do for now," he stated, emphasizing the second-person pronoun that Ikos hated. The scowl on Moore's face regarding the lost evidence jab was worth the cost of losing any cooperation he might have gotten, and he didn't even bother to look at Ikos. The two agents didn't seem in a cooperative mood anyway, he thought.

It took a few minutes to make the copies, during which time the agents must have exchanged a change of plans, or so Carlton thought later. When he pocketed the original slips and handed Ikos the copies comprising four sheets of paper, the mood in the room turned less contentious.

"Be sure to hang on to the originals," Moore said as he accepted a couple of the sheets from Ikos and scanned down the information. "We'll contact these motels and the park to see if they got you on camera. You'd better hope they did," he added, "because anybody can get receipts in the mail."

"I doubt that, but I got these in person, so I don't have to worry about it," Carlton countered, hoping he was right.

"If this checks out, you may have cast some doubt on this murder, but not the others," Ikos warned, making sure his view was aired, as usual.

Carlton had to grit his teeth to remain civil. Trying to be accommodating, right here in his own domicile, and he has to deal with Stan Ikos, one of those people who see the dark cloud behind every silver lining. "So now you have *two* copycats mimicking me—on something I didn't do? Isn't this getting a little absurd, Ikos?" Carlton fired the questions at him, angry at the agents, Diane, himself, the murderer, and just about everyone else at the moment.

"Just letting you know where we stand. This will open up a new phase of the investigation, though, and for the moment, you're on the back burner. If your story checks out, that is."

"Nice to be in that position for once," Carlton said dryly, keeping his voice calm while he made his wishes known with his next quip. "But would you look at the time? My, how it does fly!"

"Don't worry, we're just leaving Westerfield," Moore said. "And I don't need to remind you not to leave town, do I?"

"Why should that make a difference? Somehow, you're always keeping up with me, no matter where I go. Your source just made a boo-boo this time."

"Just do it, wiseass," Ikos said, standing in unison with Moore.

When the pair got to the door, it was Moore who stepped out first, giving Carlton the opportunity he had waited for since the men had entered. "I hope this gives your task force something to work with," he said cheerfully. "Oh, and Agent Ikos? You're from Minnesota, aren't you? Where is Bloomington located?"

Ikos turned in the doorway and glared at him suspiciously. "It's in the Twin Cities."

Moore took another step, but slowed to a stop and followed his partner's glare to Carlton's face.

Carlton nodded. "Mall of America, right?"

"Yeah."

The killer didn't mind the job on the raghead. There were plenty of them where he came from, and their ingrained cultural custom of living in close quarters made for normalcy in pushing, shoving, and talking incessantly. All of those traits got on his nerves, so getting rid of one of them while reducing the list was like a bonus.

Popping the camel-herding sand crab as he exited from his smelly grocery store just off of Wurzbach had been simple enough, as was loading him into the trunk of yet another boosted car. Then, a long drive toward Houston, but he didn't have to go into the city itself before finding a back street in a western suburb of the city on which to dump the stiff. The return trip was uneventful except for the highway cop who had followed him for over forty miles before exiting at Seguin. Either the stolen car hadn't been reported, or the cop wasn't close enough to read the tag number. It made the killer wonder if the other burgs along IH-10 didn't have any donut shops.

Back in San Antonio, the killer had quickly ditched the stolen car near a convenience store, then Ubered back to his hotel. It was well after midnight, but the job was done.

And the best part? Only one more to go, his despised handler had informed him. Whatever list the bastard was using had finally been completed—almost. The last one might prove difficult, he'd said, but the killer had handled tough jobs before, so he didn't sweat it.

That is, until he got word on who the target was.

"This one's going to take some planning," he announced. "I'm not getting my ass in a sling over the last one."

"Your ass is already in a sling, in case you've forgotten," came the reply. "And I'm the one controlling the sling. I'll see that you get the information you need on his movements, and you start planning accordingly. But it's going to happen when I give the word."

CHAPTER 19

Diane texted to let Carlton know she wouldn't be back for the weekend. Instead, Reynaldo had her working on a project which would entail some Saturday work, and the three of them would probably be back in San Antonio for the following weekend, June 12. Otherwise, the message didn't say anything, and Carlton answered accordingly with a vague "*Ok, c u then*." He followed it with a text to Reynaldo, asking if he could keep the pickup until their return and got an instant reply of "*certainly*."

The delay was a good thing, he thought, giving him time to examine every possible scenario. Currently, he was uncertain, and didn't want to ask Reynaldo if the weekend work story was true, since such a question would deserve its own explanation. Perhaps she would text or call later with something enlightening. For now, she was either waiting to gauge his reaction to being set up, or she was innocent, having passed along the fake trip information to Paula. That would point to Paula as the killer's informant, something Carlton simply could not accept, despite her history of erratic behavior and the still-unexplained link to Bert Morris. Or, a third possibility might exist, but he could not come up with a scenario that completely absolved Diane Martin from blame.

Of one thing he was certain: he wanted to confront her with the damning story in person to see her reaction. Steady, hypnotic look or not, the woman would have to display some readable response when he told her he had lied to her about his driving destination in order to find a leak. A possible plus to his plan would be for the story of the Katy murder to show up on her phone screen or laptop, giving her confidence that it had come off without a problem. Hopefully, there was no way she could know of the contradictory physical evidence he'd given to the agents.

Meanwhile, Carlton did his best to blend back in with his former life of delivering rental cars, making several trips in a van with other drivers in order to bring back vehicles rather than exchange them. It seemed Ralph Lopez had rented every available car out on one-way trips, and he needed inventory recovered and brought back to San Antonio, no trading. It was one of the odd variables of the job, not knowing when a trend would necessitate a different driving assignment.

At home, pastimes included reading, TV, and a renewed workout program. Also, his favorite diversion of trying out new dining places expanded to other parts of the city. With the spotlight off of him, at least temporarily, things became relatively calm, almost enough to forget the entire debacle. However, on Friday he rented a garage at the apartment to house his Cadillac. As a precaution, he began leaving the pickup in it every minute he wasn't behind the wheel—just in case.

He went to the apartment manager and had the lock mechanism on his door changed. As expected, she charged him fifty bucks, but promised him the new design was tamper-proof.

Sure. Professional wrestling is real, some politicians are honest, and the new lock is tamper-proof.

Pocketing both keys, he thanked the guy who installed it and went inside to search his apartment again for anything he didn't personally place there. Finding nothing didn't surprise him, but it made him feel better anyway. The old Carlton Westerfield, the overly cautious one, was back.

The only outside reminders of his recent troubles were a couple of texts from Heather informing him that the investigation's new direction had not yet produced an alternative suspect; however, the copies of receipts from his trip had been closely reviewed in Tuesday's meeting, along with a couple of time-stamped motel security camera photos, which effectively ruled out Carlton's participation in the gruesome murder/mutilation of Mr. Mohammed. He grinned to himself as he envisioned the dog-and-pony show prepared by young techies trying to impress the bosses. No doubt it had included a PowerPoint presentation with a highway map of Texas, red dots denoting his stops, mileage figures and driving times at various speeds between designated points, coordinated to an on-screen clock placed strategically next to a graphic labeled "Time of Death." Great, he thought, since it got him off the hot seat for a while, but of no value to Mr. Mohammed's advocates who wanted the killer caught and justice served.

As the second weekend in June approached, Carlton was feeling almost normal.

On Thursday afternoon, Heather called his latest phone using her older phone, and Carlton gave up trying to keep phones and calls straight. Not that it would pose a problem; both his and hers were unregistered burners, and each usage was immediately deleted from his phones. He had considered going to a two-phone arrangement, using one for incoming calls and another for outgoing, but that required cooperation from every contact, not a likely situation. In any event, he was pleased to hear the ring, hoping for an informative update.

"Hello!"

"Hello yourself. Where are you?"

"At my apartment. Aren't you working at this time of day?"

"Took an afternoon off. I've had enough bureaucracy for one week."

"How goes the investigation? Or can you tell a former person of interest?"

"Still don't have another viable suspect, if that's what you're asking."

"Yes, it is, since I'm tired of having that position all to myself. Mr. Mohammed's crime scene didn't yield any clues, then?"

"'Fraid not. But it turns out, he was involved in some human smuggling, fake passport stuff, and even a bit of money laundering out of his grocery store. Seems he attracted way too much cash for a neighborhood grocery and waltzed into his local bank with it, raising hell when they made out a report, as required by banking law."

"So the FBI and Treasury Department were onto him, not the DEA."

"Yes, like a duck on a grasshopper. And like the other victims whose main occupation wasn't drug-related. Then, when he became the sixth victim in the serial killing spree he got the joint task force's attention."

Carlton was quiet for a minute, then shifted gears. *"Thanks for the heads-up about Moore and Ikos, by the way. They came to my apartment last Thursday and grilled me for a while."*

"So I heard. Ikos claimed he had your undivided attention. Darren just said you were more than willing to cooperate."

Carlton snorted in disgust. *"Yeah, that's me, Mr. Attentive Cooperation."*

That got a laugh from her. *"Sure, Carlton, that's you, alright! Everyone looked at Ikos like he was nuts after that remark.*

"Anyway, the presentation on Tuesday had all your trip receipts set out in a PowerPoint presentation, complete with a timeline running concurrently with a mileage table overlaying a highway map of Texas."

Carlton nearly burst out laughing at his earlier correct assessment. "I'm sure that was entertaining."

"Pretty nifty, really. And the results are what's keeping you out of the spotlight for now, so don't knock it."

"I'm glad your boss was duly impressed with my documentation. And I hope the PowerPoint techies get a raise."

"Yeah, well, lately Stan's been acting like a rabid dog in a meat packing plant. This investigation has been driving everyone crazy, because it's so haphazard, and there's been no results. There's been no real focus on anything but you and the MO, and that hasn't played out well with everyone. I think it's run out of gas, but there still hasn't been an arrest, and that's what always signifies progress. Without an arrest, an investigation is a failure. It won't be long until the DA calls for another agency to come in on the murders, probably a state investigative unit."

"The Texas Rangers? I mean the law agency, not the baseball team."

"Maybe both. They'd both love a chance to outshine anyone in Washington."

Carlton thought for a moment. *"Six murders in a period of what, three weeks? That's got to be getting someone's privates in a vice."*

"Yes, no doubt about that. The news media is tired of keeping the lid on this thing. At Ikos' request—make that <u>insistence</u>—the newspaper articles simply report the individual murders, not the identical MOs and the serial killer angle. As you can imagine, there are a few reporters who want to make a big splash for themselves, and they're chomping at the bit."

"It would be a lot worse if the victims weren't all criminals. If upstanding citizens start getting hit, there will be hell to pay for your agencies."

"That has been aired at the meetings, but neither Darren nor Ikos has a good answer."

"Can't say I feel sorry for them. Moore and Ikos have wasted weeks chasing me around while they could have pursued the real killer.

"But how is ol' Darren doing otherwise?" Carlton added, unable to curb his curiosity over Heather's love interest.

"He's hanging on for the moment." The reply was sharp, not inviting further discussion.

"Okay, well, tell <u>neither</u> of them I said 'hi.'"

She laughed at that and abruptly snapped her phone shut, the usual end of their conversations.

After the call, Carlton remembered he'd wanted to approach the subject of Bert Morris, if gently. The oddball miscreant, who had shown up with bad timing, still lurked around the fringes of his consciousness. Without further information on him, it was impossible to place him in the scheme of things, if such a thing existed at all. He was thankful for the help Heather gave him, though still unsure of why she was doing it. And as for getting any more help from Diane…

Instead, he had gotten nothing new beyond his in-limbo status, and it sounded like Darren Moore was in the same boat with the pretty Agent Colson. It also sounded like the entire task force was muddling through an investigation that was producing no results, and with no prospects in sight for solving the crimes. In all, not much learned, but he couldn't shake the feeling that Heather was trying to keep him poised for…something.

The next day, Friday, Reynaldo called and told him they would be flying into the Hondo airport at ten a.m. on Saturday, and asked if he could pick them up. Not a problem, he assured his friend. He would be at the flight service office at ten sharp and hoped someone had enough money to buy breakfast, a proposition Reynaldo readily agreed to.

Carlton snapped his phone shut, then took a deep breath and considered how to approach the upcoming meeting with Diane Martin. Strangely, he didn't feel anger toward her, just a sense of betrayal after being attracted to her and spending some *really* nice time with her. He had only recently met the woman, so whatever incentive she had to betray his whereabouts couldn't be personal. More disturbing was her connection to the killer. *Who? Why?* Neither question had a ready answer. People were compelled to do things due to circumstances, money, or forces beyond their control, so until he confronted her, he would withhold judgment—at least, that was his plan.

As promised, at ten sharp he was sitting just inside the flight service building where Reynaldo had dealt in past fly-in visits. It was almost ten-fifteen when he spotted Reynaldo's sleek Beechcraft on final for a nice landing, and within another ten minutes, he had made arrangements for the aircraft to be fueled, serviced, and hangered, while Carlton helped the women with enough luggage for a two-week tour of Europe.

Once at the pickup, Reynaldo took over driving, and Carlton and Diane got in the back, where an exchange of pleasantries gave him no indication of his suspicions being correct. Up front, Paula was in a talkative mood, excited about some archery contest she'd participated in. The camaraderie between the four lasted through breakfast and on to the ranch, leaving Carlton to wonder if he'd passed through a time warp in which the betrayal, the murder, the trip to Amarillo—none of it had occurred.

Then, as Reynaldo pulled into his ranch gate, he and Diane finished telling about the project that had delayed their trip by a week, its success measured by the signing of a lucrative contract just yesterday. Both seemed pleased by the week's efforts.

Diane turned in her seat to face Carlton, her direct, unwavering eye contact reminding him of what he liked about her—maybe.

"How was your week?" she asked. "Oh, and your trip to Houston or New Orleans—which was it? Both?"

The timing was all wrong. Reynaldo was pulling into the front of the house, Paula already opening her door. A ranch hand was waving a greeting and walking toward them, the look on his face saying he had urgent business with the boss.

Carlton held her look for a few seconds and said, "I'll tell you in a minute. Let's get the stuff inside first."

If the delay put her on alert, it didn't show. Instead, she nodded and opened her door, then headed toward the rear of the pickup, where the ranch hand already had the tailgate down, reaching for luggage handles. When he'd gotten the three he could reach, he jumped into the bed and slid the other two bags to the rear where Carlton and Reynaldo were waiting. Ten minutes later, everyone's stuff was more or less in place, and Paula began fixing iced tea while Reynaldo and the ranch hand went over some current ranch business on the front porch.

Carlton beckoned to Diane and they slipped out the back door where deck chairs lined the screened-in porch. He motioned for her to take one and moved one close to hers before sitting down and facing her. He'd tried to come up with an effective approach, but hadn't taken enough time to rehearse his lines and think through how they would be received by the woman in front of him. Now he was just going to wing it.

"I lied to you."

The statement had no apparent effect for three or four seconds. Then her gaze intensified for a brief instant, then disappeared, replaced by a wide-eyed look of disbelief. "About your trip? Why did you think you had to lie to me?"

Carlton saw where this was going and hastened to set it right. "I told you I was going to Houston and New Orleans, but I really went to Amarillo. I wanted to see if another murder would take place, and where."

He paused, watching her face for any sign that her betrayal had been uncovered. Nothing.

Eight or ten seconds went by as she searched his face equally, as though more information would be forthcoming. Then she spoke, her voice soft, tentative. He'd not heard the tone since he'd met her. "Did another murder occur?"

"Yes. A local man of middle-eastern descent was maimed and murdered, exact same MO as the others. His body was found in a ditch in a suburb west of Houston."

"Oh my God. Carlton—" She stopped before she got started, her eyes wide, not with fear or surprise, but something like disbelief. "I told her about your work plans, your drive to Houston and New Orleans. I told Agent Martinez."

"*Who?*" Of all the possibilities, he hadn't expected to be confronted with another player he didn't even know about.

"Agent Sondra Martinez. One of the agents who questioned me at the FBI building, when, two weeks ago? She called me while I was at the airport and asked me where I was going. I was so taken by surprise, I looked around to see if she was in the terminal watching me. She said they had been watching all of our movements, and saw I had purchased an airline ticket, but their automated program only gives an alarm that a ticket has been purchased at such-and-such airline. It's up to the agency to call the airline and get all the info. Instead, she just called me and asked point-blank."

"The FBI is keeping up with movements of all four of us?" The disbelief in Carlton's voice matched the earlier look on her face.

"That's what she said, and I had no reason to doubt her, not after the grilling she and her unpleasant cow of a partner gave me."

"And my name just came up?"

"Yes. She asked me where you had gone, said Agent Moore instructed her to check on you too. She made it sound like she was killing two birds with one stone, saving time by just asking me. I hedged for a minute, but figured they would just go to your workplace and cause a scene there." She spread her hands in a helpless gesture. "So I told her what you'd told me. God, Carlton, I am so sorry! I didn't—"

"Why didn't you tell me?" he asked, a tinge of anger flaring as he realized he could have changed his plans in mid-stride, had he known of the agency's persistence in keeping up with everyone's movements.

"I tried twice to call you on my new burner before my flight left, but got no answer."

"Your *new* burner?" he asked absently, cursing himself for being absorbed in his plan that he had turned off his phones as soon as he dropped her at the airport.

She looked at him oddly. "Sure, I figured she would be expecting me to warn you immediately, and would check my contract phone for outgoing calls with my provider, Verizon. I was afraid my old burner was compromised, so I bought a new one at the airport and used it to call you.

"Oh, and I tried as soon as I landed in Dallas, then again when I got to Wichita Falls. I couldn't reach you, so I thought you had a reason to be out of touch. When you didn't contact me for the last ten or twelve days, I figured you wanted to be left alone, or maybe you had something else going on, maybe another woman. I'm aware that we're not at some exclusivity point in our relationship, Carlton." The last statement came with some force.

Carlton nodded, then took a deep breath and let it out, exasperation showing in his face. "I stayed out of touch while I was on the road, naturally. I turned my phones back on and saw the missed calls, but didn't recognize the number, of course.

"I made sure I got receipts at every stop, and even a security camera or two got me. When I came back and learned there had been a shooting, I had evidence to prove I was between here and Amarillo, Texas for over three days, so—"

"I guess that's nowhere near Houston?" she interrupted.

"Oh, sorry. No, it's the opposite direction from Houston, a few hundred miles up in the Panhandle. Even my boss at the car lot didn't know which car I took and where I was headed. So of course, when I learned the victim was found near Houston, it told me the only person who could have dimed me was you. You're the only soul who heard me utter the word 'Houston.'"

"Carlton, I am so sorry! I know that's inadequate, but I don't know what else to say."

"It's okay, Diane. I simply outsmarted myself. I had no reason to think you were the leak, but I wanted to check everyone, and I had to start somewhere, do it one at a time. You happened to be first, and all I accomplished was accusing a friend of deception. If there's an apology owed, it's I who owe you."

She nodded, her eyes lowered. Carlton thought she might be on the verge of tears, but when she looked up, her face suddenly brightened. "It accomplished something else, though. It tells us the connection is the task force. The DEA or the FBI has a killer on their payroll, or somebody near the task force is bent."

He looked at her with surprise. "I hadn't even thought of that. All along, I've been wondering who you were connected to that could be the killer, and why. I haven't known you very long, so the possibilities were endless.

"But you're right, the feds got the info on me and the next vic shows up near my presumed destination, just like the others."

Both of them sat quietly for a moment before Carlton went on to tell about Moore's and Ikos' nighttime visit to his apartment, their smug attitude fading when he presented ample irrefutable evidence that he'd been far from Katy at the time of the latest murder.

He also told her about Heather's phone call and her siding with Carlton's story, along with confirmation that he was, for the moment, out of the spotlight, although another viable suspect had not been uncovered. When he had finished bringing her up to date, he spread his hands in a "what now?" gesture.

She shook her head, the first time he recalled seeing her lacking an idea or a plan to computer-snoop in another direction. He wondered if she was truly out of ideas, or if his ill-fated plan to expose the leak had irrevocably changed her opinion of him and ended her drive to help him out of his predicament. Thinking back on the occasion of their introduction—what, only three weeks ago?—she had claimed to fully understand his stance on keeping his life very private. So it didn't seem logical that she would be upset by his attempt to do some research for himself, but he wanted to clear the air. He opened his mouth to ask, but she was already talking.

"Don't think I've changed my mind about trying to get to the answers," she said, the laser-look back on her face. "I know you felt you had to try something on your own, especially since my methods haven't been coming up with anything."

Unsure of how to respond, Carlton said, "It's not only the prospect of getting no more help from you. I truly feel bad that I doubted you, especially since it worked out in such a bizarre fashion that it made you the bad guy for the last three days. I hope we can get beyond it."

She smiled. "Beyond what? It's over, Carlton, let's get on with finding out who the bent cop or cops are."

"Okay, fine by me."

Whether by design or chance, Paula took that moment to emerge onto the porch carrying a tray of drinks, followed by Reynaldo, and the mood shifted back to four friends enjoying a summer afternoon in South Texas. Sipping his tea, Carlton was feeling relief at having the ugly incident behind him when he remembered the three other maiming/murders that had mysteriously culminated with the victims showing up uncomfortably close to him in Houston, Corpus, and Sabinal. Diane Martin had been present at two of them.

CHAPTER 20

The weekend was peaceful. Reynaldo took pleasure in driving around his small ranch, pointing out cows, fences, pens, and regaling his guests with stories of their background and usage on this, purely a hobby ranch. After lunch on Sunday, they all piled into the pickup for one of his "pasture cruises" as he had begun labeling the jaunts.

"It's not like I can make any money doing this," he explained as he pulled away from the ranch house onto the outer perimeter road. "In fact, it costs me a lot to fool around with this stuff, pay the hands, the land taxes, veterinarian bills, and upkeep. But everyone has to have a hobby, and this one at least represents an appreciating investment in the land and ranch house. That's more than a guy with a bass boat or golf clubs can say."

Paula turned in her seat to look at Carlton and Diane in the back. "And it keeps him in a better mood than dealing with contractors, suppliers, and home owners all the time."

"And employees," Diane added jokingly, nudging the back of Reynaldo's seat.

Reynaldo grinned, agreeing with her observation. "Like most businesses, it would be a great one, if not for customers and employees."

The talk then turned to recent construction jobs, progress on various locations (and lack thereof), interspersed with Reynaldo's running ranch commentary, this time given for Diane's benefit. She seemed interested in learning details of the agricultural operation, asking pertinent questions and appearing to grasp the answers. Listening to the exchange, Carlton figured it was the same attitude that made her valuable in Reynaldo's real business.

After a while, he tuned out the chatter and watched idly as the scene slipped by his window at a crawling pace. Something about the land, with its thorny vegetation sprouting up among stands of lush grass, was relaxing to him. Out here, there was no deceit to be found, no subterfuge lurking behind the prickly pear clumps. Everything was pretty much as it appeared: the livestock needed food, water, some basic shelter, and the land provided that, along with Reynaldo and his ranch hands. In return, the herd bull saw that the cows had calves to be taken to market and sold, so the cycle could begin all over again.

Carlton smiled inwardly at his unrealistic assessment of the ranching industry. He knew there were market fluctuations, drought, disease, payrolls, taxes, drunken ranch hands...all the same pitfalls that went with life in general, including the home construction industry. Oh, and the prickly pear patches were prime locations for rattlesnakes, big ones. Looking at it through the window of an air-conditioned vehicle just glossed over the problems. Still, those problems paled beside being in an illegal industry, with every law enforcement agency hounding after the scofflaws day and night, as it had been with Reynaldo and Tino in the drug importation and distribution business.

Clearly, Reynaldo had made the right decision after Tino's death, as had Carlton. The trouble was, Carlton was having a hard time making a break from criminal life. His past continued to haunt him, and it would until he was able—with help from Diane—to uncover the *who* and *why* of the heinous crimes being committed in his name. For the umpteenth time, he groused over his punishment of Clive Millstone, wishing he had just put a single round through the traitor's forehead. That *modus operandi* was pretty widespread, and copying it wouldn't single out anyone.

He put the nagging train of thought on the back burner as Reynaldo pulled into the ranch house area, the ranch tour over. Everyone got out, headed into the house, and made plans to depart for the upcoming week. It was going to be work for Reynaldo and Diane, an archery contest for Paula. For Carlton, a week of...not much of anything, he thought.

"Why don't you stay out here for a few days?" Reynaldo suggested, as though reading his friend's mind. "You can help Francisco repair those places we saw in the northern pasture, while he helps you with your Spanish."

Carlton thought about it for a minute, then agreed. "I'm getting the better end of the deal, then, because Francisco's Spanish has to be better than my fence-building skills."

"Good! He won't be back from Laredo until Tuesday, but you can manage to find something until then, can't you?"

"Sure. I brought a couple of books. I'll stay occupied."

At Diane's suggestion, the three discussed heading out to Wichita Falls soon, in order to get a jump on Monday morning's heavy agenda. Reynaldo shrugged and agreed, always keen to start the workweek well and quit early on Friday. Carlton sensed something else might be driving the decision, and he made a feeble attempt to find out.

"That's a good idea for y'all, but I'll have to drive into town for coffee in the morning," he intoned gravely, looking from one to another of his friends. "All by myself," he added sadly.

Reynaldo and Paula stared at him blankly, but his announcement got an eye-roll from Diane, followed by a recounting of his complete lack of culinary skills. Her story gained him nothing but ridicule and laughter from the others, so he decided he'd been wrong. Given the merriment in her face, it didn't seem she was having second thoughts about their relationship—whatever *that* was. It was just a good idea to get the unavoidable workweek started.

At mid-afternoon, the three loaded up and left for Hondo. "The pickup will be in the airport parking lot if you want it," Reynaldo told him.

Carlton shook his head. "Thanks, but I've got my Cadillac here. I rented a garage at my apartment, so I'm good on that."

"Well, stay all week if you want to. We'll be back next weekend. In fact, probably on Thursday, since we're getting a head start on the week."

"Francisco will have two more hands here by then, and we've got to pen some cows for the auction on Saturday. So try to learn some Spanish and get the fence fixed, okay?"

"The fence will be fixed, Boss, but I can't make any promises on the Spanish." He gave a mock salute and walked around the vehicle to open the doors for the women, a good move, since it got him a hug from each of them.

Watching as they pulled out toward the front gate, he had to wonder again at their hasty departure, but decided he was being overly critical of every movement of every person in his life—and several who weren't. He went back in the house and dug a book from his bag. The front porch was on the east side, now sheltered from the falling sun. It was a perfect spot to sit and read and put his workaholic friends out of his thoughts for a while.

By seven that evening, he had read enough to tire his eyes and figure out who the culprit of the book was. He stood and stretched, thinking how still and quiet it was, the absolute serenity being broken periodically by a chorus of white-winged doves cooing in a grove of small oak trees beyond the barn complex. Back in the city, there was never complete silence; the sound of vehicles on the freeways permeated every minute of city life, no matter the time of day.

The relative quietness made it especially bothersome to hear an approaching vehicle, the tires crunching loudly on the gravel drive. He turned to see a plain, older sedan, drab gold in color, still over a hundred yards away. He was unable to see the driver or passenger because of the falling sun's glare on the windshield, but the overall appearance of the car left no doubt of the occupants, or at least, their occupation. For a few seconds, he considered his chances at disappearing into the house and out the back door, but the car had drawn too close, so he opened the screen, stepped out, and steeled himself for yet another visit with members of law enforcement.

As the car rolled to a stop, all the suspicions he'd harbored earlier returned. How had he been cornered out here like a rat in cage, without these guys being told of his whereabouts? And what did they want? The ugly questions didn't get prettier when the heavily tinted window rolled down partially and SAC Stan Ikos beckoned to him. Carlton was unable to see beyond him to identify the other occupant, if any.

"Get in, Westerfield, we need to talk."

The strange setup seemed all wrong to Carlton. Why would the head of the local DEA office drive over sixty miles out here to talk? Apprehension building, he did the only thing he could think of to stall while he learned the answer—the straight-forward approach.

"What do you want to talk about?"

"You want to know who the killer is, right?"

"Of course. So tell me, there's no one within miles to overhear what you say."

"That's not the way it works, Westerfield!" Ikos yelled. "Get in the damn car!"

Tired of the mindless game and angered by the shouted demand, Carlton made another poor choice in diplomacy and communication. "I was taught not to get in a car with a stranger, and I don't know many people stranger than you, Stan."

Red with rage, Ikos turned in his seat to speak with an unseen occupant. The back door on the opposite side of the car opened, and an outstretched hand holding an automatic pistol appeared immediately over the roof of the car, followed by a man's head and upper body. From thirty or more feet away, Carlton could see the unwavering muzzle locked onto him, aided by the gunman's forearm resting comfortably across the car roof. The move had been swift and fluid, obviously one made by the gunman many times before. Shocked, Carlton realized he was already covered, not a chance of moving without being shot. Even more shocking was the face behind the outstretched arm.

"Carl, do what the man says," Bert Morris ordered, his tone only slightly more civil than Ikos'.

Carlton evaluated the situation as swiftly as possible. Getting in the car would result in a one-way ride to his death, of that he was certain. Though mystified by this strange turn of events being carried out by even stranger traveling companions, the pair was not going to take him for a ride, discuss whatever was on their minds, then return him to the ranch house, holster the gun, and bid him a good evening.

But it appeared that Bert Morris was skilled with a handgun and could easily kill him from his current stance. So if killing him was the idea, why hadn't he done so already? There was no need to take his next victim elsewhere, away from this secluded ranch property. And how was Stan Ikos caught up in this part? Carlton didn't know Bert Morris, so maybe this was his method for forcing a conversation with everyone, but Ikos, for all his faults at social graces, had to be horrified by this action. No matter how it turned out, this couldn't be good for the SAC's career path.

Or maybe this was a kidnapping. But if this was a kidnapping attempt, the show of lethal force wasn't a great tool for gaining cooperation from the target while still thirty feet away, and able to break and run. That would leave no choice other than killing the fleeing target, a bad way to get top ransom money. Besides, what would kidnapping Carlton Westerfield accomplish?

His analysis had taken way too much time, and the impatience was showing on Morris' face. Carlton knew he had to stall for time, get some type of reaction, some hint of what was going on without dying in the process. He decided to turn the tables on these two, give them something to think about.

"Think it over, Mr. Morris," he opened, working to keep his voice a lot calmer than he felt. "Would you get in the car if I were holding a gun on you? Wouldn't you think your chances of coming back here for the evening were pretty slim?"

"We just need to talk to you, Westerfield!" Ikos said again, loudly, but not shouting this time.

"Well, you two have picked a good way to gain my confidence. Tell you what, Stan: you can get out of the car and tell me whatever it is that's so important, because I'm not getting in a car with someone holding a gun on me."

Ikos turned and said something to Morris, and the gun disappeared from the car's roof, though Bert remained standing, car door opened. From his previous lightning-quick maneuver, Carlton knew he hadn't gained much as far as personal safety was concerned. Also, he didn't like the way Bert Morris had gone silent and now stood staring at him as though contemplating his next move.

Ikos opened his door and got out, grumbling something Carlton couldn't hear, apparently directed at Morris from the way he stepped back and closed his door, then began stalking around the rear of the car. Only then did Carlton think about the man's odd dress style in previous encounters and noticed he was now dressed in casual slacks and an open-neck shirt. The riverboat gambler look was gone.

"I came to tell you about the murderer, Westerfield," Ikos began again.

"Tell me you're convinced it's not me, and I'll be happy."

Ikos seemed confused by the statement. "But I thought you'd be happy to learn who it was."

He looked to his left as Morris rounded the car's trunk and stood beside the rear tail light. Both men now faced Carlton, about twenty-five feet away. As he had feared, Morris reached into his jacket and pulled the auto-pistol again, cocking it at he brought the muzzle directly to Carlton's chest. An expert move; no wasted time, no wasted motion, instantly on target, the muzzle unwavering.

A movement beyond the car caught Carlton's eye, a flicker of something against the side of the maintenance barn, which stood about fifty feet beyond the car. The movement disappeared, and Carlton couldn't take time to look for it or even think about it; he had to move now, and move quickly. He tensed to throw himself backward, onto the porch, then try to roll out of danger. With no weapon, he had no further plan beyond that, but getting out of the line of Bert Morris' gun muzzle was a priority.

"I guess you know now who the shooter is." It was Stan Ikos, his voice changed from the business-like, informative tone to one of gloating. He turned to address Morris. "Alright, get it done."

"I plan to," he answered calmly, swinging the muzzle to his right, bringing it to bear on Ikos.

The look of confusion on Ikos' face lasted only a second, replaced by anger. "Dammit, Morris, do what I told you to do, or I'm finished with you—"

"Shut up!" screamed Morris, interrupting him and startling Carlton. The gun muzzle wavered slightly and, for a second, he thought Morris was swinging it back to him, giving him all the incentive he needed to propel himself backward.

He landed on the wooden plank porch hard, jarring his back and forcing his head to snap back with the momentum. When the back of his head smacked the porch, bright lights flashed behind his eyes at the same instant the gunfire reached his ears, telling him he'd been hit in the face with a large-caliber slug. He didn't feel anything, but slumped back anyway, knowing the effect it would have as soon as his brain could process the fact that its owner was dead.

He'd seen the effects not long ago, when Tino's head had disintegrated against the window glass of his pickup door, while parked on a side street in Laredo. Reliving the scene now gave Carlton a sense of failure; not only had he failed to protect his friend from a horrific death that day, he had fallen into the same scenario and talked himself into getting a bullet in his head, dying instantly. But he couldn't reconcile what he knew to be the results of such an impact on a human face with what was going on in his mind. He was still able to think, to process what was happening, to hear a second shot without feeling anything. But he had never died before, he reminded himself; this must be the norm. Curious about seeing his own death, he opened his eyes and raised his head. It didn't take nearly as much effort as he'd expected, and he decided dying might not be such a bad deal after all.

Bert Morris had indeed shot again, this time hitting Stan Ikos in the chest as his already-dead body angled toward the ground beside the car. After completing the classic one-two killing shots, Morris was now swinging the big automatic back toward him, and Carlton realized he'd not been shot—yet—but without being able to see the man's finger tightening on the trigger, he knew exactly what was taking place twenty-five feet away. The tightening finger, the trigger tripping a spur of metal, releasing tension on a spring, the spring driving a nail-like pin toward a primer cap in a brass casing, which would ignite a load of gunpowder…all in a small fraction of a second.

But before the finger-tightening squeeze on the trigger took place, Carlton's eyes were drawn to a flash of silver and crimson on the gunman's shirt. The paralyzed shooter looked down at the silver blur and the blossoming crimson surrounding it, unable to squeeze the trigger to start the sequence of firing the next round. The look on Bert Morris' face was one of amazement, complete bafflement at seeing what had just killed him.

The broad-head hunting arrow protruded about five or six inches from his left pectoral muscle, indicating it had missed the sternum on its flight through the body, having entered just beside the left shoulder blade, but it probably passed through a good portion of his heart and its surrounding vessels, judging by the steadily pulsing stream of blood pouring from the exit wound and running down the shirt front, spreading to his pants in a broadening pattern as gravity did its job. The dying man leaned back against the car, his eyes never leaving the sight of the arrow's business end a few inches below his chin.

To a bystander, it would have been difficult to tell who was more horrified by the sight, but the smart money would have been on Morris, for the obvious reason. Still, Carlton found himself unable to tear his eyes from the sight of a slow-motion death being played out before him. Like the sight of Tino's head exploding against the glass of his pickup door, the sight of the big-game arrow emerging from Bert Morris's chest would remain with him forever.

A movement behind the car got his attention, and he tore his eyes from the sight of the sagging man to see Paula and Diane approaching, with

Reynaldo a few feet behind them. For some reason, the unexpected sight of his three friends walking toward him instead of being airborne to Wichita Falls confused him greatly; he couldn't fathom how they had ended up in the maintenance shed when he'd seen them drive away hours earlier. The inability to come up with a logical answer made him wonder if the blow to his head had caused a concussion, or worse. It took a few more seconds to recall Paula's recent affinity for archery and connect it to the scene in front of him. Only then did it become less surreal, but just as shocking.

Wordlessly, the two women came around the car just as Bert Morris slumped to the ground. Diane went toward him while motioning for Paula to check on Carlton. After only a few seconds of standing over Morris, she moved on to kneel down beside Ikos and feel his neck for a pulse. Paula moved quickly to Carlton, who noticed for the first time she was carrying a compound bow in her left hand and wore some type of gloves on both hands. He started to ask her about it, but she beat him to the conversation starter, one of her own choosing.

"Are you hurt?" she asked, kneeling beside him on the porch and reaching for his head.

"I don't think so, but—well, I smacked my head pretty good when I fell back, but I don't think I broke anything. Sure going to have a knot on my noggin, though," he added as he gently massaged the impact area on the back of his head.

"I didn't think I could get the shot off in time," she said. "We were hoping it was going to be a conversation only, since you wouldn't get in the car. But when he shot Ikos, I was so surprised to see you fall back, I had no idea what had happened."

"Which was a really good move on your part." The comment had come from Carlton's left, where Diane was approaching them after checking on both dead men in the driveway.

"I guess a knot on my head beats the alternative, doesn't it?" he said, managing a weak grin at the two women before turning serious. "Thanks to both of you, I didn't have to face the alternative. Paula, that was incredible. I can never begin to thank you for that."

"You already did, Carlton. You saved Celia, remember?"

At that moment, he heard the screen door open and turned his head to see Reynaldo coming out of the house. Evidently, he had gone to the back to check for anyone else and walked through the house from the back door to the front. Seeing Carlton sitting on the porch planks, he rushed over and knelt beside him. "You okay?" he asked, concern lining his face.

"Think so. I'll know more when I hear how all this took place."

Reynaldo grinned, relieved to hear a coherent statement. "It's a long tale, my friend, but Diane will have to tell it, since she's the only one who knows the complete story. Right now, we're just glad you're alive, because it didn't look good a few minutes ago."

"How did you end up back there?" Carlton asked, nodding toward the maintenance shed.

"There are two gates farther up the road, small ones that access the perimeter road we drove this afternoon. It's a little closer to take the second one, and the pasture road leads to the back of the shed. I had to drive way too fast, but we figured that was our best approach to get into position if the car was already in the driveway."

Carlton nodded, understanding that part, but still remained confused. "But what made you decide to come back in—"

Diane cleared her throat to speak, and Carlton turned to look at her. He was instantly on alert, steeling himself for an explanation he wasn't expecting, something that would change his opinion of the attractive woman kneeling beside him. He was right.

"I was notified by a text that Agent Ikos had left the city and was heading west on Highway 90," she stated. "This thing has been drawing to some kind of conclusion, and I thought this might be it."

"This *thing*?"

"Sorry, the investigation. And not the investigation of your involvement in the six murders, but the investigation into SAC Ikos'…uh, enforcement practices.

"By the way, I work for the DEA, Carlton. I work in a division that's much like Internal Affairs in most law enforcement organizations."

"So you knew all along that I wasn't…"

"I couldn't be positive about the first three, but obviously I knew you weren't doing the next three murders yourself. But all the information from the task force pointed to the Miller thing, so that recurring MO kept you on the radar. It was *theoretically* possible for you to have engineered the shootings, but I doubted that from the beginning. Why would you call

Reynaldo for a read on it and explain the situation to me, a stranger? *Maybe* to cast suspicion elsewhere, but that would be a stretch, a risky one at that.

"Anyway, you didn't fit the profile of a man who has someone else do his dirty work, and the more I got to know you, I became sure you weren't involved."

Her assessment of the facts told Carlton she had gone over things in her analytical mind and arrived at a logical conclusion—something he'd tried to get the other agents to consider, but with no apparent success. That led to his next question. "And when did Ikos' obsession with it being me lose its credibility with the task force?"

She shook her head. "It was losing steam for a while with Agent Colson and Agent Bales. But not until you made the trip to Amarillo did Ikos' theory come unwound. You really threw a curveball with that one. No one knew where you were, but it turns out you weren't committing a murder here or in a Houston suburb. Even your boss at Superior didn't know where you had gone."

"That's exactly what I intended!" Carlton reminded her, his tone harsher than he'd wanted it to be. Seeing her flinch, he softened his delivery for the next part. "I explained that to you, Diane. I had to limit the people who knew my whereabouts to one person—you—to find out if you were the leak. Turns out, you were."

"I know, and I'm sorry, Carlton, I really am. It didn't start out to be running a scam on you, but as Ikos' obsession with taking you down grew, his over-zealous investigation of you turned into the perfect vehicle to expose him. And it finally did, when you were nowhere near here or Katy, Texas to do the job on Mr. Mohammed, even though I'd put you in place with my report to Sondra Martinez.

"Look, it's a very long story. I want to tell you every single detail, I promise, but first I have to call in and report all this so the right people can get out here. Can't have the local Sheriff's Department out here investigating the murders by themselves."

That made Paula look at her sharply. "*Murder?* I wasn't going to let him kill Carlton, even if I couldn't stop him from shooting Ikos. I tried to get close enough to—"

Diane interrupted her with a gesture and head shake. "Don't worry, Paula, it was the only way we had to stop another murder, and under the

Texas Penal Code, a person can use deadly force to stop an imminent murder, certainly the situation here.

"As to any federal law, which I don't think applies here, I'll testify that I asked you to do it—which I did. That puts this on me, and I can handle it, believe me."

Her lengthy explanation and tone of authority lent credence to the statement, but Carlton was becoming wary of the word "believe." He wished she had used different verbiage as well as a less take-charge tone. Although he realized he was now seeing the real Diane Martin, this one was less appealing to him than the smart, introspective one he'd met a few weeks earlier. This one would take some getting used to, he decided.

Paula nodded and rose to walk back toward the car and the bodies in the driveway. She stopped and squatted few feet from the man she had killed and stared at his lifeless face for a long moment before turning back to the group, where Diane had a phone out, studying it as though she didn't use it often.

"Diane, I hope you can explain all of this to me, as well as the people you answer to."

Diane looked up at her quizzically. "I can, Paula, I *told* you. Plus, all three of you saw Bert Morris kill a U. S. government agent, and he was about to shoot an unarmed civil—"

Paula interrupted her, pointing at the body. "But that isn't Bert Morris."

CHAPTER 21

After about fifteen minutes out in the driveway and five or six calls on what looked like a satellite phone, Diane walked back to the group on the porch and announced that she had contacted the necessary parties to come to Reynaldo's ranch and take over sorting out the "complicated events" that had occurred in the past half hour. Again, Carlton was put off by the change in her overall demeanor, and had to remind himself of her new position on the game board. She acted like she was pretty high up the ladder, so she had to sound like it, right? But it didn't make it any easier to think about how she had fooled him and Reynaldo into thinking she was simply a bright computer geekette whose skills could prove useful in the construction industry, or for researching background information on shady individuals committing crimes and getting popped in Carlton's name. That train of thought made Carlton wonder if she got to keep the paychecks from Reynaldo's construction company while she drew pay from the DEA.

Why not? She <u>did</u> put in a lot of hours!

Despite Paula's warnings, Carlton had gotten up and walked around some, feeling he'd be alright except for a lump on his head and a slight headache. His back seemed to have survived its collision with the porch planks, though he didn't want to try it again—ever.

Noticing Reynaldo at the end of the porch, he walked over toward his friend, saying nothing, a wan smile plastered on his face. A full minute went by as the pair stood together, barely hearing Diane and Paula quietly discussing things in the background. Carlton finally clapped a hand on Reynaldo's shoulder. "We really know how to pick them, don't we?" he said softly.

"*We?*" he answered with a brittle laugh. "Hell, this is on me, Carlton, just like that son of a bitch Millstone! Although she picked *me*, not the other way around. Still, you'd think I'd be smarter than that by now.

"Her original assignment was to check my construction business for any sign I was still in the drug importation racket. So when this came up about Ikos being a loose cannon, it was a natural fit for her to carry on with their Internal Affairs group. Besides, she had been with me long enough to tell I wasn't involved in the drug industry anymore.

"But I just can't believe she suckered me in to begin with," he added shaking his head, a frown on his usual smiling face.

Carlton laughed at his friend's distress, trying to assuage his guilt and naivety. "At least you didn't fall for her the way I did. You'd think I could spot a DEA agent by now, especially a pretty one who gets *real* close and personal, wouldn't you?"

Reynaldo looked at him in disbelief. "Yeah, but men are allowed that screw-up when they look like Heather or Diane!"

Both men laughed. Carlton nodded in agreement and thought for a minute. "When did you find out all of this? Have you known all along?"

Reynaldo shook his head again and put up his hands in defense to assure Carlton he'd not been a party to the deception. "Only about an hour ago. She got a call while we were on the way to Hondo. When she hung up, she asked me to pull over, she had something important to tell both of us. She explained the call and proceeded to give us a quick rundown on what's been going on for the past several weeks, and her part in it. Then she said Ikos was on his way to get you, and could I get back to the ranch really fast. So I did, and used that back gate to get to the shed without being seen."

After a moment's reflection on the recent revelation, he smiled and amended his recounting of it. "I can't imagine how shocked Paula and I must have looked as she started telling us who she was and what was happening."

At that moment, the two women walked to their end of the porch. Paula asked Carlton how he felt, and Diane reached for the back of his head to confirm the diagnosis.

"You can't make a habit of throwing yourself backward like that," she scolded him. "Agent Colson told me you used that move in the parking garage when you two punched Brujido Ramos' ticket."

Carlton looked surprised, which he was, and he wondered when Diane and Heather had had such an interesting conversation. Stan Ikos had long been suspicious of the exact events of that day, and both he and Heather had hoped that Ramos' bullet-riddled body wouldn't get too much scrutiny on the ME's table. Carlton had indeed fallen backward onto the concrete and put the finishing touches on Ramos when Heather's gun ran out of ammo; however, that move would have been frowned on by authorities, so…

He tried to turn the comment aside. "I don't recall any acrobatics that day," he lied. "I was younger then, at least a few months, but I just fell down."

The trip down Memory Lane didn't last long. Diane got information in the form of a text, and she relayed it to them. "Bertrand Gayle Morris has a brother, Brendon Garth Morris. They have the same birthdate, so they're twins. Brendon goes by Brent." She glanced out to the driveway. "Make that *went* by Brent. That Morris brother wasn't in the pawnshop business, he was in the *suspected murder* business in Minnesota. Oh, and get this: questioned a few times, but never indicted or even held overnight, according to this."

"In the Twin Cities area, same as Stan Ikos," Carlton added. "I checked and found Bloomfield is just south of Minneapolis, so that was where Ikos and the Morris brothers were hooked up."

Diane was nodding in affirmation as she scrolled down her phone screen. "Seems that Ikos had the Morris brothers in his sights for years. Every time they had a run-in, Stan managed to get them untangled, but his help came with a price tag. At least, that's the theory in this report written by a Minneapolis State Police investigator. The report was rejected by the local IA department, by the way, as 'unsubstantiated.'"

"He used the Morris brothers as his personal button men?"

"Almost certainly Brent did some work for him, but as you recall, Bert doesn't have a history of violent offenses, not that I could find. The only things are a few pawnshop-related dings concerning fencing of stolen goods. Bert never caught much heat."

"That good fortune may have been a result of his relationship with Stan Ikos, too. Or Darren Moore. I wonder if anyone has checked to see where Agent Moore hails from."

Diane seemed concerned by his last statement. "What makes you say that?"

Carlton shrugged. "Moore and his partner, Dave Fowler, braced me at breakfast on May 20. They already seemed convinced I was the doer because two hits had been made with the same MO, the one Ikos harped about all along.

"Then, Moore and Ikos came to my apartment on June 3, the Thursday evening after I returned from Amarillo. Both of them were on me for the Katy murder like two dogs humping a sofa—that is, until I showed them receipts from the other end of the state for the previous three days. So it seems Moore and Ikos were on the same page a lot. In fact, every time I spoke with either of them."

Now Diane's eyes widened in genuine surprise. "You have the dates of those meetings down pretty well. Why didn't you—"

"You would too, if it were your neck in the noose," he interrupted, irritation in his tone.

The DEA investigator stepped back, surprised at the retort. She had intended her remark about his memory of the events as a casual observation, even a compliment, but now she struggled for an adequate response. "I'm sure everyone who operated with the joint task force will be investigated and the notes of their meetings reviewed," she said with more certainty than she felt.

"Oh, I'm sure," he countered in a tone that said the opposite. Then, seeing the look on her face, he added: "Sorry, didn't mean to take it out on you personally, but I've had quite enough of the DEA and FBI."

She waved off his apology. "Forget it. Remember, I went through one of those interviews myself, and the two female agents had no idea I was on the job, working undercover. It doesn't take many of those encounters to last a lifetime."

It was almost midnight before the first of an investigative team from Washington showed up. Apparently, the aircraft they had used was unable to land at Hondo and had to backtrack to San Antonio, where a couple of Suburbans picked them up for the sixty-mile drive. By then, local DEA assets, plus Uvalde County law enforcement had converged on the scene and secured it pending the bigshots' arrival. Of course, when that occurred, personnel of the various agencies were bumping badges like bantam roosters fighting in a barnyard. Watching the melee from a distance, Carlton figured it was the biggest thing to happen in Uvalde County since the Newton Gang ran amuck there early in the twentieth century.

Reynaldo and Paula stayed up for the ordeal that followed, but Carlton retired to his room just after ten, citing his advancing age and the trauma of hitting the porch with his head. He managed to corner Diane and promised he would be there in the morning if anyone wished to speak with him. "Until six a.m., they can leave me alone. And they can wake me up *only* after somebody makes coffee."

Agent Diane Martin laughed, the first time she'd done so since mid-afternoon. It sounded like the old Diane and almost made Carlton start liking her again. *Almost.*

CHAPTER 22

The crime scene investigation went on for two more days, replete with yards of yellow tape, spray painted areas labeled and grid-marked, tiny cones marking the landing spots for brass casings (there were only two), three crime scene photographers, eight or nine agents, and interviews… lots of interviews. The only thing missing was any sign of news media.

When the Uvalde County Sheriff's Department arrived soon after the shooting, a Uvalde TV station crew followed within minutes and were given a sparse rundown of the event by Agent Martin while being held at bay just inside the front gate. No film or photography was allowed, and no interviews beyond her basic statement, which was followed by a terse suggestion that the matter be dropped until such time as further information would be made available to them—first and exclusively, of course. Then the crew was ordered off the property with a stern warning not to try aerial tactics via drone surveillance under penalty of federal law. Apparently, this bloody scene wouldn't make the news until the feds were good and ready.

Carlton lost count, but later estimated he was braced by six different agents, to whom he told the same story six times. Paula and Reynaldo didn't fare any easier, with Paula getting special attention due to her timely physical intervention in the shooting. Even Diane got a good share of interviews, during which she tried to get some pressure taken off of the other three, but without success. The next agent in line always insisted that all four be kept separated until he or she could speak with them. Hearing the barked orders from the self-important agents, Carlton wondered if they'd thought about the hours the four of them spent together between the shooting and the arrival of God's gift to law enforcement.

Throughout it all, meals and sleep were irregular, but between the ranch house and the outbuilding designed for occasional cowhand use, everyone managed. A few of the East Coast agents actually seemed to be enjoying their visit to the Wild West, a source of entertainment for Reynaldo. Finally, late on Tuesday, the action was winding down, and all witnesses but Diane were cleared to go. The out-of-town agents packed up equipment and prepared to leave, while the local agents made arrangements to stay in Sabinal's single cheap motel or a better place in Hondo. Seeing the exodus, Reynaldo and Paula elected to stay at the ranch and try to return to some degree of normalcy by going forward with the cattle sale; the business in Wichita Falls could wait.

Though officially released, Carlton stayed, hoping for an opportunity to speak privately with his new agent friend, Diane Martin. He wanted to hear the story from someone who knew the full background as well as what had taken place on Sunday, but as the evening wore on, the likelihood of that happening looked slim. She was constantly on one of her phones or talking to a fellow agent. Carlton retrieved his book and propped up in a chair on the porch, where he could read and check Diane's progress from time to time. Reynaldo and Paula retreated into the ranch house. Francisco arrived late in the day, tired from his journey to visit family in Mexico. After talking to Reynaldo and Carlton about the fence repairs and the cattle sale for about five minutes, he headed for the bunkhouse. Everyone was exhausted.

It was well after dark when Diane came into the ranch house to find Carlton on the couch watching TV. He looked up to see the tired woman cross the floor and plop down in the recliner with a muted groan.

"Are you finished for a while?" he asked. "Or is this just halftime?"

"God, I hope we're done here on site! Of course, there will be weeks of work in the office over this mess."

"Thanks for turning Reynaldo around and heading back out here. Oh, and for bringing Paula, too."

She looked at him and smiled. "I tried archery once, and couldn't really get the hang of it. But I stayed with it long enough to learn the basics—and that was an incredible shot. She was too far away when we walked out of the maintenance shed door, so she had to cut the distance by running to the drive before setting up and taking the shot. It's not something one can do very well on the run, or after a sprint, I'd guess."

Carlton shook his head. "I was surprised when Reynaldo told me she was taking archery lessons, and now I hate to admit that he and I were poking a bit of fun at it.

"I don't know anything about archery, but the results speak for themselves on this one. Morris was partially obscured by the trunk of the car, and from that distance, she didn't have much of a shot opportunity."

Diane nodded her agreement. "I was really concerned about what Ikos would do, and from where we were standing, the roofline of the car almost completely blocked him from our view. If he had planned to kill you himself, she couldn't have saved you."

"But save me she did," Carlton said quietly. "I don't know about Ikos, but I could tell Morris was no stranger to handling a gun. If he hadn't taken the time to shoot Ikos first, I'm not sure Paula or my acrobatics could have saved me.

"And speaking of *saved*, are you okay? I've never seen anyone look so wiped out."

She managed a tired grin. "You mean I've been ridden hard and put up wet?"

"Something like that."

"That doesn't sound very lady-like, but I may include it in my report anyway."

The pair fell silent for a moment, Diane resting her tired eyes and brain, Carlton gathering his thoughts in order to ask a few key questions, things he really wanted to know. A full explanation would have to wait, he knew; Diane looked like a zombie who was going to nod off in about five minutes.

"Is this the end of it, Diane? You think Ikos had simply wandered off the reservation, gone round the bend, or whatever cliché fits a crooked federal law enforcement agent?"

She hesitated, then hedged when she responded. "That seems to be it on the surface, but we need to uncover a lot more information about the past several years of his career before we can say for sure. Or come up with a reason for him to blackmail Brent Morris into killing the perpetrators in cases where there was no indictment. That was the common thread, by the way."

"It took a while, but we figured that out by process of elimination."

"*You* figured it out," she corrected him. "You're pretty hard to fool, you know it? She added with a sly grin."

"You mean you were sandbagging a bit on the research?" he asked with a smile to soften the accusatory question.

"Some, but not altogether dogging it. The common thread between the victims had already been discovered, but not linked solely to Ikos. As you said, their crimes were different, not all ones to be prosecuted by the DEA, FBI, or Homeland Security. And just because all of them had avoided indictment, that didn't automatically mean much, because hundreds of arrests are made where no indictment occurs. Many times, it's because the prosecuting attorney quickly sees a weakness in the case, like an illegal search or tainted evidence. Or, a defense attorney spots it and points it out. Either way, the prosecutor knows that it will fail the grand jury test, so the scumbag is back on the street in no time.

"And I wasn't sandbagging on some of the individuals' backgrounds. For instance, the Morris brothers really *haven't* left many cookie crumbs on the trail of life. That doesn't mean anything criminal, but it also doesn't exonerate them. But remember, that can be a good thing."

"How so?" he asked, missing the point.

She smiled at him. "As I told you about sparse-information citizens; Carlton Westerfield fits that category, as well as the other Morris brother, Randall."

"Oh, yeah, I forgot. I guess it *is* a good thing, not leaving many tracks."

She continued her tutorial. "But now the real digging is going to be centered on Stan Ikos, Agent in Charge, and his interaction with Morris."

"Going to be harder to find out the rest of the story without Ikos or Brent Morris to explain, isn't it?"

"True, but solving difficult cases is what we get paid the big bucks for," she reminded him, arching her back in a tired stretch. "Because if it were easy to do—" she stopped to yawn.

"They'd get Girl Scouts to do it," he finished for her.

The conversation lagged for a moment, and Carlton took the opportunity to let her off the hook. "You've had enough questions. Now go get some sleep," he ordered. "You're exhausted, and I'm not much better, so I'm going to sleep right here on this couch."

"Good idea," she said, the laser beam look in place, if briefly, then supplanted with another stifled yawn as she rose from the recliner. She stopped at the hallway leading to the bedrooms and turned to look at him. "Oh, one other thing you should know: the times we were, uh…"

"Sleeping together?" he suggested, smiling at her embarrassment.

She laughed. "Yes. God, why do I feel like a schoolgirl talking about it? Anyway, I wanted you to know that wasn't in the plan. It just happened because I wanted it to."

Carlton didn't say anything for a long moment. Since learning who and what Diane Martin was, he had had thoughts about their nights in Corpus Christi and here at the ranch house, and not very charitable ones. Seeing and hearing her in her true element for the past two days had painted a picture of someone as focused as her penetrating stare, one who would use all the resources at her disposal to accomplish the task at hand.

He had wondered—make that *accepted*—that she had used her appeal to get close to him, and he was chagrined with himself for once again letting the little head think for the big one. However, recognizing it was not his first time for that mistake, he had endured it and gotten over his anger with her even before she made the confession that it happened because she "wanted it to."

He considered telling her his initial thoughts about the matter, but settled for giving her a smile he truly meant while responding. "I don't quite know what to say, but I'm glad it worked out that way. And that you told me."

"Me too. Goodnight."

The killer looked at his phone. 3:00 a.m., Wednesday, June 16. Today would be the third day in the cheap motel in Uvalde. He'd only left for brief periods to get meals, then returned to watch TV and check the internet for any more news about the shooting at a ranch in the east end of the county. But so far, there had been no other mention beyond a blurb on Sunday evening saying "a shooting involving a federal law enforcement agent and another man, as yet unidentified, has resulted in two deaths. No other details are known at this time. Stay tuned to..."

Even without hearing further news reporting, he sensed it was over... almost. He wasn't even sure why he was staying here in this dump waiting for news that wouldn't change anything, not really. He had done exactly as ordered, but the thing had come unraveled anyway. In any event, he felt a need for a tidy ending to it all—everything and everyone—but for now, all he could do was contemplate various scenarios that might present themselves as the facts became clear—that is, if the unreasonable bastard in charge didn't screw up.

Over the past seventy-two hours, the killer had spent far too much time going over and over every single facet of the string of murders, at least what he knew of them. All of the replaying had done nothing to improve his outlook for the future; nor did it improve his chances of getting out of this without the unthinkable happening, the event that would completely turn life upside down.

Meanwhile, if he had to surf the damn channels one more time for something besides bad Mexican soap operas and game shows, he'd go nuts anyway—the knock on the door interrupted his disjointed thought process and made him flinch involuntarily. He went to the door and checked the peephole, seeing exactly who he expected, glaring at the door like some sci-fi monster because of the fish-eye perspective of the curved peephole lens. For a few seconds, he considered one of the scenarios he'd envisioned earlier, a particularly violent one, then thought otherwise and opened the door a crack.

CHAPTER 23

Diane had to leave the next morning to continue working on the shooting investigation after learning she would be operating from the San Antonio office until further notice. Carlton stayed behind and spent the week with Reynaldo and Paula, and worked for a couple of days with Francisco. Cow/calf pairs were selected for the sale by Reynaldo, and Carlton got speedy lessons from Francisco on how to separate them from the rest, herd them into the only pen with a loading chute, then slam the gate before the surly cow could reverse course and run over him. Those lessons were hard-learned and rough, and he swore off being a rancher long before the last pair was penned. Nevertheless, Francisco praised his work and taught him colorful phrases to describe the unruly animals, the high point of the entire exercise.

By Friday evening, he'd had enough cow punching and begged off going to the Saturday auction sale. He waited until well after dark to drive home to avoid rush-hour traffic, and it was after ten when he got to his apartment, tired, but relieved to be home and done with the ordeal in Sabinal. A heavy load had been lifted from his shoulders, and he was delighted to be looking forward to something as mundane as performing his Saturday cleaning ritual, then nothing else on the horizon but rest and recovery from his brief stint at being a rancher. Oh, and there was the matter of Agent Heather Colson, whom he hadn't heard from all week…

Checking his phones, he had a missed call from her on each of them, both made while he was battling stubborn cows. He tried calling her, but got no answer, and after a hot shower, he settled in for a night of TV, feeling better about things than he had in a month. The mysterious murders had begun almost exactly a month earlier, with no relief until the climactic shootout on Sunday, which resulted in two more deaths. Despite all the unanswered questions surrounding the case, it was good to know he wasn't involved any more, at least as a suspect. But he still wanted to ask Heather some questions, ones he hadn't wanted to ask Diane. During the past week, it had occurred to him that he was truly walking a minefield between the two female agents, and he wondered how to negotiate it without becoming a casualty.

When the newer phone rang just after eleven, he checked the number and couldn't suppress the slight unease it caused as he recalled the events since getting her first call back in May. Then he relaxed, deciding the feeling was due to the bad news she had delivered to him in recent weeks. With each call, she'd informed him of another murder, another body found near his location, and mounting suspicion of his involvement. That was all past now, he thought, and he looked forward to talking to her and thanking her for being a dissenter in the task force mob mentality.

"Hello there! Sorry I missed your calls, but I was busy being a cowboy."

"So I heard. You going to hire out as a full-time cow puncher?"

"Nope. Today was the last day of my career. All I want to do with cattle is eating an occasional hamburger."

"How are you feeling?"

"Fine. A little stiff, but that may be from trying to take on a thousand-pound cow."

She laughed, but it sounded forced. *"Maybe, but I heard you took another backflip dive onto a hardwood floor."*

"Guess I'm a slow learner."

"I told Diane about your previous experience doing that while saving my bacon in the parking garage."

"She mentioned it. Do you think that was a good idea, telling her about that?"

The pause told Carlton she was considering how to answer, and for a moment, he wished he hadn't questioned her risky disclosure to the IA agent. But when she spoke, he could picture her shrugging it off.

"That was only a problem with Stan Ikos. He kept pushing for another autopsy on Ramos' body, but no one else cared. Three agents survived that day, in large part because you were there and shooting."

The mention of Ikos was an opening Carlton had hoped for. *"Guess his days of worrying about that event are over,"* he said, hinting for her to give some insight of how the SAC's death was being viewed by the San Antonio office.

"Yes, that's for sure," she answered, her voice slightly unsteady at the end.

Carlton sensed a need for diplomacy in his response, maybe even some compassion. *"He and I had our differences, but no one can say he wasn't devoted to his job, I guess. Seems he really hated seeing scofflaws getting away with their crimes.*

"And I saw him killed by someone he apparently trusted. I've been in a similar situation, and it's not a pleasant one."

Again, she was quiet for a moment, comparing Ikos' death with Tino's. *"I hadn't thought of it that way. Of course, I wasn't privy to his connection to Brent Morris, but he apparently had something going with him that will take a while to figure out.*

"He was a difficult boss from time to time, but no one wished that kind of retirement for him."

Carlton thought it time to change gears. *"Speaking of that, I want to thank you for the heads up you gave me during this ordeal. For a while, you were the only one who had any thoughts about my innocence, and I appreciate it."*

"Carlton, you and innocence usually don't belong in the same sentence, but I know you pretty well, and I just couldn't see you for those hits on scumbags you never heard of."

He laughed at her observation of him. *"Yeah, I guess innocent is the least-suitable adjective for me—most of the time.*

"But this time, I got a real lesson in how people can be accused and railroaded by law enforcement."

The conversation went silent, and Carlton thought she'd ended it. When she spoke again, her tone was different, and he perked up to catch unspoken words as well as spoken.

"That may still be going on in some quarters," she said carefully.

Carlton took a stab at it, fairly sure he was right. *"Does that mean Agent Moore still has me down as a bad guy? What does it take to convince him?"*

"Well, he's read the reports and attended all the meetings, so he knows the details of the shooting at Reynaldo's ranch, including your status as a back-flipping survivor.

"But to him, it doesn't take you off the list for doing a few of the murders yourself, with Morris doing the others. He still likes you for Peters and

Crenshaw, with Morris popping Pembrooke and Mason. The other two are open in his mind, but your proximity makes him think you and Morris were in it together, sharing the hits. He thinks that's why Ikos and Morris came out there—to silence you."

Carlton sighed, seeing the logic, but angry at Moore's obstinate tunnel vision. *"I didn't even know there were two more Morris brothers until a few days ago! Where the hell does he come up with the connection?"*

When she answered, she used her patient, teacher-to-student one, the one that made Carlton grit his teeth. *"Carlton, are you forgetting all the material that was gathered on you and Randall Morris? That may seem a big stretch to you, but these guys are—were—brothers, remember?"*

"Yes, Agent Colson, I remember," he said icily (through gritted teeth), immediately regretting it and trying to make amends. *"Sorry, I don't mean to shoot the messenger, but we've been through this before, and there is no connection between me and Randall Morris that makes me good for being a hitman partner to his brother."*

"Carlton, with me, you're telling Noah about flood water. But I'm telling you how it appears to an experienced investigator looking at the information compiled by other experienced investigators.

"Oh, and not to piss you off further, but there's the matter of Paula Hendricks working for Randall Morris and meeting Bert Morris a few years ago, all of which she told Agents Maris and Belk. Therefore, it's ended up in the written reports, the ones everybody reviews."

Carlton took a deep breath and exhaled slowly. Now he understood why seeing Heather's phone number come up always caused an uneasy sensation in his stomach. The savvy agent had a good overview of the case and was able to see all points of view objectively, unlike himself. Still, he thought Darren Moore might have another agenda, and he decided to press it.

"You think your boyfriend might be chasing me around for personal reasons?"

"I wouldn't know, but since he's not my boyfriend any more, I'm not in position to ask him."

To that, Carlton relied on his stand-by, catch-all response, the clever one intended to impress her with his knowledge of the situation at hand.

"Oh."

As he feared, that ended the conversation, but at least he didn't look at his phone screen for answers. Instead, he flipped it shut and tossed it onto the kitchen counter with a clatter, replacing it with the TV remote. It was almost midnight, time for reruns of *The Twilight Zone*. After talking with Heather Colson, he felt a close kinship with Rod Serling.

Rod, that gal could have provided material for a dozen episodes!

Saturday turned out to be a normal clean-up day. By mid-afternoon, almost everything was done, so Carlton decided to finish up at his favorite car wash on West Avenue before getting a late lunch at one of several *taquerias* in the area. He spent an hour on the Cadillac, and had it looking so good he promised it a wax job...soon. As he pulled onto West, he noticed a black mid-size Ford sedan pulling across the lot quickly, and he braked to let the idiot get past without incident.

Another day in the big city, he thought, and drove to a *taqueria* on the east side of the street, near its intersection with Bitters Road. As he got out, he glimpsed the Ford tooling by at normal street speed. He headed for the entrance to the taco place, but kept the car in his peripheral vision as it turned left onto Bitters and disappeared. Two beef tacos and one *Dos Equis* later, he had forgotten the careless driver.

Back in the apartment, he saw the phone flashing on the counter and opened the text, a single-line message consisting of three words: *black ford fusion*. He sighed and wondered, not for the first time, why the woman couldn't simply send a comprehensive message. But at least she had given him another heads-up, this one timely and accurate, if incomplete. He didn't know what he could do with the information besides keep an eye open for the car...of which there must be a couple thousand in this city, he thought. Still, it was better than blowing off the incident, as he had already done.

By Sunday morning, the soreness of his physical exertions and mishaps had eased, and he went to Hardberger Park to walk a few miles, maybe even run a bit. When he pulled in to park, he scanned the lot quickly for the Ford, but saw only a few vehicles scattered throughout the sparsely occupied area. It appeared the only park-goers were in the dog off-leash area on the south end, leaving the walking and bicycle trails empty. That suited him just fine; it was already getting hotter by the minute, so a quick three-miles out and back would log him six miles before breakfast, enough for anybody, he thought.

The walk/run took almost an hour, and he was wringing with sweat when he huffed back to the lot. He popped the trunk to get a towel, then the driver's door. At that point, he sensed something wrong; the usual click was muted, as though the lock plunger hadn't moved the internal mechanism. Opening the door carefully, he glanced inside before entering, but saw nothing amiss. Remembering the strange encounter with Bert Morris, he stooped to check under the car.

"Don't bother looking, Carl, nothing's been added. I just wanted you at a nervous disadvantage while we spoke this morning, so I unlocked the door to get your attention. You're very attentive, by the way. Not many people would have caught that."

Carlton straightened up and stood in the open doorway of the car before turning to face Bert Morris. "I thought we had an understanding about your coming near me, Mr. Morris."

"We did, but things have changed considerably, as I'm sure you know," he said, easing his right hand across his mid-section toward the gun in the shoulder holster concealed by his jacket. His hand hovered just inside the jacket, telling Carlton all he needed to know: this Morris brother was as well-versed and comfortable using a handgun as Brent had been. Without whipping out a piece and shoving it in his victim's face, his intent was quite clear and somehow more threatening than a maniac pistol-waver. Like Brent Morris, Bert was a pro, Carlton thought, his mind instantly jumping to the conclusion that Bert and Brent had both been committing the shootings, which explained the rapid occurrences.

"Indeed I do," Carlton answered evenly, hoping to match Morris' professional move, then gain some psychological advantage as he delivered the punch line. "Your brother killed Stan Ikos and was then killed by a hunting arrow about two seconds later."

If Bert was worried about the same thing happening to him, he didn't show it by looking around for a ninja archer, dressed in black, arrow pulled back to release point. Instead, an involuntary flinch, followed by a pained look on Morris' face told Carlton he hadn't heard the details of his brother's death, even if he was aware of Brent's demise. As he watched the man closely, he saw the results of stress and lack of sleep: red-rimmed eyes and a two-day stubble made the oddly-dressed man look even more like a character in a well-produced stage play. Clearly, things had been going poorly for Bert Morris, and the harsh description of his brother's end might have been the wrong approach, Carlton thought, and he took steps to explore the extent of Bert's involvement, if any, without being shot in the process.

"You knew about the connection between Ikos and Brent, right?" he asked, knowing the answer and keeping his tone almost gentle.

The man laughed harshly. "Oh, I knew, alright! And I knew it would come to this one day, I just didn't know when. Or *how*, but it doesn't surprise me. We've both hated that son of a bitch for a long time, so I'm glad Brent took care of that piece of business.

"Unfortunately, you are also a piece of unfinished business, which I have been commissioned to take care of. You should have taken me up on the job offer, and this wouldn't be necessary, Carl."

Carlton hesitated, trying to follow his logic. "I'm not sure I understand, Mr. Morris. You wanted me to help you carry out your assigned hits? Or your brother's? And that would have done *what*, exactly, except make me a bigger suspect than I have been? Ikos and Moore went for that plan?"

Morris shook his head. "I didn't exactly get a go-ahead from Ikos and Moore, but they wouldn't have cared, as long as the jobs came off like they wanted. Brent and I were getting a bit overworked, and I thought the idea of you actually *doing* the deeds you were getting framed for had a real ironic twist, don't you?"

"Oh yeah, what a great idea! I'm surprised I didn't think of it myself, but since I didn't, what now?"

"So now we'll just be getting in your nice car and taking a little ride."

Carlton was shaking his head before Morris was finished speaking. "What is it about you two? I told your brother I wasn't getting in a car with him so I could be murdered and dumped in a ditch. He responded to that by putting two hot ones in Stan Ikos.

"Now, I'll tell you the same thing, but in a different way: *Bert, I'm not letting you get in the car with me!*" he said forcefully while jabbing a forefinger toward his face.

The bold stand would have looked good in a movie, but Carlton knew it was a good way to die immediately, without even a chance to get away, or change the odds against himself by following Morris' orders, at least in the short-term. Still, he clung to the logic that the only reason an adversary would force a change of locations would be to go somewhere more convenient to kill. Even with the sparse crowd in the park on this early Sunday, the setting presented more risk to Morris than being together inside his car, heading for who knew where. For the moment, Carlton was determined to keep Bert Morris feeling at risk—and himself alive.

Bert responded to Carlton's push-back in an unexpected manner: he smiled. "You know Carl, that sounds like something Randy would tell me about you."

The blank look on Carlton's face was soon replaced with a nod when he remembered Paula's rendition of the brotherly reunion years before, but Bert explained anyway.

"Oh, sorry, I mean *Big Mo*, as everyone around here knew my older brother. He was always telling me about your work, your penchant for complete honesty in your accounting to him for the vics' money and credit cards. He said you were the most stand-up button man on earth, and probably the smartest.

"Anyway, it doesn't surprise me that you don't want me in your car, driving off to a quiet spot. So, for that part of it, I'll have to call in my own shithead boss to convince you."

Still smiling, he used his left hand to extract a phone from his jacket pocket while his right hand never ceased hovering over the shoulder holster beneath his jacket. He flipped it open and pressed a single button, no doubt a speed-dial designated to Shithead. The murmured conversation took only a few seconds, then he flipped the phone shut and turned his head slightly toward the park entrance. Within a minute, the black Ford appeared. It cruised in and turned sharply toward the two men beside the Cadillac, but stopped well short, about thirty or forty feet away, engine idling, the dark tinted windows obscuring everything inside, despite the small opening at the top of the back one on the driver's side.

Carlton didn't like the way this was shaping up, and his mind raced to figure out a way to turn things in his favor before Bert and Shithead decided to kill him here and now. Bert could easily jump in the Ford and be gone before the dog walkers could figure out where the shot had come from. Carlton's body would be found beside his car, then the park would be closed and taped off with yellow crime tape, police swarming over everything…

"Tell me Shithead's number, Bert," Carlton said, extracting his own phone from the car door's storage compartment.

Looking mildly surprised, Bert shrugged, then pulled his phone back out and read off the number, giving Carlton ample time to punch in the digits. Carlton hit "Call" and raised the phone to his ear. The call was answered on the second ring, but no verbal response was made. It was exactly what Carlton had expected. What he hadn't anticipated was Bert Morris walking up to stand facing him, not three feet away. Backed up against his car, Carlton tried to ignore the man poised to overhear his phone conversation, but the hand still hovering over a weapon made it difficult.

"Agent Moore, how nice of you to join us in the park! Unfortunately, as Bert probably told you, I'm not going anywhere with either of you, just as I didn't go anywhere with Ikos and Bert's brother."

"Westerfield, you think you've got this all figured out, but you don't. And I intend—"

"I've figured out you and Ikos had your own button man to take care of people you couldn't get indicted," he interrupted.

"Shut up and listen, wise guy! You're just like all the scumbag bozos I've dealt with through the years—you're always convinced that you're a step ahead of everyone around you, especially law enforcement. Of course, in order to learn that, I had some inside information on you, right after I met you. A certain young woman already had you pegged in that department, and she was anxious to share her insight with me."

Carlton was uneasy with the direction of the conversation and he wanted to steer clear of it by claiming his standard position, even if Heather had related her own take to Agent Moore, her POC at the FBI during a task force meeting—or to Darren, her boyfriend during a pillow-talk session. The comparison would have been funny under different circumstances. *"I think you misunderstood. I have great respect for law enforcement and its capabilities, and I told Agent Colson that—in those very words."*

Moore laughed at his remark. *"And she told me that's what you would say. But she also mentioned that you put law enforcement and their criminal targets in the same category, 'not any different than the bad guys you chase' is the way she put it. She said that was your 'jaded observation' when she first met you in Galveston. That was a couple of years ago, right?"*

Carlton was surprised at the accuracy of the last part, but forced a laugh anyway. *"Well, Darren, having people murdered sounds like it makes a good case for my observation, jaded or not! And that makes you two no different from the criminal types you're chasing after, in case you need to check your FBI rule book. So no, I don't have any respect for a cop who uses a mechanic to make up for weak criminal cases. But normally, I wouldn't even care, because I don't give two shits about scumbags; plus, I understand your motives, you and Ikos. Both of you had the incentive to save your incompetent careers."*

Moore started to say something, but Carlton cut him off. *"But you and Ikos took it one step further. You instructed your mechanics to use an MO that would point to me, even though that was based on another pipe dream of Ikos. He kept trying to connect me to old murders here in San Antonio, from years ago. He couldn't do it, so he considered me one of his failures, a case he failed to get an indictment for. So you two formed a hokey 'joint task force' to chase me around the block a few times, interrupt my breakfast, plant a gun in my apartment, and drag us all in for questioning that didn't even address the alleged crimes.*

"But the tipoff was coming to my apartment after the body was found in Katy. Trouble was, you didn't count on my non-cooperation—like not being where the body showed up."

A long silence ensued while Moore was apparently digesting the news that Carlton had made the connection between him and Ikos, their in-house hitman, the poorly-disguised task force, and the slip-shod investigation that concentrated on the wrong suspect. Having just recited the very events he'd experienced, Carlton was again reminded how easy it would be for such tactics to intimidate a normal, everyday citizen, just a guy with a family, a job, and a home mortgage. Whether right or wrong regarding his life's decisions, right now he was sure the only reason he had been able to see the scheme was his own sketchy past, his connections to people like Big Mo, Tino Perez, Clive Millstone, and the recent tutorial he'd had from Diane Martin, plus the ongoing heads-up calls from Agent Heather

Colson. Oh, and his jaded observations regarding law enforcement went hand-in-hand, he reminded himself.

As though reading his mind, Moore chose that instant to speak again, this time to counter Carlton's accurate analysis by playing his trump card. *"Okay, try this one on for size, Westerfield: black ford fusion. That's a description of the car I'm sitting in, right? Coincidentally, it's the outgoing text I'm reading off of a certain burner phone."*

In a flash, Carlton now understood the short, cryptic messages, the abruptly cutoff conversations, and the overall inconsistencies in Heather's communications over the past weeks. Apparently, Moore had always been near, or had walked in unannounced at a crucial moment. Those were circumstances Carlton couldn't imagine Heather Colson enduring, and he wondered what had transpired to enable Moore to exert such dominance over the independent, self-assured female agent. This time, he had hacked her latest burner phone—or worse, had forcibly taken it from her. His next words told him which, and it was the worst scenario he could imagine.

"If you don't believe me, you can ask her yourself," he said, followed by a rustling sound, then a muffled voice and sounds of a struggle, followed by a slap, none of which Carlton needed the phone connection to hear. Instead, the sounds coming through the open window of the car carried Moore's intended message to him loud and clear. His next words only clarified it.

"Get in the fucking car and drive Morris exactly where he tells you! If you don't stay right behind me, I'll pull over and finish this part myself. And you, the recently jilted boyfriend, will look good enough for it to short-stop any investigation."

CHAPTER 24

Bert Morris must have known their destination, since he didn't have any more communication with Darren Moore during the drive. Instead, he sat on the passenger side, looking relaxed and issuing directions for every lane change and exit until they were headed toward Corpus Christi on IH-37. For Carlton, that was a relief, since he'd been unable to stay "right behind" the black Ford Fusion in the rapidly increasing morning traffic. Instead of mimicking Mario Andretti he was able to concentrate on ideas to extract himself and Heather from this, a one-way trip to their deaths.

The problem was, no options were readily available, not with two experienced gunmen, both killers, holding them captive. Though trained by different methods and at different schools, it made little difference whether it was Quantico or the back streets of Minneapolis; both were street-savvy, and it wouldn't be easy to change the outcome they had in mind for them. Worse, Moore's last words to him revealed that he, Carlton, would be accused of killing Agent Heather Colson in a fit of jealousy, while Darren Moore would be a hero for killing her murderer in some bizarre love triangle shootout. With Ikos dead, Moore would be clear of any pesky loose ends.

Not for the first time, Carlton cursed the day he'd lost his solitary life as a private contractor, working solely for Randall "Big Mo" Morris. But the choice hadn't been his, he reminded himself, and it opened a train of thought that might be useful...

"You know, Bert, things were a lot simpler when I worked for your brother," he said casually, knowing he might not have much time to accomplish anything before arriving at the scene of his and Heather's death.

Morris didn't even turn in his seat to answer. "Yeah? How so? This seems pretty simple to me. We're just taking a little Saturday morning drive to the country."

Carlton managed a laugh. "Oh, sure! You heard Moore. He's planning on setting me up for Agent Colson's death, then becoming a hero by killing me at the scene. But he left out any mention of your outcome, didn't he? That ought to tell you something."

Bert laughed, more like a short snort. "You think I'm going to fall for that crap, Westerfield? You turning me against Moore? Come on, Westerfield, you're a pro, you know how this works—I get paid, somebody gets dead."

"I don't think I have to turn you against him; he and Ikos already did that. I don't know what they've got on you and your brother, but it must be a real grip on the short hairs," he said, letting the crude remark soak in and hoping for the best. After a few seconds of silence, he tried again. "When I found out you were both from the Twin Cities area, I knew there was an old thing going on between the two of you, and a score to settle. Then I found out about Brent and his occupation as a button man—but no indictments appeared on his sheet. I knew the leverage had to come from his activities, but it wasn't drug-related, so I couldn't see the connection to the DEA."

"You're in the business. There's all sorts of ways."

"How did Ikos do it, anyway?" Carlton persisted "What did he threaten you with? And Moore's FBI. How did he get in on the deal? Does he have something on you, something the FBI would prosecute?"

The volley of questions made Bert shift uncomfortably in his seat, giving Carlton a glimmer of hope. A full minute went by without a word, and Carlton was frantically trying to come up with a different approach when the Minneapolis hitman spoke. "That's the worst part; *he* doesn't have anything, never did," he said, gesturing toward the car in front of them. "Neither did Ikos, because me and Brent were careful. But it was the *threat* of what they could reveal that kept us in line."

Carlton nodded, trying to appear genuinely interested, but not so nosy as to ask for details—and not rude enough to correct his clumsy grammar. It was excruciating, waiting while Bert Morris did some soul-searching before continuing the long, convoluted tale. He could only hope the gangster beside him felt compelled to continue soon, but it was two minutes, two miles closer to death, before he offered his next tidbit.

"I—we—have another brother. He's big in politics, of all things. Plus, our parents are still alive. Both are way up in their nineties, but living in a nice place and doing okay, not senile or anything. In other words, they keep up with everything our younger brother does."

He paused for a moment, and Carlton chanced a sidelong glance to determine its cause. A look of emotional pain was plastered on Bert's face, and it took a few seconds for Carlton to realize he was probably contemplating how to break the news of Brent's death to his elderly parents—or not. Or was it something else, a looming threat to the aspiring politician brother? The answer came soon, and Carlton had never been so glad to hear the phrase "long story short," since it might keep his and Heather's lives from being as short as they currently appeared.

"Long story short, Ikos didn't really have anything, but he kept telling us he could come up with enough evidence to indict the Pope and pin it on anybody he wanted to. To us, that meant he could plant dope or dope money in the pawnshop or on the books. He made us believe it, too, because he was pretty successful in Minneapolis. He got convictions left and right, so we knew he had the juice.

"Anyway, to keep him quiet, all we had to do was pay him. So we did—two grand a month for almost two years. It wasn't too bad, not at first. He let Brent keep doing his button work for a local contractor, a guy that Ikos knew and was probably tapping for a piece of every job at the same time. And the pawn shop did okay in those days, so it was worth the bite when Ikos got me off of a fencing beef with a small fine.

"Then the price went up—doubled—and that's when I came down here and talked to Randy about it. He told me all about you, and how you and him did business for years without a hitch, no bite from anybody. He made it sound so easy, so good, because of your secrecy and privacy hang-ups. I just gritted my teeth, listened, and wished me and Brent had done it differently.

"But it was already too late for us, we were fucked and locked in for four large a month, which we didn't have, not even the first month. Randy was pissed, but he gave me the bite money for that month, and said he never wanted to hear from either of us again. I went home and paid Ikos for the month, and that's when he told me we had to do some other stuff for him, but we could cut back to two grand, as long as we did every job he threw our way. That's when we figured out the real reason for the price increase—it was just to force us to take the next step, which was doing takeouts for him.

"The hits were always on some thug who'd gotten off an indictment. Ikos hated that shit, especially since those guys can't resist giving a middle finger to anyone they get over on. And as you know, those hits don't get much attention from cops; they don't give a shit about some scumbag dead in an alley.

"Anyway, for us it sounded okay, since we got back to the original two grand."

Again, the story faltered and Morris went silent, seeming to shrink back in the seat as he pondered the sordid history between his family and the crooked federal lawman. Carlton thought he might have re-ignited enough hate to throw a wrench in Moore's plan, but he couldn't be sure. He hesitated, then moved forward a notch, even if a bit timidly. "So you two are doing the jobs, and when Ikos gets transferred to Texas, he forces you to come down here and continue taking out his failed indictments?"

Morris nodded. "Yeah, and it was bad enough that he kept making us to do his dirty work for the past few years, but then he got nosy, started checking out the rest of the family. That's when he uncovered our youngest brother, Allen, who took a different path in life than his older brothers. He's a state legislator, and since he was elected the first time, me and Brent made sure we maintained our distance from him. But Ikos had contacts— like Shithead up there—so he found out we were brothers of the big-shot politico, Allen Morris.

"So right away, he reminded us that he could put the pinch on *anybody*. And we knew that *anybody* happened to be our brother, the legislator. And we also figured out Ikos and Shithead weren't even the top of the heap. Somebody's gotta' be greasing *their* chains, we thought, giving out information on Allen. It had to be somebody who's got a special connection to him, and a way to squeeze him.

"So I go visit Allen and asked him who was squeezing his balls. Turns out, it was a woman, an analyst who worked for a lobbying firm, or so he said. She spent a lot of time in the state capitol, schmoozing with every bigshot in sight. I guess she had some ax to grind with him, maybe banging him and he dropped her. I don't know the details."

Carlton was stunned as pieces started to fall together. Several mysteries were clearing up; however, this was a poor time to worry about something he and Heather wouldn't live to read about in the newspaper. He didn't want to interrupt the rambling tale, but the hated DEA guy was already dead, so pushing the Ikos story wasn't helpful. Nor was Allen's problems with some woman who had decided to get even by joining the shakedown game—not right now, anyway. No, he had to move the story along and arrive at a pressure point he could direct at the driver of the black Ford in front of them—and soon.

He forced his brain into high gear, trying to get the words just right. "Let me guess—Ikos could plant evidence of a drug beef on your brother, but Moore had something even better to use that would kill his political career. And your parents along with it," he added, hoping he was pushing the right button and not crossing some invisible line human beings held for their loved ones that might make Bert Morris clam up.

"Oh, yeah, with Ikos, it was drugs, of course! He's DEA. But with Shithead up there, it's even worse, if that's possible. Besides all the other shit they do, the FBI prosecutes child pornography passed across state lines, and he claims he can come up with a child porno sting that's infallible— irrefutable evidence just shows up on the target's computer from an out-of-state server. The feds' IT department gets an alert at the same time, which makes it easy to convince a judge for a search warrant, and boom, it's all over. And it's worse than drugs, because no matter the outcome of an investigation, just try explaining naked kids while you're on the campaign trail.

"And to answer your other remark, yeah, it would kill my parents. All us other kids were fuckups, but Allen distanced himself from us and became somebody. They're really proud of him. Hell, I am too," he added, looking over at Carlton, as though to convince him of his fraternal admiration.

At that point, the story dropped dead in its tracks. Morris shifted in his seat and craned his neck to see farther up the interstate. Carlton knew they must be approaching the appointed exit off the highway, and he couldn't keep from thinking about an alternate connotation of the word *exit* when it came to his and Heather's lives. There was no other reason to get off the interstate here than to pull over and kill them both. A mileage marker said it was just over a hundred miles to Corpus Christi, and Carlton was thinking he'd never see it again. Then he had an idea; a long shot, but it was the only chance he and Heather had to see another sunrise.

Time to make a deal, Carlton, even if it's with the Devil over there in the passenger seat. Don't screw this up!

"Do you know the name of the analyst gal?" he asked.

"Nope. Allen wouldn't say at the time, and I couldn't dig too deep, or he would be in worse shit. She's sharp, though, I gathered that much when Shithead told me she was concerned about Allen's brothers making her disappear. He said she'd better not have any accidents, or we'd regret it before God got the news."

"You get me her name, and I'll guarantee she'll quit leaning on your brother. And you won't need to do a thing but stay out of sight for a while after taking care of Shithead."

Bert issued another of his harsh laughs. "You can get this gal to stop squeezing his balls? How you plan to do that?"

"If Big Mo were still alive, he'd tell you I can handle the job," he said, pulling out all the stops to convince his prospective customer. "And you and Allen could start sleeping well."

Now Bert Morris turned in his seat to stare at Carlton while precious seconds ticked by, the two cars headed for execution detail at sixty-eight miles an hour. "I'll need a head start to get out of Texas. And I can get the name to you within a couple of weeks.

"You do this thing right, Carl, and I'll see that you have an old dog to kick around when you retire. But if you fuck it up..."

Bert's admonition regarding failure went unfinished when Carlton turned his head to stare back at him. "Big Mo must not have *fully* informed you about me, Bert," he said, his voice so quiet it barely carried across the car.

The hokey performance worked on his fellow button man. Bert relaxed his stare and turned back in his seat to watch the black Ford again. Carlton started breathing again, but barely. He hated theatrics, but convincing Bert Morris that he could resolve his brother's problem was necessary—if he wanted to live more than another ten minutes. He had to hope the Clint Eastwood, tough-guy delivery worked.

When the Ford's turn signal came on, he felt his pulse go up dramatically, and he wondered how Heather was faring in the car ahead. No matter the outcome, he had put all his efforts into a verbal goading, one he hoped generated enough doubt and hate in the man beside him to produce a different result than Darren Moore had in mind. He'd find out soon.

The exit serviced a parking pullout and picnic area. Short of being a true rest area, there were no restrooms; a paved road wound in and out of small stands of live oak trees, with short driveways forking off to provide picnic tables with some degree of privacy and protection from the bright-lighted eighteen-wheelers, which were the most frequent users of the facility. At this time of the morning, all the truckers had gotten back on the road, leaving the area completely deserted. Though only yards from the freeway, Carlton knew they were unlikely to be interrupted. Even a car stopping for a break would simply pull to another part of the park before stopping; it was the unwritten protocol for this type of pull-out. The only exception would be the occasional state trooper pulling through to check for illicit activity. The thought of that occurring now, when a citizen really needed a cop, made Carlton laugh, despite the situation he faced.

"Whatcha' laughing at?" Bert asked suspiciously as he reached for his phone. It must have been set to "vibrate only," since there had been no audible ring. Carlton just shook his head and wondered how the phone call would set things in motion.

"*Yeah?*" Morris barked.

"*We're walking both of them out to those trees on the right. The ones about thirty yards out.*"

"*Got it.*" Leaving his phone on, he barked at Carlton. "*Get out, Carl! And then don't move until I say so.*"

He snapped the phone shut and looked at Carlton. "Play this out, and don't fuck up!" he hissed. "Just do what I say and you'll both live. *Don't,* and you'll both die."

Carlton felt he should say something in acknowledgement, but he was too frightened to speak, so he just nodded. Opening his door, he got out and stood stock-still as Bert exited, his hand again inside his jacket, poised over his gun. In his peripheral vision, Carlton could see movement at the Ford. He strained to shift his eyes to the left without moving his head and saw the driver's door opening. A figure emerged; a man, who now stood facing the opposite direction. Only after shutting the door did he turn toward the Cadillac and glared at the pair standing in its open doors. About twenty feet separated the two vehicles.

Darren Moore was dressed for work, and Carlton had the absurd thought that he'd never seen the man in any other attire. Moore straightened his tie and stalked around the car to open the passenger-side rear door. Reaching inside, he jerked Heather from the seat, gripping her wrist so hard Carlton could see the pain on her face when she emerged. She was barely able to retain her balance as he dragged her in the direction of the trees, stumbling and nearly falling while Moore cursed her and jerked her arm even more savagely. She appeared to have been drugged, which Carlton thought might be a blessing under the current circumstances.

"We're gonna' walk over there, and don't even think about stumbling!" Bert commanded in a street-slang style that matched his riverboat gambler appearance. "You do, and I'll drill your ass before you hit the ground," he added, using the same savage tone as Moore and making Carlton think he'd misunderstood his fellow hitman's earlier remarks about living or dying. Before leaving the car, Bert remembered something else. "Gimme your phones. Come on, I know you got two of them, so hand them over! The car key fob, too."

Carlton retrieved both phones from the door compartment and handed them to Bert, along with the key fob, then shut the door and turned to see Heather continuing to struggle unsuccessfully against Moore. The FBI agent now had twisted her right arm against her back, pushing it upward under her shoulder blade to an impossible angle. The sight made Carlton wince, and he wondered how she kept from screaming with pain, drugged or not.

Moore guided Heather around to the far side of the grove and Carlton followed, now with Bert's automatic shoved into his back. When the group had all the trees between them and the main drive, Moore stopped abruptly and stepped back, shoving Heather to his right and bringing his service weapon to bear on Carlton's midsection. From seven or eight feet away, it wouldn't take much marksmanship to achieve what he'd promised.

"Do her first," he instructed Morris, nodding his head toward Heather. The look on her face expressed more terror than Carlton imagined a human being capable of, and he had a momentary urge to scream or cry at the sight. Fortunately, what happened next didn't give him time for shrieks, tears—or anything else.

Bert Morris quickly raised his pistol to her face, then shifted the muzzle to his right about twenty degrees. Darren Moore's face had just enough time to register the look of panic and astonishment before exploding in a shower of blood and tissue. Watching, Carlton flinched involuntarily, while an insane question formed in his mind: why hadn't he heard the shot? At their closely-grouped proximity, the muzzle report should have been deafening. Instead, he'd heard only a muffled pop, like a plastic bag being run over, its trapped air causing a minor burp.

He dared to turn his head and saw that Bert's pistol now had a sound suppressor attached to the muzzle. Though a poor time for reflection on past events, he recalled that when Brent had shot Ikos, the big auto pistol had been loud, so he'd not used a suppressor at the remote ranch—possibly because such an attachment can inhibit aiming the weapon, and he had not known what range to anticipate. However, here close to the highway and at very close range, Bert was quick to employ exactly what was needed. It told Carlton that the Morris brothers had taken their craft seriously.

He shifted his vision to Heather. She was trembling so badly it was difficult for her to stand, and she wobbled downward until her knees met the leaf litter carpeting the ground. He made a move to help her back to her feet, but Bert's harsh voice brought his attention back to the killer standing beside him.

"Don't move!"

With those two words, he withdrew a different gun from his trouser pocket and shot Carlton before getting in the Ford and driving away, leaving one very dead FBI agent, one very frightened DEA agent, and a wounded guy who didn't know what to expect next.

CHAPTER 25

Barely able to think, much less react, Carlton shook his head to clear the cobwebs and confusion. At first, that accomplished nothing beyond making him acutely aware of the sharp pain in his upper arm, where the .22 round had scythed a path through his bicep. Ignoring the pain, he focused on heading toward Heather, who had sunk down to the ground and was on hands and knees, shaking uncontrollably. He stooped beside her and cradled her clumsily in his arms, ignoring the wound and its trickle of blood making its way down to his wrist.

It was several minutes before either of them could speak or even think clearly. Finally, Carlton was able to form words into a question. "Are you able to stand up?"

She didn't reply at first, just pushed with her hands and managed to draw her feet under her body, then pushing hard to straighten her legs. Wobbly at first, the closer to upright she got, the better she moved. Carlton moved with her, and both of them finally managed a full upright position. Another minute passed before they staggered, arms entwined, toward the Cadillac.

About halfway to the car Heather chose that moment to answer his earlier question. "I guess I can stand up. It feels like it, anyway."

Carlton laughed without knowing whether the answer was intended as a joke or if she wasn't yet fully in control of her voice or actions. Either way, he thought, they were both alive, the killers were gone, and it appeared they would survive this ordeal, much as they had after the shootout with Brujido Ramos.

When she spoke again, he knew she must have had the same thought. "We've got to stop meeting like this. We don't have enough blood to survive any more shootouts with bad guys," she added, choking on the weak laughter her joke caused. She stopped to cough and clear her throat, then seemed much better.

Carlton found that hilarious, and they both collapsed onto the hood of his car, giggling insanely for almost a full minute. Five more minutes went by as their emotions steadied, their thoughts cleared, and both were able to contemplate their next move.

"Bert took my key fob, but there's a spare underneath the car. I'm not sure we should leave, though, not without Diane or somebody coming out here and doing the onsite part of the investigation."

Heather still seemed to be a bit foggy, and she thought about it for a long moment before responding. "I guess we need to stay put and get somebody out here? Maybe we can flag somebody down and borrow a phone?" she suggested in the form of questions, as though she didn't quite comprehend what was happening.

"Okay, let's walk out together. Nobody's going to stop and help a bloody man, but everyone will stop for you."

The pair walked up the narrow pullout toward the main drive, where both were stunned to spot a state trooper SUV parked about a hundred feet away, facing their direction. Already dreading the long process that would follow, they walked quickly to the vehicle, each raising a hand in greeting when the trooper, a thin black man, ran his window down and began a quick, methodical appraisal of the couple. It only took seconds for him to fall into his training and get to the point.

"Sir, how did you get injured?" he asked sharply, pointing at Carlton's bleeding arm.

"I was shot by a man named Bert Morris."

"*What?* When?"

"About nine or ten minutes ago. Another man was shot and killed. He's over there behind that grove of trees."

The trooper got out of his vehicle quickly, his eyes never leaving the pair, while his hand stayed near his service weapon. Clearly, he had taken his training seriously. His name tag read "Simpson," and he was all business. "I want both of you to step over here. You, sir, put your hands on the vehicle door. Keep them where I can see them. And you, miss, step down here and do the same.

"Do you have any identification?" he asked, looking from one to the other as they headed toward their assigned points against the patrol vehicle.

Heather shook her head. Carlton motioned in the direction of his car. "I do. It's in my car, parked just down that narrow driveway. It would be quicker to contact Diane Martin of the—"

"Sir, just keep quiet and let me ask the questions. And move to the vehicle like I instructed you."

Both did as instructed, but not without Heather giving it a try. "Officer, I am Agent Heather Colson with the Drug Enforcement—"

"Miss, please just do as I instructed you!" Simpson repeated, his voice going up in volume.

When both were planted against the state vehicle, Simpson demanded their full names, then got on his phone and called in the situation (omitting any mention of a second shooting victim) including a request for onsite medical treatment. Watching and listening as he recited the information to someone, somewhere, both of them figured it was the best outcome they could hope for. Their names, especially Heather's, would elicit a response from her agency at some point, and the long, torturous process would be sped up considerably—or so they hoped.

Meanwhile, Carlton had to resist the urge to ask Officer Simpson if he had any donuts left over. He could have repeated the question a dozen times over the next twenty minutes as patrol units from SAPD, Bexar County, Wilson County, ICE, and the nearby Border Patrol station descended on the spot. No one inquired about the other shooting victim, leaving both Carlton and Heather to wonder if the trooper had forgotten about it, or had simply dismissed Carlton's claim. They also considered what the outcome of this debacle would be if, by some miracle, Darren Moore were still breathing—for the moment.

Last to arrive was an ambulance, its lights and siren going full-tilt. Shrugging off Simpson's assistance, Carlton walked to it feeling like a complete idiot, even though his arm hurt like hell. The personnel were on him like ants on honey, and within minutes he was washed, rinsed, scrubbed, sterilized (the wound, that is) and given a couple of shots. Carlton asked if the shots prevented lead poisoning, but got only a blank stare for his efforts at comedy. Standing at the open back door and watching the procedure, Heather rolled her eyes, telling Carlton she was back to normal.

However, when the medics descended on her, it was time for Carlton to grin at her predicament.

As the medical team finished up examining Heather, Officer Simpson strode toward them and asked about the other victim. Both turned and pointed toward the body's location, while Simpson looked back and forth between the pair suspiciously. Refusing their offer to accompany him, he bade them to "stay put" and headed toward the grove alone. Within minutes, he returned to report his findings, and several other officers started toward the spot, again reminding Carlton of picnic ants.

Almost two hours later, both had told their stories several times to several different people, when an unmarked sedan rolled into the pullout, going faster than Officer Simpson apparently deemed appropriate. He put on his angry face and stalked out into the driveway, holding up his right hand in a "halt" gesture.

The sedan's brakes squealed as Diane Martin came to a stop and opened the door before the car quit rocking on its suspension. Dave Fowler emerged from the passenger side as Simpson headed purposefully toward the car. Just as he opened his mouth to begin a long scolding, both agents converged on him and proffered their badges while simultaneously citing their names and respective positions and agencies. Simpson's mouth stayed open for several seconds before he remembered to close it.

Before Diane had finished her self-introduction, Simpson opened his mouth again, but she didn't give him a chance to talk. "Officer, thank you for your on-site actions and your prompt reporting of this. We appreciate your help and your professionalism, since I can see it must have been quite unusual to encounter this pair in such a state of disarray, telling you about a murder.

"However, Agent Colson and Mr. Westerfield are indeed who they say they are, and the investigation into the events of the past few hours will be handled jointly by the DEA and the FBI. We will be in touch with you for your report as first responder."

She went on to explain the previous weeks' events, including the shooting at the Sabinal ranch and the relationship between those occurrences and today's shooting. In the end, Trooper Simpson was nodding thoughtfully, thankful this mess was to be handled by someone else.

Abandoning Simpson, she moved toward a knot of officers from various agencies and repeated her spiel about Heather and Carlton, then thanked them and added, somewhat forcefully, that they could all leave the area. As if to underscore her request, two more plain sedans arrived, occupied by plainclothes officers, a couple of them agents from the questioning session at the FBI building two weeks earlier.

Beyond Simpson's patrol SUV, Agent Fowler was carrying out the same exercise with another group of law enforcement people. Still, it was over a half-hour before the local and state patrol cars began leaving the pullout. Watching the exodus, Carlton wondered if the nearest Starbucks could handle such a rush.

Escaping their new captors, he led Heather toward Diane's car, where they stood waiting for whatever came next when the others were effectively shooed away. "I've never been so glad to see two *more* cops arrive on the scene," he quipped to Fowler and Martin as they watched the last of the state and county patrol cars pull onto IH-37. "I thought we'd never get to explain anything beyond our names and what we were doing here. They weren't even interested in knowing there was a deceased victim beyond my car."

Diane smirked and Fowler grimaced at his cynical report, accurate though it was. Apparently, the two of them weren't in any mood for levity, and with good reason. The death of a senior FBI agent, even though it marked a critical milestone in the ongoing corruption investigation, would set in motion more weeks of work for the Internal Affairs section of both agencies. However, for the moment, Heather and Carlton didn't share their somber mood. Carlton, having experienced Agents Moore and Fowler on occasion, did wonder briefly about Dave Fowler's presence at the scene of his partner's murder, or if he would soon become a subject of the ongoing investigation regarding his partner's misdeeds.

Heather seemed to drift in and out of varying states of fright and relief, one emotion changing into the other every few minutes, making Carlton wish the medics had checked her for administration of a drug by Moore. Just when he started to ask her about it, she switched to the relief mode and a normal demeanor, leaving him unsure if he should say anything. Above all, both were elated at being alive, and all they wanted was for the immediate stressful experience to be over so they could leave.

It was not to be.

Diane morphed into Special Agent Martin of the Drug Enforcement Administration, the local lead investigator. As such, she made sure Carlton and Heather had minimum contact with each other "in order to protect the integrity of each one's recounting of events." From the Sabinal debacle, Carlton knew it was coming, but it didn't make it any more palatable when he and Heather were isolated in separate agency cars for "integrity's" sake. It gave him time to worry about his car, parked a couple hundred yards away with agents swarming around and through it, and Heather, who had no one to keep an eye on her during her mysterious mood swings.

Just as in Sabinal, it was a long time before the main investigative team arrived. Luckily, several of its members were still in San Antonio, so the ball was rolling much quicker. And just as before, Carlton told the story over and over, making sure he included every detail, every time. In particular, he recounted with certainty the vague reference to Brownsville that Morris had made to Moore during the phone ordeal:

"I could only hear Morris' end of the conversation, but he said *'yeah, I know how to get to Brownsville, and I know the place we're supposed to be picked up.'* Yes, those were his exact words, I'm sure of it. So Moore must have used the specific word to elicit that response, a repeat of their destination. They were headed to Brownsville, and didn't care if I overheard. After all, I was going to be killed."

After the third telling of the outright lie, Carlton had almost forgotten the blurry aftermath of the shooting and his brief glimpse through the trees of the black Ford cutting across the median, then turning north on IH-37, headed back to San Antonio…so, by the fifth rendition of the story, he was *certain* that the Ford, driven by the nattily-dressed Bert Morris, had pulled out of the rest area and headed *south*—toward Brownsville.

It's always best to tell the truth, but it's rare that anyone can tell what it is!

CHAPTER 26

It was late afternoon before the murder scene was cleared by the DEA and FBI. Carlton fished the extra key from beneath his car—which had been searched at least four times, with none of them finding the key fob—and helped Heather into the passenger seat. She seemed to be doing alright in the emotional department, but as the hectic day progressed, she looked and acted extremely tired—no, *exhausted*, as though she could barely make her muscles do her brain's bidding. Carlton again wished he had informed the ambulance personnel that she may have been drugged so they could have checked her system. However, at the time, she'd seemed to be recovering, so it hadn't felt right to butt into her medical help. Having been kept separated during the questioning, he didn't know if her interrogators had inquired, but suspected they hadn't—they only wanted information to further their investigation, not to worry about an agent's health. The whole sorry mess reminded Carlton of his last conversation with Agent Darren Moore, during which he had chided him about his "jaded opinion" of law enforcement...

Gosh Darren, wonder how anyone would form such an opinion?

Now, he didn't want Heather to be alone...and that went for himself, too. "I'll take you home if you want, but if your place doesn't feel right, you can stay at mine for as long as you want," he offered while buckling his seat belt.

"That's really nice of you, Carlton, but you don't have to do that. I'm a big girl—a cop, for cryin' out loud, so I can handle it."

"I know you can, but that's not the point. It's been a helluva day for both of us—for you more than I. I'm your friend, and I want to help if I can. So think about it," he added.

She nodded and remained silent while Carlton was maneuvering his car out of the tree grove and onto the main driveway of the pullout area.

Accelerating onto IH-37, he exited at the next off-ramp and turned around, back toward the city. Approaching the crime scene from the opposite direction made it no less ominous, he realized, looking across the median while the pain in his arm reminded him of the day's violent events. He glanced over at his passenger and saw that she had her eyes shut, but not in a fashion that indicated she was trying to sleep; instead, he got the impression she simply didn't want to see anything that would recall the day.

After they passed the pullout, she spoke up without opening her eyes. "I think staying at your place might be a good idea. Can you take me by my apartment so I can get some stuff?"

"Of course."

It was late evening when they arrived at Carlton's place. Heather had showered and changed at her apartment, and all he wanted was the same for himself. Thirty minutes and a long, hot shower later, both were sitting on the couch, feet propped on the coffee table, and beverages in hand— wine for her, a *Dos Equis* for him. For the first time in hours, they were able to relax, and Carlton hesitated to open a conversation regarding the day's nasty business.

He didn't have to.

"It's hard to believe all that's taken place in the last two months," she began. "Make that three months, if I count meeting Darren."

"Where'd he come from, anyway? Did he and Ikos already know each other?" Carlton asked, trying to get the conversation going in an informational direction without prying into her personal relationship with a man who'd been gunned down before eyes her a few hours ago.

"I got the impression they knew each other from somewhere else, but I asked one time and got snubbed. That was after Jeffrey Bales and I started seeing inconsistencies in the investigation, things that weren't going like they usually do. He got the same treatment when he asked on his end—it was like no one wanted to be questioned about their motives, previous relationships, and duty postings, nothing."

"Which only made you and Bales more suspicious."

She nodded.

"Did Ikos approach the local FBI office about forming the joint task force, or does that kind of decision come from above?"

She shook her head. "The higher-ups have to approve ultimately, but it's always after the fact, and they hardly ever refuse implementation of one, or call for a task force to be disbanded. So Ikos was the one to put it in motion."

"Another reason for you and Bales to think something wasn't right."

"Of course. That, and my—our personal relationship. Darren was always high-strung, but he began to show some tendencies that reminded me of my ex-husband—some verbal outbursts at first, just to emphasize a point he was making. But the verbal abuse became physical when I outright confronted him about you being good for the Ruiz murder, which had happened the night before.

"We were at his house, just discussing it at first, having a meaningful conversation—I thought. Then he started railing on about the body being dumped onto the railroad track in Sabinal, how you seemed like exactly the kind of perp who would do something like that, blah, blah. I asked him how he had formed that opinion, and what information he had on your psychological profile. He grabbed me by both arms and told me to shut up, I didn't know anything, leave the profiling to the FBI...then he shoved me, really hard. I fell back and hit the dining room table hard enough to bruise my back pretty badly.

"That's when I knew something wasn't right in his motivation. It wasn't just trying hard to do his job well; he and Stan were both *obsessed* with putting you away for the murders."

"Which ended up getting both of them murdered," Carlton concluded. "By the very guys they forced into doing the dirty work for them. There's a certain poetic justice to that, I guess."

"You think so?" she asked. "Will justice be served completely when they catch up with Bert Morris? You know, the *final scene* kind of justice?"

"Maybe so. I'm not much of a philosopher, but I know the Morris brothers had plenty of reason to hate those two guys."

Her questioning look led him to tell her the history as related to him by Bert Morris, on the way to their execution. At the end of the tale, she was shaking her head in disbelief at the long, ongoing extortion racket being carried out by her boss and her former boyfriend. She played over the setup in her mind a few minutes before commenting. "You think that's an accurate take on it?"

Carlton shrugged. "I don't know. But when he mentioned how it would destroy his parents if the brother was publicly besmirched, I think something snapped in him, he made the decision to do what he did—use the privacy of the scene to kill Moore, then shoot me to make it look a little more believable before hauling out of there."

She shook her head again. "My God, I can't believe I couldn't see how Darren was so twisted. I mean, in Stan Ikos, he was my boss, so I always took issue with whatever he said. It's the American way to disagree with your boss, or think he's a jerk.

"But with the relationship with Darren...I should have been able to see he was an outright criminal, not just a guy who pushes women around, like my husband did. But both of them tried to convince me they were right each time we had a disagreement, so I should have seen the parallel, especially the outright *malice* each of them displayed."

"Well, you didn't need Darren any more than you needed your husband," Carlton said, immediately regretting the condescending tone. "I mean, there are degrees of malice in everyone, but why should you put up with any at all? Life's too short—make that too *long*—to put up with much grief."

She thought about that a moment before answering. "I hope I've finally learned that. And I hope I can spot someone who keeps trying to make me think they're right all the time, or that they're more capable than what they are." She paused again, then looked at him before continuing. "I guess that's what appealed to me about you. You never tried to sell yourself as anything but who you are."

"If that's a compliment, I'll take it. If not, I'll live with it anyway, because I think that's a fair assessment of yours truly."

The tinny ring that passed for a doorbell interrupted them. Carlton went to the door, then looked through the peephole when he remembered Bert Morris was still on the loose, his final intentions still a mystery. There was always a possibility that the professional gunman had had second thoughts about letting anyone from the recent murder scene survive.

It was Diane Martin, looking tired from her long day. Carlton turned to raise his eyebrows in question and silently mouthed her name. Heather looked confused at his poor charade technique. The doorbell rang again, and Carlton simply opened the door.

What worse can possibly happen after the last two Morris brothers failed to kill me? Well, I suppose Paula could show up!

"Hi, there! Mind if I come in?"

"Not at all. Come on in. Something to drink?" He opened the door fully, not knowing what else to do.

As expected, both women were embarrassed by the situation, but Carlton did his best to alleviate any discomfort. "Heather and I just going over the chain of events that led up to today. I was telling her about the Morris bro—"

"I'm sorry, I didn't realize—I tried to call, but both of your phones went straight to voice—"

It was Carlton's turn to interrupt her interruption, first by laughing at the dilemma the three of them shared, then explaining why their phones went unanswered. "Diane, it's not a problem, you're not interrupting anything.

"But as to the phone mystery, the last time I saw mine, Bert was stuffing them in his pocket. When they catch up with him, he'll probably surrender just to avoid hearing any more ringing phones. Anyway, I'd sure like to get both of mine back."

Heather spoke up. "I think mine is somewhere in the car that Morris escaped in, too. Darren—Agent Moore—took mine away when he saw I was texting a warning to Carlton.

"So he's got all of ours," she added with a nervous laugh, still uncertain about the *debacle á trois* they'd landed in, especially with the lead of her employer's Internal Affairs division gazing at her as though evaluating every move she'd made with the sole man in their midst.

Carlton, for his part, did a good job of fetching the wine, filling glasses, and turning attention away from their awkward fix and onto something less…sticky. He motioned Diane toward the recliner and retreated to his usual perch at the breakfast bar before speaking.

"You had a long day, I see," he said, nodding toward the window, where dusk was in full swing, darkness not far off.

"Yes, another one. This is unlike any assignment I've ever handled, and I've had some doozies."

"Will today's events make it worse, or does it tie up some loose ends?" Heather asked, stifling a yawn and leaning back. "Or can you say?" she added, then closed her eyes to wait for the answer.

Diane laughed. "If I knew, I could say. It's not like I need to keep you out of the loop.

"As to the two rogue agents, Ikos' actions are being uncovered pretty rapidly. A review of every psych exam he's had throughout his career has already begun to determine why his behavior wasn't suspected or even foreseen as remotely possible. When it's all over, that may bring about a new method for periodic testing for all agents.

"But Moore's involvement with the Morris brothers may open up a whole new box of worms. It will probably entail opening an entirely separate investigation, but I just don't know at this stage. If so, it will be the same at FBI as at the DEA: full career review from the day he started.

"A lot will depend upon apprehending Bert Morris, and that's not looking too promising right now."

Carlton marveled at her command of the overall story, her ease of discussing all aspects of the case. He recalled something from a long-ago conversation and decided this would be the time to air it. But first he wanted to lay out some bait from a very recent conversation, while she was tired and not entirely on top of her game.

"What about keeping an eye on Allen Morris?" he asked casually. "You think Bert is likely to contact him?"

"Probably not a bad idea," she answered quickly, her information-rich mode of the past few minutes slipping easily into the take-charge boss mode. "I can contact some help in the Minneapolis office—"

Her voice stopped short as she realized she'd stepped into the trap Carlton had laid. The look on her face told him that she knew a lot more than she was telling him and Heather—and probably a lot more than would appear in her reports—those reams of paper concerning the extortion scheme being carried out by senior agents of two high profile agencies.

She recovered quickly, maybe too quickly for Heather to see it, since she was almost dozing and not directly facing her as Carlton was. "How did you know about Allen?" she asked quietly, casting furtive glances over at her fellow DEA agent, who now had her head back, eyes closed.

"Bert Morris told me. How about you? How did you know?"

Diane saw her best defense was a strong offense. "Wait a minute. I went through the transcripts of your interviews today, all six of them. I didn't see any reference to...that particular subject. Please don't tell me you withheld information from a federal investigator."

Carlton smiled. "I didn't withhold anything. I was asked dozens of questions, and I answered every one of them to the best of my recollection and as fully as I could—under stressful circumstances, I might add, since no one seemed concerned that I'd been shot.

"Not a single one of the agents asked me the specifics of what Bert Morris said, but I told them about his accosting me in the park, calling Moore to force me into going where told, and his driving instructions to the picnic area. I told each one about Agent Moore's actions and remarks, including his plans to kill Heather and put the blame on me. I think I covered those conversations almost, if not completely, *verbatim*.

"Oh, plus, I told them what I'd overheard about their plans to get to Brownsville. Does that sound like withholding?"

By now, Heather was picking up on the change in tone of the conversation. She opened her eyes and swiveled in her seat on the couch in order to look more directly at Diane. Then she turned to Carlton to speak. "Who's going to Brownsville? What's there?" The look on her face said she wasn't keeping up with the conversation very well.

"That's where Bert and Moore were headed after they finished with us," he informed her.

"So you think he went there anyway, without Darren?" Heather asked, looking from Carlton to Diane, then back.

Now worried about coming under fire from two directions, Diane squirmed to retake control. "Yes, but that's an area I have to avoid talking about, even with you, Heather. Or, for that subject, I guess I have to say *Agent Colson*." She managed a nervous laugh at the fake formality.

Heather responded with a yawn. "Suits me. I've had all the intrigue I want for one day—*Agent Martin*."

Diane, relieved at seeing an escape, took that as her cue. "Well, I need to be going, so the two of you can get some much-needed rest."

She rose from the couch and headed toward the breakfast bar where she placed her empty wine glass. Passing in front of Carlton on his barstool, she leveled her now-trademark gaze on him and winked. He gave her one in return, the first time he'd winked at a woman since that time in Vietnam…it had seemed normal then, but pretty lame now.

EPILOGUE

September came with only slightly cooler temperatures, so sitting on the front porch at Reynaldo's ranch house was the perfect end to a long day of helping with ranch work. Carlton was sipping a *Dos Equis* while Reynaldo and Paula had iced tea. The evening's discussion had been of the events of almost three months ago, and Carlton had been able to fill in the blanks for his friends, who had wisely stayed in Wichita Falls for the past two months.

Of all the players in the action, one name had kept coming back into play, and it did again, this time with a big surprise for Carlton.

"Diane's retiring from her government job and coming back to work for me," Reynaldo declared. "In fact, she will be showing up here pretty soon. I told her we were out here and to come out for the weekend so she and I can go over some things."

Paula leaned forward on the swing she was sharing with Reynaldo. "You noticed Reynaldo didn't confer with you first, didn't you?" she stage-whispered. Then, laughing, she added, "You don't really mind, do you?"

"Of course not," he said, meaning it. "I've talked with her a few times, but it was always some point or another that she was asking me about for the investigation. It'll be great to have a normal conversation with her."

"We think she's a good fit for you," Reynaldo announced, getting a nod of agreement from Paula. "A better fit than Heather."

His proclamation got a shrug from Carlton. "Yeah, I guess…uh, she's okay. I mean, Diane's great. Well, *both* of them are. I'm just not sure I'm the guy for her—either one, I meant," he added, hedging in order to avoid the uncomfortable conversation and botching it in the process.

His rambling answer and obvious discomfort got a laugh from Paula, who reached over to pat his arm. "He's just ragging on you, Carlton. He knows it's none of his business, but somebody—"

"Somebody has to do Tino's lines for him, and who better than Reynaldo Gomez?" Carlton finished for her, and all three smiled at the memory of their departed friend and his gossip antics.

The placid scene continued while the sun sank behind the house. Just at dusk, a car came through the gate and pulled to a stop in front. Diane Martin got out and retrieved an overnight bag from the back, while her hosts and Carlton converged on her. By the time she had gotten settled into the house, Paula had snacks ready, and the four enjoyed a meal together for the first time since breakfast at Max and Louie's, some three months prior.

Afterwards, the four migrated back to the porch and talked until full darkness had set in, interrupted when the moon began rising. As if on cue, Reynaldo and Paula soon claimed sleepiness and abandoned the couple, leaving them alone together for the first time in months. It should have been an ideal arrangement, but Carlton was unsure about what to say or do and figured Diane was of like mind, judging by the lag in conversation.

So much of their words and actions of recent weeks had been dictated by events around them, it seemed as though they were meeting on a personal basis for the first time, or starting over in a relationship that had held some promise when they had first become acquainted. At least, that was how Carlton was viewing this...*date* arranged by their mutual friends. Plus, there remained some unanswered questions regarding the ongoing investigation, questions he didn't want to ask— and he wasn't sure he wanted to know the answers to them, anyway. Oh, and the unfinished job he'd promised to handle...

While he had spent two or three minutes mulling over the touchy situation before him, Diane made a decision to get to the heart of the matter by clearing the air about something she felt important. "Carlton, are you sleeping with Heather Colson?"

The question surprised him, but he hid his astonishment pretty well by shaking his head before verbally responding, which gave him a few seconds to formulate his answer. "No, I'm not. I think she and another agent have a thing going, but you didn't hear that from me."

"Does that mean you would be sleeping with her if it weren't for Jeffrey Bales?"

Carlton laughed. "I should have known not to try to fool an IA cop by leaving out his name. Internal Affairs hears all, sees all, knows all, right?

"But no, that's not the reason. We had a short…uh, *fling*, but it ended at about the right time, I'd say. We both moved on."

"She moved on to Darren Moore. And you…?"

"I just moved on."

"You've always been pretty good at that, haven't you?"

"It seems I get lots of practice."

That got a laugh from her. "I think we all practice what we like doing. And I think you like moving *on* better than moving *in*."

"It always happens when I've just renewed my apartment lease, and I don't want to lose my deposit."

Another laugh, this one a bit nervous. "I'm not proposing that you move in with me, Carlton. I don't even have a place to move into myself, not yet. I'm just trying to understand you."

"Good luck with that. Let me know when you figure me out, will you? I'd like to understand me, too."

She got quiet after that, for several minutes. When she spoke, her voice sounded different; inquisitive but firm, almost to the point of demanding.

"You figured me out, didn't you? My connection to Ikos and Moore. The Morris brothers. Eventually, even Allen Morris. How did you do that?"

Carlton shifted uneasily in his chair, uncomfortable with disclosing things about her he wished he hadn't learned. But it had to be done—tonight.

"The night we met at Ernesto's. I was explaining my trepidation at revealing my past, and you told me—us—that you weren't judgmental and didn't mind exploring both sides of the law, and I wondered what you'd done on the other side. Whatever it was, I was impressed and more comfortable after your saying that.

"So, the next day at the park, when I noticed you spoke of Ikos and Moore, I thought you might be hooked up with them already, or knew them better than you let on. I just didn't know what it meant, what *they* were up to."

"What made you think I already knew them?" she asked, confusion on her face.

"You used both of their first names. To my knowledge, I had not called them by their first names, but you somehow knew it was 'Stan' and 'Darren.' At the time, I dismissed it, figured I was mistaken about not using their names.

"But when Bert Morris was riding with me to my execution, he told me about Allen, which brought up two more points: one; when you searched data bases for the Morris brothers—right out in that driveway, with Paula looking on—you surely should have found a brother who is a state legislator, and maybe a blurb on Randall. Instead, you found only Brendon Garth Morris, twin brother to Bertrand Gayle Morris. So I figured you sandbagged on that computer search."

"And point number two?" she asked, clearly interested in Carlton's low-tech methods of simple mental deduction, instead of digital wizardry.

"Bert suspected Allen was susceptible to extortion, so he went to him and flat-out asked. Allen admitted that a woman—an analyst for a lobbying firm he was suing—had something on him, or could put something on him that Ajax wouldn't take off. Whether personal or business, he didn't say. But since you worked in the Midwest as an analyst for a lobbying group, I figured it was a good bet you were that woman."

Diane laughed at that. "Carlton, Texas isn't the only big area in the world! The Midwest covers twelve states, and has thousands—"

"I know, I was excellent in geography. I can even name all twelve of them.

"But only Minnesota has a state legislator named Allen Morris, who got in a flap with a lobbying group about three years ago. He sued the lobbyist and won his next election easily due to popular support for bucking the system. The lobbyist's name is—"

"How did you find all this stuff?" Her interruption query was delivered about two octaves higher than needed.

"—and the analyst working for that group was a woman named Diane Martin."

"Dammit Carlton, tell me where you got that! Otherwise, I can be sure you're just making it up as you go."

"Same answer as before: Bert Morris told me. He recently got the entire story from Allen, then texted it to my phone—the phone he took from me on Sunday, June twentieth, then mailed back to me at my apartment. I got it about a month ago, with the text already entered on it in draft form, ready to be sent."

"You've been in touch with Bert Morris?" she asked incredulously. "Exchanging information with a wanted felon, across state lines? Do you realize telecommunications across state lines brings the RICO statute into play?"

He shook his head. "I'm not sure about that. I said it was entered on my phone in a text draft, *ready* to be sent, but was never sent. He wanted me to have the information, but he didn't want it drifting around in cyberspace. So, it was never *telecommunicated.*"

"Still, it was mailed to you across state lines." She paused for a moment before letting her cop voice kick in to emphasize the final line of her scolding. "Do you realize you could go to prison for that?"

It was exactly the threat he'd been waiting for. He leaned forward in his seat and smiled at her. "Sure. You think we could get adjoining cells?"

She stared at him a long moment, the laser beam unfaltering. Carlton matched her look with his own direct eye contact; not threatening or intimidating, but steady and confident. Finally, she sighed and leaned back in her chair. A look of defeat replaced the laser beam, and it was almost a full minute before she spoke. "I contacted Allen soon after the night I came to your apartment. He said he had already heard about Ikos' being killed. I told him about Moore meeting the same fate, but I dodged his question about who killed them. He probably knew, or at least suspected, his brothers had something to do with both deaths.

"As to my part, I told him that our relationship was finished. He didn't say anything to that, but I'm sure he took it in the right context, since Ikos and Moore were out of the picture."

"I'll bet he was relieved to get off the hook," Carlton said, genuinely surprised that she had interpreted his wink from their last encounter as a warning that he could, at the least, wreck her career and, at the most, get her imprisoned with what he knew. He hadn't been sure the wink would do anything—it hadn't worked that time in Vietnam.

Once again, Diane was reading his mind. "When you mentioned Allen's name, I knew you were onto something; I just didn't know how much you had. Ikos and Moore were both dead by then, but I was concerned that you'd let Heather in on it, and she'd do anything to get me sacked and indicted for extortion and blackmail. She's not a fan, you know."

Carlton shrugged. "At that time, I just had a strong hunch. Everything was circumstantial, but taken as a whole, I was pretty sure you were in the game with Ikos and Moore. But the confirmation came when I got my phone from Bert. But I'm curious: how'd you get started?"

She shook her head disconsolately. "It's a long, ugly story—but I'll bet you've got a theory on that, too."

"Sort of. Allen got cross-ways with your company. They gave him money, and he didn't produce or reject the legislation as needed. Your boss knew you had the ability to rattle Allen's chain, or maybe you already were. Anyway, he or she offered you a bonus to shake him up, so you did. When you saw how easy it was, you decided to harvest some for yourself. But Allen's no pushover; he sued the lobbying firm and won. You lost your cushy job, but you held on to Allen with your extortion play. So, I'd say the shakedown was personal business—you had pictures, videos, letters—something that would taint his career.

"But you still needed a job, so Ikos probably got you the gig with the DEA, maybe with an endorsement from Moore at FBI. I'd guess they even figured out a way to get years of retirement shifted from your lobbying job to the new position. Afterward, the three of you stayed in Allen Moore's pocket for a long time. Then, you got scared when Ikos and Moore started using the other Morris brothers as their personal goons.

"Then Ikos gets transferred to Texas. I'm not sure how Moore ended up here, but he and Stan took up where they left off, imported the Morris boys to clean up their losses here and frame me at the same time. Meanwhile, you're on assignment, tasked with checking Reynaldo for drug activity. But soon you ended up investigating your former partners in crime, right after wedging yourself into Reynaldo's Construction business under the pretense of checking on prospective customers and employees, while scanning his operation for drug smuggling. My, you stay busy!"

Diane smirked and gave a tiny round of applause. "As the saying goes, that's close enough for government work—which it was—so you win the prize.

"As to my assignment, I worked for a lobbyist, remember? So I lobbied hard to get the assignment to investigate Ikos, so I could direct things to a favorable conclusion. Turns out, I didn't have to worry. Brent took care of that problem. Then Bert took care of Moore and left the scene, whereabouts still unknown. I never thought I'd have to worry about..." Her voice trailed off as she searched for the right words.

"An old guy who can barely *spell* computer? Figuring out a high-profile extortion gig?"

"You said it, I didn't," she answered, laughing good-naturedly.

"Diane, you're an ambitious girl, I'll give you that. Oh, and I wasn't about to tell Heather anything, because she's pretty ambitious too. Too ambitious to sleep with me, by the way."

"Thank you for that. She'd like nothing better than to see me crash in flames.

"So at this point, you've saved my career—what's left of it, my vested pension—what little there is, and saved me from going to prison. You're the busy one. But what are you going to do with that juicy information you have?"

"The same thing you're going to do with the juicy information you gathered on me—absolutely nothing."

She nodded, relief showing on her face. She knew that the damning information he held on her was a lot more relevant and useful to law enforcement than the old hearsay tales about Carlton's long-past occupation, the parties to which were no longer around to testify.

The silence between them lasted a few minutes. When she spoke again, it was apparent she had been thinking about her recent job activities, the legitimate ones. "The investigation has unearthed some interesting things, you know. Mostly lies, but a few truths came to light. Aren't there a few unanswered questions in your mind?" she asked, powering up the laser beam look again, to full agent mode.

"Just one," he said, making a show of thinking about it. "Could we go to bed?"

She responded by rising from her chair and reaching for his hand. When he stood, they embraced, and Carlton felt a release of the tension brought about by the previous months' suspense and worry. The tedium of worrying about who, how, and why began melting away like South Texas snow in April, leaving him to wonder if it really had happened at all.

She pushed away just enough to look at him. "That's exactly what I'd like, and that's the truth."

Carlton smiled. "Good, because we both know how rare the truth is, don't we?"

ABOUT THE AUTHOR

Hanes Segler was born in San Antonio in 1949. Son of a career military man, he lived in Germany for three years as a young child before returning to Central Texas where he attended school. After a decade of odd jobs, he entered the commercial banking industry and remained for many years. Upon retirement, he returned to San Antonio where he continues to work occasionally and travel at every opportunity; however, writing remains his true passion.

Traveling extensively throughout South Texas and Mexico, he observes and enjoys the culture, history and people—good and bad—of the Border Region. *The Truth, Very Rare* is his ninth novel set in the region and the fifth of the Carlton Westerfield Series.

See the author's entire body of work and contact him with questions or comments at www.hanessegler.com.

Printed in the United States
by Baker & Taylor Publisher Services